BLOOD BOUND

DINERO DE SANGRE BOOK 3

LANA SKY

Blood Bound

Blood Bound By Lana Sky

Cover Design and Interior Formatting by Charity Chimni
Editing and Proofreading by Charity Chimni

ACKNOWLEDGMENTS

Thanks so much to everyone who supported this draft along the way, including the many beta readers who provided encouragement! Please keep in mind that this story includes dark, graphic and explicit content matter that is not suitable for readers under the age of 18—or for readers who are uncomfortable with the following subject matter: explicit sex, mentions of sexual abuse, mentions of child abuse, mentions of eating disorders, graphic depictions of violence, and mentions of self-harm.

CHAPTER ONE

I've never felt hatred like this before—it devours me. My head pounds, my vision blurred by tears. At the back of my mind, I know I'm being irrational.

Insane…

But all I can do is approach her in a way I never have, snatching a slender arm the second I'm close enough.

"Ada? What the hell?" She turns, fixing those green eyes in my direction. They blaze irritation and that smug confidence she always possessed. Like nothing in the world could ever hurt her.

And no one.

"Finally come to show your face?" She wrenches her arm away from me, her teeth bared in a snarl. "I know what you did, you little bitch. Though should I be surprised? You're just like them. Evil…"

The memory fades as I startle to awareness, unsure of where I am. All I know for sure is that I'm lying on something soft. A bed?

The air is so heavy, scented with an acrid stench reminiscent of beer. I think… The harder I try to get my bearings, the dizzier I feel. It's like I'm underwater. Every sound echoes, muddled and distorted.

Except for one.

"You shouldn't have come here." The hostile tone sends alarm shooting down my spine.

Something's wrong. What, exactly? I'm not sure.

I think I should be with someone…

"She needed medical attention," another man replies as if answering my unspoken question. His name comes to me with chilling recognition. *Domino.*

"And you did too, I suppose," the first man replies.

We must be in a room. I think I hear the whirl of a fan, and cool air teases my skin every few seconds, lessening the overall heat that has sweat dripping down my forehead. The voices sound nearby, but I don't see a thing. Belatedly, I realize my eyes are closed, too heavy to lift.

"I see the way you're shaking like a fucking leaf, Dom," the first speaker continues. "How long has it been, huh? You think you can go toe to toe with Jaguar while you're fighting through withdrawal? Spit it out and ask what you really want."

"Her arm. How bad is it?" Domino demands. I shiver as his voice runs through me. For once, it contained some vague emotion. Concern?

Her arm.

A wave of memories washes over me. *My wrist. Pain…*

"I set it," the man replies with a sigh. "She'll heal up fine enough. I might even have an extra brace around here somewhere. Now, let's talk about *you*. How much longer do you think you can go on without a dose?"

"I need you to keep an eye on Inez while I'm gone," Domino continues. "I mean it, Luis. If anything happens to her—"

"She knows the risks of going against Jaguar better than anyone. Hell, she practically raised the bastard."

"You think that will stop him from killing her if he gets the chance?"

"Of course not," Luis replies gruffly. "I'll see what I can do. But like I said, she knew the risks. The same risks that come with going off painkillers cold turkey without a backup supply."

A low sigh teases the air before Domino finally bites out, "So do you have any?"

"Not much," Luis admits. "Enough to get you over the border, at least. Can I ask what your plan is from there? Fuck around and hope that you can traipse through the city unnoticed with Ada Pavalos in tow? What?" he scoffs. "You think I didn't recognize the face that's plastered all over the news reports? If you want to buy yourself more time, I suggest you cut her hair, at least."

Domino's reply is muffled, as if he moved further away. I find myself straining to hear him. My eyelids twitch, but even that amount of movement is a struggle. More sweat drips down my forehead by the time I manage to pry open one eye enough to see through.

It's blindingly bright. Only snatches of my surroundings register. White walls. Yellow sunlight. A sputtering ceiling fan, and…

A shadowy figure who looms just out of sight, his silhouette chillingly familiar.

"She should be good for some light travel at least," the other man, Luis, continues. "But I suggest you get her to a doctor soon. Only a crazy motherfucker could cause that kind of a break with his bare hands. You really want to go up against that alone?"

"I…" As he speaks, Domino finally comes into view. He's pacing, his back to me, shoulders rippling with tension, straining the black shirt he wears. With a tilt of his head, his eyes cut in my direction. It's like I've been holding my breath, instinctively waiting for his acknowledgment.

Once I have it, my mind goes blank, unsure of how to process him. Friend?

Or foe.

"She's awake," he says, frowning. "Give her another dose. Enough to buy me a few more hours, at least."

Another dose of what? I attempt to speak—say anything—but I can't. All I can do is frantically try to meet his gaze, but he looks away. Almost as if he's deliberately avoiding eye contact.

"Don't you think you've put her through enough?"

"Trust me." His lips twist into a grimace. "She'll enjoy the ride."

"You haven't said what you're even after?" Another man appears at his shoulder, fumbling with a small glass vial. He's relatively short, with graying brown hair and piercing eyes gazing from behind wire-rimmed glasses. I don't recognize him, but I assume he's Luis.

"Breaking your cover after so long. Taking on Jaguar directly," he harrumphs. "You must have friends in powerful places. Rumor has it you've been working with the feds to cover your ass when Pavalos' little empire falls. I shouldn't have to be the one to tell you how fucking bad of an idea that is if true."

"Just get her ready."

"I will… But I hope you haven't forgotten the only reason I'm risking my neck for you in the first place. Because of Lia—"

"I haven't," Domino replies, advancing closer to me. Still frowning, he palms the side of my face, radiating an addictive warmth. "But don't forget *your* end of the bargain either."

"I've already secured a truck you can use, and my contact is ready to ferret you across. The only catch is that you'll be on a tight deadline. You need to reach him within two days, not a second later. Understood?"

"I just need to make one detour. Then I'll be there."

"And where would that be? Plan to go sightseeing before you catch a bullet in your skull? Oh, don't give me that look, Dom. I could have called Jaguar by now if I wanted to turn you in."

"North," Domino says cryptically.

"Through Mateo's territory? He won't like that."

"Which is why you won't inform him," Domino warns.

Luis shrugs. "Mind if I ask exactly how you plan on traveling anywhere with an injured woman in tow? Besides, what I can spare regarding your little problem will last you only a few days, at most. Then you'll have to find your own supply."

"All you need to worry about is making sure your contact holds up. As for the rest… Once I return to Terra Rodea, not even Jaguar can stand in my way."

He steps closer, and I try to speak. Move—anything—but I'm paralyzed as a sudden wave of exhaustion washes over me.

Was I drugged already?

A violent high could certainly explain the last thing I see as my lids flutter shut—Domino Valenciaga, looming above, the devil, ripped right from my nightmares.

When I regain consciousness, I'm still floating in that dreamy state of awareness. Not awake. Not asleep. I hate this feeling. The stupidest things come back to me—memories that should have died a long time ago.

Like Pia…

Her face haunts me, ripped right from the last night I ever saw her, her blazing eyes fixed in a hateful glare.

"You're just like them," she hissed. *"Evil!"*

She lunged for me next, nail drawn. All I could do was throw out both hands, pushing back as hard as I could. The move was impulsive. Instinctual.

But the sickening thud that followed was way too loud. Too heavy.

You're evil, Ada…

Perhaps, we are; everyone cursed with the last name Pavalos. An insidious nature infects my father's bloodline, doomed to corrupt all who follow in his path. A Pavalos will do anything to survive—a tenet I embodied in every way—

until Domino Valenciaga weaponized that tried-and-true creed against me.

I remember now. Everything responsible for the pulsing anxiety building in my gut, at least. When given a choice between Domino and another monster, I was stupid enough to trust that, even for a second, he had my best interests at heart.

Perhaps it's a blessing in disguise that I'm too exhausted to face what I've done—not that I find much reprieve in unconsciousness. Sleep continues to come in broken fragments as the noisy, violent world beyond fights for my attention. One persistent sound rises above the rest, giving me some clue of where I am. Near a radio or a television broadcasting a news report:

"...politician Roy Pavalos is still hospitalized in critical condition, while a search is underway for his daughter Ada-Maria. Arriving at the Terra Rodea international airport early yesterday morning, Rodrigo Pavalos declined to comment on the status of either his brother or his deceased sister-in-law..."

Rodrigo? It's seconds before I finally make the connection—Rodrigo Pavalos—my uncle. I haven't seen him in years, but any hope I feel is immediately swallowed by horror. If he's in Terra Rodea, then it's further proof that at least one of Domino's claims is true.

My father is alive...

And the broadcaster confirmed another horrifying claim of his—my mother is dead. The sick part is I haven't found the space to mourn her amid the chaos my life has become. Even now, someone else takes precedence—the owner of the masculine scent flooding my nostrils with every breath.

Domino.

No one so cruel should smell like he does. Like sin. One inhale, and some twisted part of me ignites, despite the million other ways the man repulses me. He's a liar for one, and a murderer...

More memories return by the second, reinforcing each menacing descriptor—but any real fear is kept at bay by a dreamy, warm cloud separating my brain from the rest of my body. I recognize this feeling. I'm high. But not high enough. What lurks beneath this dizzy euphoria is still recognizable, though dulled and distant. Pain. A lot of pain.

Along with that unshakable sense of unease.

For now, I ignore it all to reassemble more of my scattered thoughts. *Think.* The most pressing issue, of course, is where am I? My hazy memories provide a clue, uttered by Domino himself, *I'm taking you back...*

To Terra Rodea—but not in the hopes of a joyful Pavalos family reunion. No. He wants me to find Pia's body.

The low rumble of a vehicle's engine reinforces that very scenario. We must be in his car, jostling over an uneven road. Hell, for all I know, we could be in Terra right now.

The noise that first woke me—definitely a radio—continues, fragmented and disrupted by static.

"...no further news on the whereabouts of Ada-Maria Pavalos, but a nationwide search is currently underway. A press release by the office of Roy Pavalos stated that—" Suddenly, the sound cuts off, replaced by a guttural rasp.

"I know you're awake. Open your eyes."

His voice serves as the catalyst needed to jumpstart my exhausted brain. I can move again. Warily, I blink, wincing as my vision adjusts to the blinding hot sun spilling in through the windshield. My first observation is that we aren't in the car I remember. This vehicle is higher off the ground, sporting a narrower cabin and tan, fabric seats instead of leather. A truck?

The landscape visible beyond the windows differs slightly from the desolate fields surrounding his estate. Instead, tan grasses and cacti speckle the earth beyond a poorly maintained dirt road.

Domino doesn't seem alarmed by the remoteness. With a steely calm, he manipulates the wheel to navigate the rough terrain. His hair hangs loosely down his shoulders, his eyes narrowed with determination. A hot jolt of jealousy shoots through me. I hate how unfazed he always manages to seem.

"Where are we?" I croak, wincing as my throat aches. I'm thirsty.

The last thing I can coherently remember is him putting me in a car after nightfall. Then waking up, though in a room. He was speaking to a man, Luis, referring to my arm, and a "dose" of something I assume is responsible for my current high. Who knows how much time has passed since then?

"On schedule," Domino cryptically replies. "We only have time for one break, so make it count."

"On time for what?"

Abruptly, he pulls onto the side of the road and parks. As he wrenches open the door on his end, a burst of acrid air slams into me like a battering ram—followed by fear.

Weakly, I turn in his direction. "What are you doing?"

"I suggest you stretch your legs now," Domino continues, unconcerned by my discomfort. "That is, if you want to piss without getting bit by a rattlesnake. They come out in droves to sun themselves on the rocks this time of day."

I don't know what disarms me more. His uncharacteristic calm—or that his statement doubles as a thinly veiled threat.

"Where are we?" I demand a second time, testing my sore limbs. In the end, I manage to slump closer to the nearest window, but the low hills don't enlighten me on our location one damn bit. There isn't a house or building in sight.

"Luis," I rasp. A glance behind me reveals no one in the back seat, either. "Where is he?"

Appearing on my end, Domino raises an eyebrow. I've surprised him.

Without supplying an answer, he yanks my door open so suddenly I nearly pitch over, too weak to hold myself upright. His grip on my shoulder is the only thing keeping me from falling out of my seat—my *right* shoulder.

I gasp out, recalling at the same instant that my wrist is broken. Panic surges down my spine as I tense in anticipation of the agony that never comes. Looking down, I realize why—my arm is immobile, supported by a black brace made of sturdy material. It extends from my shoulder to my wrist, lessening some of the pain.

"Look at me." Domino grips my chin, impatience radiating through his fingertips. "You've had one hell of a ride," he murmurs, tilting my head for inspection.

"What do you mean?" I ask.

Only as his eyes narrow do I realize what he's doing. Checking how dilated my pupils are. Whatever he finds makes him purse his lips in disappointment. "It's a damn good thing we aren't trying to cross now. You'd get us flagged the second any agent takes one fucking look at you. I suggest you take my advice and try to piss while you have the chance. Hold onto me."

He offers his arm, and I blink.

"You're wearing your costume," I croak.

Gone are the casual loose shirts and slacks he sported around his estate. Both have been swapped for jeans and a denim shirt with the collar buttoned. All he's missing is the wide-brimmed cowboy hat, and he'd be the spitting image of my father's faithful bodyguard.

His scowl, however, disrupts the façade, proving what it was all along.

An act.

"What you call a costume, I call practical in the heat, Ada-Maria. Now move." He lunges for me, and I wince, too weak to push him off.

Pain is the only thing I've come to expect from him, but all he does is loop his hands around my waist, hauling me from the truck himself—gingerly. The second he sets me on my feet, my knees buckle.

"Lean back," he growls, shoving me against the vehicle itself. I was right to guess it was a truck. Painful nostalgia brings back bittersweet memories of watching him drive off in a battered pickup. Unlike his old navy model, this one is red.

I'm so caught up in observing it that I miss the moment he palms the front of my jeans.

"W-Wait!" My belly flips, my thighs tensing as I try to bat him off one-handed. Images flash through my brain of the last time he had me in this position, and all I can do is ask, "You'd fuck me now. Like this?"

He chuckles, but it's not malicious or mocking. Dare I say it even sounds genuine? His teeth flash, bared by a smile that lasts a heartbeat. Then he's scowling again, focused on the task at hand.

"I want you to *piss* like this." He kicks my legs apart, drawing my attention downward. I'm still wearing the black sweater and jeans I took from his closet—but someone added a new component to my outfit while I was unconscious—sturdy black hiking boots.

My first impulse is reckless—all I'd have to do is push past him and make a break for the scraggly hills surrounding us. With proper footwear, I'd probably last longer than my previous escape attempt.

The second feeling washing through me is just more confusion. Kindness is so unsettling from him.

In my experience, it's only ever followed by violence. A smart woman would run now—though there is the small dilemma that I can barely hold myself upright. My knees tremble, straining to support my weight.

"I need a hospital," I insist.

"You need to listen to me," Domino snaps back, shifting so that my shoulders are braced against the side of the truck. Then he crouches, continuing to drag my jeans down my legs.

"W-What are you doing?" My cheeks flush as hot air teases the skin of my thighs, melding with his body heat. The sensation reinforces the reality that I'm at his mercy, helpless against whatever he has in mind. When his fingers twitch over my hip, I suck in a breath. "S-Stop—"

"Relax." Anticlimactically, he stands and grips my shoulders so that if I did happen to pee, I wouldn't wet my pants or the shoes.

Or him, for that matter.

Rather than gratitude, his rare display of thoughtfulness spurs my unease. So I retaliate the only way I can. With spite. "Are you going to drag me all the way to Terra?"

"I could." He lets that statement hang menacingly in the air. "Or I could leave you here as a tempting decoy."

I don't miss the underlying threat—yet another reminder that, according to him, I have no one else to rely on.

But he's wrong.

"My uncle is looking for me," I blurt, merely to gauge his reaction. I so desperately want to see him flinch. Frown. *Something.*

His eyes narrow, but I can't tell if it's out of irritation or amusement. "I wouldn't go looking to Rodrigo as a savior."

A part of me quivers. I know my father is no hero, but is my uncle no better?

"If anything happens to your father, who do you think will be next in line?" he adds, feeding on my doubt without me voicing it. "Your uncle. Your brothers. They aren't your allies—merely claimants to the throne. Loyalty means nothing when power is up for grabs."

"You should know," I hiss.

"I *do* know. Which is why I suggest you don't take my protection for granted."

He sounds so damn smug—as if he's dancing around something unspoken, daring me to voice it. Rather than ask outright, I deflect, "Because you're the one who has my best interests at heart? Would that be before or after you had me kidnapped?"

"Because I'm the one with your life in his hands." He flexes said hands at his sides, cracking the thick knuckles one by one. "After all, you're the one who put it there."

"Not by choice," I bite back—but it's a lie.

Gradually, bits and pieces of that last night at his estate return, putting the truth into blinding focus. I *did* choose him over Jaguar—but Domino made a monumental choice of his own. He left the estate without Jaguar's permission, taking me to only God knows where for only God knows what.

Though, to be fair, he did give me a hint. He's aiming to get back to Terra Rodea, a task that involves a border crossing. Suddenly the fake passport I discovered in his closet makes more sense.

I wonder if that's how he smuggled me here in the first place.

"Who is Luis?" I demand a second time, changing the subject. "A friend of yours?"

"You have four seconds to piss before we need to move." As he angles his head toward the sun, I see a genuine hint of alarm cross his gaze. He's worried.

"I could always leave you here," he adds in the same breath. "Cutting the deadweight would keep Jaguar off my scent for a few more hours. At the rate you're going, he'll catch up by lunch, just in time to break more than your wrist."

As much as I try to suppress the fear, I can't. Neither can I ignore the pressure in my bladder and the million other pressing concerns my body chooses now to make known. I'm starving—but this hunger isn't the same bastion of control I've clung to for the past decade. It hurts. The gnawing ache in my belly makes it harder to think. Harder to reason. Harder to find the strength needed to resist the man before me.

Shame sears my cheeks, but I close my eyes and relieve the one discomfort I can on my own.

"It's about damn time."

I open my eyes again as Domino advances, withdrawing something from his pocket that he unceremoniously swipes between my legs. A dry rag. Satisfied, he yanks my pants back up and fastens them. Then he retreats, waltzing toward a thicker patch of grass—presumably to follow his own suggestion.

Alone, I inspect our surroundings more closely. This landscape varies from the region around his mansion in more ways than one. It's drier, the air liable to suck every ounce of moisture from my throat. Given the rugged terrain, I don't think Domino's quip about rattlesnakes was merely to unsettle me.

"Come on."

I jump as he reappears near the back of the truck, zipping his fly. My gaze tracks the motion, and I swallow hard as he draws close. Easily, he lifts me into my seat before returning to the driver's side. When he reclaims the wheel, he slams his foot on the gas, kicking up a swell of dirt as we go.

I inspect the truck's interior, noting that on the back bench is a black duffle I recognize from his estate, along with an unfamiliar burlap sack.

"What's in there?" I ask, eyeing him guardedly.

He doesn't even take his attention off the road. "I suggest you put your energy into preparing to walk." Apparently, he isn't in a mood to reveal any more secrets.

"Don't you think you owe me answers?" I ask, trying a different tack. "Something? After everything you've done—"

Abruptly, he flicks the dial for the radio, triggering a barrage of upbeat mariachi music. "It's at least a six-hour drive where we're headed. Then we'll need to move on foot. Focus on that. Here—"

He reaches across me, wrenching open the glove compartment. From it, he snatches what looks like an energy bar and tosses it onto my lap.

"Eat."

The question of how—with only one hand—crosses my mind. Rather than ask for help, I grab the bar with my good hand and bring it to my mouth. Thankfully, I manage to tear the package open with my teeth, but then I hesitate.

I wait for the disgust. The nausea. The desperate need to cling to this gnawing, aching hunger and seek that fragile grasp on control I've come to rely on.

Instead, my stomach growls, and in three bites, I consume half of the bar outright.

"Where are we going?" I demand after swallowing, raising my voice above the noise.

If he hears me, he doesn't bother to answer.

Good. He had a point—I should focus—like on what the snatches of the broadcast I heard as I woke up revealed. My uncle is in Terra. While he lacks the political pull of my father, Rodrigo has influence and money of his own. If I could find a way to contact him…

"There is a search for me," I say carefully, watching Domino's reaction from the corner of my eye. "My uncle. The police. How do you plan to get me into Terra without drawing notice?"

He makes a show of scanning the road, still silent, but I know he's listening.

"Either you talk to me, or I leave." To bolster the threat, I muster enough strength to swipe at the door handle.

"Stop." He shuts the music off, leaving only the hum of the engine to fill the quiet. Finally, he sighs. "Do you have any idea what I've done?"

He lets the silence resonate for a handful of seconds before answering his own question, "Jaguar claimed you. I took you anyway. He'll see that as a direct challenge. Do you have any idea what that means?"

His tone chills me to the core. I swallow hard, weighing my response before replying. "That you're a selfish bastard?"

"No," he says softly. "That I let five goddamn years of planning go down the shitter because of you. He won't stop. Not if he feels I need you—that I want you for some other purpose. *Fuck—*" he strikes the wheel so hard I jump. "If you'd waited another fucking day at least to have your petty little outburst…"

I must be more out of it than I thought—either that, or he's lost his damn mind. "So, this is my fault?"

Riling him is a dangerous game, but I'm too exhausted to dance on eggshells anymore.

"You did this," I remind him in a hiss. My eyes burn. I frantically blink, but there's no stopping the tears that fall. "You sold me to that sick bastard! What the hell did I ever do to deserve that?"

"You haven't been listening." Real emotion colors his tone; he's angry. Furious, in fact, though he's managed to disguise it until now. "I suggest you pay close attention, Ada-Maria.

Jaguar will kill you if he thinks your death will affect me. Congratulations. You did the one fucking thing sure to provoke him."

"What?" I demand.

"You chose me over him," Domino growls. "You might as well have wrapped a noose around your neck."

"What was I supposed to do?" I ask, genuinely curious. "Hop onto his cock?"

"You were supposed to shut your fucking mouth and do what I say."

"Oh really?" I watch him, but fury isn't what I find straining those handsome features into a frown. This is something far more unsettling. My pulse surges as if warning me to back down. I don't think I want to know the answer to this riddle.

"Maybe I should have stayed with Jaguar?" I suggest, choosing to play with fire. "At least he was upfront about what he wanted from me."

"Damn you."

The truck veers off the road in a cloud of dust, and we stop so suddenly I jolt forward, forced to brace my good hand against the dashboard. Any pain I feel vanishes in the face of his cold scoff.

And terror instantly replaces it.

"So fickle are your affections, Ada-Maria," he snarls. "I guess pain is what truly gets you off. Maybe I shouldn't stop myself the next time I feel the urge to wrap my hands around your fucking throat—"

"You've done that," I counter breathlessly. Reaching up with my good hand, I trace the flesh in question. It's still tender, smarting from his use of a collar. "You think you're so different from him?"

His eyes flash, and I recoil against my seat. The way he looks at me… It's an expression somewhere in between shock and hate.

"You don't know how many fucking times I've gone against my better judgment when it comes to you." Gone is the false calm. *This* is the Domino I remember.

The same twisted figure who held me captive for weeks.

"I could have let you die a million different ways by now, Ada-Maria. Don't think I haven't considered it. From that very first day your boyfriend offered your head to Jaguar on a silver platter, I could have let you go to him then, and I can tell you for a fact that more than your wrist would be in pieces by now."

"So why didn't you?" My heart pangs, betraying just how badly I crave an answer to that question. Why? Even if it's a cruel, selfish reason—which it must be—I still need to hear him say it.

"Why?" He lashes out, fisting his hand in my hair so hard stray hairs rip from my scalp. Pain isn't his motive.

Control is—he wrenches me toward him, bringing my face within inches of his.

"I told myself how easy it would be. To watch you die. To see him fuck you. Hurt you. Sell you." He ticks the horrors off one by one, his voice devoid of any emotion. But when he brings his free hand to my jaw, it trembles—and that rare hint of instability chills me to the bone.

"Some men have to commit horrific crimes to know they've crossed some moral line, Ada. Kill men. Women. Children. Not me. I'll let you in on a little secret. *You* were always my gauge—"

"What does that even mean?" I snap.

Irritation radiates from him so fiercely I can feel it on my skin, hear it bitten into every word.

"My pretty, Ada-Maria... As long as I didn't give a fuck as to what might happen to you, I could face Don Roy on even ground. No one could stand in my way. Not even his daughter with the perky ass and Bambi eyes. God, you make it so easy to hate you."

As if to prove it, he drags his fingers through my hair, tugging on random strands as he goes. Hard. Harder. I wince, and he changes tack, stroking my forehead with terrifying care.

"I knew that I could step aside and let Tristan play his little games at your expense. I could use your body to settle an old debt and never think twice. You meant nothing to me."

I hate the tears that spring to my eyes. It's one thing to experience his hatred firsthand—but it's torture to hear him state it so plainly.

"Then why not kill me?"

"Why? Five years," he says hoarsely. "Five damn years. That's an odd time to plot revenge, Ada. Have you asked yourself why I would act now? Or why *that* time frame? After everything I've done for Don Roy, what could make me finally act against him? Believe me or not, five years wasn't anywhere near long enough—" the look in his eye cements the conviction in his voice. He means every word. "I would have worked for that bastard for ten decades if that's what it took. Why ruin the life I built up, huh? I knew Jaguar's stupid ass stunt wouldn't kill him. I had to beg that bastard to help me in time. I had to scramble to get the resources in place to bring you to me. Why? What might force me to tip my hand? I'll tell you…"

He flicks his tongue across his bottom lip. Then, in a voice like sin, he grates out the answer, "*You*."

He adjusts his grip, grazing his nails carelessly against my scalp, using the pain to reinforce his next words. "I wanted to spare your feelings before, but no more. That bastard ordered me to kill you. Not Tristan. Not some nameless cartel. *Me*. You were meant to die that night—but by *my* hand."

Ice-cold, his eyes don't hold a shred of remorse or pity. Just endless hate.

"Do I have to spell it out for you? Your own father wasn't just willing to sell you," he says gruffly. "He wanted you dead."

CHAPTER TWO

He wanted you dead…

No. I shake my head, refusing to process the rest of his claim—it's too insane. This is just another sick mind game at my expense.

"You're lying."

"Am I?" A muscle in his jaw twitches as he releases me, settling back into his seat. "He didn't think I'd question him," he adds. The lack of fire in his voice makes my blood run cold. Though he's lying. He must be…

"It wasn't the worst act he's ordered me to commit, by far," he continues, his expression contorting into the calculating frown I know so well. "Hell, I couldn't tell you everything he's done in the name of your family. But I never thought he could order the death of his own daughter over a cigar and a whiskey."

"You're lying—"

"You don't believe that." He doesn't even put effort into his voice. "You know it sounds like him."

He's right. I can easily picture my father as he claimed, standing on the balcony, glaring out over his estate. Cigar in hand, he'd blow out smoke rings while contemplating his next move.

He was always plotting and planning.

Ironically, Domino seems to share my doubt—even Roy Pavalos isn't capable of this.

"You said he was working with Tristan," I point out. "First he wanted me kidnapped, and now—"

"Ada..." His heavy sigh leaves me paralyzed, and it takes everything I have not to slap my hands over my ears and scream just to drown him out.

"You were an obstacle in his way," he explains. "At that moment, you ceased to be his daughter—"

"No!" I reach for the door handle, fumbling with the lock. "You're lying."

"I asked him why," he adds, and I watch my hand fall, landing helplessly on my lap. "Why you. Do you want to know what he said?"

So cruel, he lets the silence hang until I finally glance over my shoulder to find him staring back. "He said, 'You've never questioned me before, Domino. I suggest you don't start now.'"

Despite everything, a laugh rips from me. And a sob. *That* definitely sounds like the father I knew—a tiny sliver of my soul can admit that.

But…

"He wouldn't."

Domino rests his head against the top of his seat. For a long, long while, he observes the unmoving road, and I can't deny how twistedly beautiful he can seem like this. As unreachable as some mythical God, detached from emotional beings. To him, the only forces that matter are power and fear.

"I don't falter," he says finally.

I flinch. His tone resembles the stern baritone that was a hallmark of his dutiful soldier façade. The voice that would make me tremble every time I imagined him at night.

The same voice that will haunt the nightmares I'll undoubtedly have from here on out.

"I don't hesitate. If I want something, I take it. If I need something, I take it. And in the name of revenge, I will become the errand boy of a man I hate for a decade if I have to. No one will ever stand in my way, do you understand that?"

He soldiers ahead without waiting for a response.

"If your father orders me to put a bullet in the brain of his only daughter, then I'd do so without question. After all, who would mourn Ada-Maria Pavalos? Your mother, perhaps, but we both knew it was only a matter of time before she joined you in the afterlife. Beyond her, you were merely a symbol, and your death would make you a martyr. An albatross your father could wear around his neck for the rest of his political career. It doesn't matter that you've spent your entire life degrading yourself for him, pining for even a scrap of appreciation. Or that you sold your body and soul in the name of his ambition. Your life didn't matter as long as you stood in his way. More than anyone, I'm sure you understand that."

My vision blurs with unshed tears, but he remains unmoving—briefly. Upon closer inspection, even I can see how his hands shake over the steering wheel.

"So why didn't you?" I ask thickly. "You wanted your revenge first? To hurt me?"

"I'll ask again. Who would miss Ada Pavalos?" He inspects the endless blue sky expanding before us as though it holds the answer. Apparently not. He has to voice one of his own, "Who watched her, day in and day out? Who watched her play with countless men like toys? Who knew every hue of gray her eyes could touch on when she was frustrated? Or sad? The way she pursed her lips when angry... Who could see through that fake fucking smile to the pain lurking beneath? Who would crave the sight of that bouncing, perky little ass of hers—" he laughs, but it resonates more like a heavy sigh, devoid of inflection. "It would have been far, far easier, Ada-Maria, for both of us, if I took my gun like I planned to and blew out your fucking skull."

He says it so callously that I know he's not lying—and that's what is so terrifying. The way he described me, the raw craving in his voice... Those tiny little realizations serve to tip me over the edge.

I can actually *feel* something inside me rip apart. I can hear it as faint as tearing tissue paper, so fragile when all is said and done.

Who knew that a few careful words would utterly break my soul? And yet, the only sound I can make is a ragged intake of air. "Please stop lying to me—"

"No. You ruined my carefully plotted timeline, Ada," Domino soldiers on, unwilling to show me mercy, even now. "You ruined every fucking thing, and I knew then and there that your father was merely testing me. Of course, he saw the way I looked at you—how could he not? Don Roy realized I'd been working against him from the start. What better way to flush me out than by using the best tool at his disposal?"

He's thinking out loud, revealing a hint of the convoluted mindset I would have given my soul to understand just a few weeks ago.

"Still, I decided to play along," he continues. "I'd arrange a test of my own. I had to scramble to get everything in place months, years before I'd planned to. I needed Jaguar, and the bastard loved having me crawl to him on my hands and knees. He thinks he has me by the balls, but I knew that I could use this moment to my advantage and punish you, Roy, and Jagger in one fell swoop. Neither would ever see it coming—and as a bonus, I would have you. Even if you were a scheming little snake in on your father's grand plan, I'd fucking have you."

"You… You sound insane," I manage to rasp.

He doesn't even hesitate. "I am."

"Why?" It seems surreal for one man to crave having that kind of hold over another.

It's demented.

A cruel obsession.

And yet…he smiles, and it's the most wickedly beautiful expression I've ever seen.

"From that very first day when I saw you in Don Roy's office, Ada-Maria, I haven't been able to get those gray fucking eyes out of my head. That smile. Your voice. I wish for your sake that I could have been one of those poor bastards you're used to playing your games with. Someone who could fuck you once and forget you. If I only wanted your body… It would have been better for you in the end."

His earnest tone makes my heart feel liable to lurch right out of my chest. I sense that he's trying to tell me something. Something important.

And horrifying.

I try to ask, "W-What are you—"

"It should have been easy to overlook you. But you were never stupid," he continues, tapping his knuckles against the steering wheel for emphasis. "Never. You were always watching, always alert. Behind those empty fucking smiles was a little viper staring back, missing nothing. You didn't follow your father's orders because he hurt you, or because you were too much of a silly fool to question. No. You obeyed him because you love him."

Love. He makes it sound so different from the dreamy way Pia and I would reflect on that term as schoolgirls. In his grated inflection, that term becomes something lethal. A weapon.

"You loved him enough to stand by him no matter what he asked of you. You trusted that every time you went into hell for him, you were earning his love in return. A fool isn't capable of that sacrifice. Idiots have no honor, no integrity. A real fool would have turned on her father the second she got the chance, but not you. You valued your loyalty to him, even if the bastard never truly deserved it. Men like Jaguar pride themselves on trusting no one. They believe there is strength in that, but it's bullshit. If it's every man out for himself, then what's the point in fighting so damn hard?"

As if seeking out the answer, he eyes his hands, pulling them from the wheel.

"I saw it firsthand. The way you'd lie for him. Cheat for him. Sell your soul to the highest bidder. You'd die for him; he knew that too—don't think for one fucking second that he didn't. He thought that it was because he had you cowed enough. Because he whipped you hard enough. Because you were terrified enough to do whatever he said with no complaint. But that wasn't it. Fear doesn't make you loyal; it makes you seethe. It makes you desperate to escape the leash you can feel around your throat. You'd lie, cheat, and steal. You'd become the monster if you have to, anything to break those bonds. So no, you didn't serve your father out of fear. You did it out of love, and in so many ways, Ada-Maria, that's far, far worse. Your love blinded you, and it made you suspectable to hope, and that hope? It will kill you faster and more painfully than I ever could."

"I don't have any hope when it comes to you," I finally spit out—but I have to strain just to hear my own voice over the harsh sound of his breathing. "Not anymore. Over and over, you hurt me—"

"You play the part of a dumb woman well, Ada, but you are far from that, aren't you? Your father is one of the most calculating men I've ever met. Together, you two have taken down mayors, and journalists, and anyone who might even dream of threatening the Pavalos family legacy. If your father suspected me even once during my time working for your family, he would have told you. He would have used you to get close to me, and you tried. I managed to resist your every attempt."

Shock cuts through me like a knife as it hits me—this is his attempt at honesty. This is why he tortured me so cruelly.

I see myself in what feels like another lifetime, preening for him, smiling, desperate to cajole him into grinning back. Something. Anything. I wanted a fraction of attention from him, and who knows what I would have done if he'd given it to me.

But all he saw was manipulation. A lying little bitch he had to resist.

"You think this changes anything?" I ask, practically wailing at the insanity of it all. "That you hurt me out of doubt? Bullshit! So much for wanting my loyalty—"

"I'll earn more than just your loyalty." His confidence rattles me into silence, my mouth still open.

What truly unsettles me is the look in his eye. It's determined. "By the time this is over, you'll be willing to put a knife in Roy Pavalos yourself," he says. "I can promise you that."

I almost laugh again. At least now I have confirmation that whatever he feels for me, is far beyond compassion.

"Oh really?" I choke out. "I'm not as stupid as you think."

It's mind-blowing how conflicting his opinion of me seems to be. A dumb, senseless whore one minute. A thoughtful, loyal woman the next, someone worthy of his admiration—as twisted as the term is where he is concerned.

"I never thought you were stupid, at least in that context," he admits. "You're so damn stubborn. You'd deny yourself pleasure just to get a rise out of someone you hated. You'd starve yourself just to make me watch you die. Don't pretend like you wouldn't."

I look down at the energy bar crumbs on my lap. "Why tell me this now?" I ask, unsure which of his confessions I can even risk trying to believe. "So I can be your lovesick puppy again and lead you to Pia's body? Then you'll kill me, won't you? Or sell me, anyway—"

Abruptly, Domino grips the wheel, and we accelerate so quickly a cloud of rust-colored dirt billows up around us.

"I'm telling you this so that you can understand the choice you made," he says darkly. "Put your trust in me, and you'll have nothing to fear. Doubt me, and Jaguar will be the least of your worries. But don't take my word for it. You want it driven home just how little your father cares about you? Fine. I'll let someone else explain it better than I ever could. In their own words, you'll learn the truth."

I lick my lips, thrown off yet again. Someone else. "Who? Alexi?"

"I'll take you to them," he says evasively. "Right now. It's not like you have a better option."

"What about Jaguar," I whisper, shivering at the sound of his name. "You sold me to that monster. How can I even begin to trust you? What if he were always the 'better option'?"

He laughs, and I'm so startled by the rich cadence that I just gape.

"If you were paying attention, Ada-Maria, you would have known from the start that I never had any fucking intention of giving you to anyone. You were always mine. Always. Mine to take, and mine to destroy. I suggest you don't forget that."

The grit in his voice guts me. As tired as I am, I don't have a chance in hell of playing his mind game—not now. Everything he said was all lies, and I'm better off not believing a word of it.

I can't risk going off on my own now, either. Not yet.

Instead, I close my eyes again, letting the hum of the engine lull me into a flimsy excuse for sleep.

He doesn't speak again, and I savor every second of silence. Something tells me it will be the only reprieve from Domino Valenciaga I'll receive.

CHAPTER THREE

"Get up," a voice I know all too well drips into my ear, jarring me awake. Gone is the unrestrained possession. He's cold again.

"We need to walk the last leg," Domino adds gruffly, sounding further away. "Get ready to move."

The last leg…

Supposedly before we meet with someone who will offer proof as to my father's true intentions. That thought spurs me into motion. Reluctantly, I blink my eyes open, but all I see is black. Then silver…

Moonlight. Gradually, my vision adjusts to the faint glow of it seeping into the truck. It's dark. The absence of sunlight enhances the remoteness of the terrain as the moon itself shifts from behind a patchwork of purple clouds. A sobering mixture of awe and dread washes over me, shattering any remnants of sleep. I can't escape the thought that this sight would be beautiful if I had someone I cared about to share it with.

Someone other than the man eyeing me from beyond the open driver's side door of the truck. "It's a long walk," Domino warns, his gaze electric in the shadows. "I can only drive so close. It's risky to take a chance on this terrain in the dark, but it will be harder to track us than during the day."

"To where?" I demand. Another fragment of memory comes back to me. "I heard you speaking to someone before. A man. Luis. He said you were trying to cross the border—"

"Get out." He circles around to my end, muscling my door open for me. He grasps for my uninjured forearm, leaning in so close his breath sears my throat.

"I can move on my own." I try to shrug him off but, aided by only one hand, I'm no match.

For all my bravado, I sway, forced to rely on his strength for stability. I shudder as my fingers latch onto his forearm, sensing the thickness of the muscle twitching beneath.

"Where are you taking me?" I manage to croak, craning my neck to see his face. Better yet, "Who do you think will convince me you're telling the truth about my father?"

He inclines his head as if surprised I remembered that much.

Good. My thoughts are clearer now. The drug is wearing off, but in its absence lurks the pain lancing up and down my right arm. Thankfully, the makeshift brace is strong enough that I can hold it against my chest without much discomfort.

"Was he a doctor?" I ask again, trying a different tack. That occupation would explain the relatively stable condition of my right wrist, anyway. "Luis?"

Maybe it's my soft tone that wrings a frown out of him. "Something like that," he grunts, slamming the passenger-side door. "We'll need to move fast to make it before sunrise. Then it will be a game of trying to cross the border in time."

I don't miss the unofficial deadline he tacks onto that statement. He's hiding something, and his posture only bolsters that suspicion. He's edgy, his jaw clenched, eyes blazing through the darkness.

"I can't carry you," he adds, lifting an object that he must have taken from the truck without my noticing—the black duffle. He slings it over one shoulder, hefting the burlap sack with his other hand. "So you'll have to keep up. Come on."

He sets off into the rugged terrain at a pace that makes my legs throb in sympathy.

Despite the rapidly growing distance between us, I don't move, contemplating what he'd do if I climbed into the truck and made a break for it. Damn him and his secretive plots.

As if reading my mind, Domino cocks his head my way. "Jaguar's men will be watching the roads, if they aren't just hours behind us already. I don't think you'd enjoy what he'll do to you if you happen to fall into his hands again."

Sufficiently cowed, I take a step. Then another. As I start moving in earnest, I have to throw out my free hand for balance. This is harder than I'd thought. Every inch I advance takes twice the usual effort, and I'm panting by the time I draw even with him.

"Stay close," he tells me, moving assuredly—but slower than I think he would if I weren't here. "It's a little over a mile before we can stop."

"Where are we going?" I ask for the umpteenth time.

Predictably, he keeps walking.

His concept of a mile is as laughable as his concept of loyalty. I'm pouring sweat by the time he finally slows, shrugging the duffle from his shoulder.

"Sit," he commands, his expression unreadable in the low lighting. "We'll rest here."

Here being a roughly flat strip of earth, riddled with unseen rocks and scraggly grasses. I'm wary, picturing those rattlesnakes he hinted at. Who knows what else might be crawling in the shadows?

Not that Domino seems concerned by either possibility. The picture of confidence, he crouches, rummaging through the items in the burlap sack. As I crane my neck to get a better view, he shifts to block me.

"I suggest you don't waste time," he calls back. "We only have an hour before we need to be on the move again, and you won't be able to sleep."

The ominous edge to his tone prompts me to ask, "Why not?"

He inclines his head, and a fraction of moonlight illuminates his eyes long enough to catch the glimmer of interest that flits across them. "I think it would be better if you listen. You're about to get a crash course in the Domingas Cartel."

I hold my breath. For all I know, the promise of information could be his way of luring me into another trap. Another mind game. More lies.

But, fuck it. I'm desperate to learn any scrap of info, and he knows it. With a sigh of defeat, I start to sit, only to realize how hard it is to maneuver with my right arm in the brace. Losing balance, I nearly pitch over—but a firm grip on my left hand saves me from the impending impact.

The second I can steady myself, I wrench my hand away, my cheeks flaming. Then I sit down on the hard earth, heedless of whatever creatures might be slithering nearby. "Start talking," I snap.

He sits as well but counters me with a demand of his own, "Let's see how well you were paying attention. Do you remember that name I told you? Who used to run the cartel?"

I swallow hard, unnerved by this impromptu pop quiz. "Carlos," I say, recalling that name. "Jaguar's father?"

"Yes. And he was just one of many players you'll need to remember. Here—" He withdraws something from the sack that he hands to me. I recognize it from feel alone—a water bottle. Eagerly, I drink from it, aware of his gaze on my throat.

As I swallow, I risk choking out another question. "Is Luis another 'player,' too?"

He looks away, scanning our surroundings with an eagle-like focus. Finally, he says, "Consider him an old friend of your family's, but not someone important at the moment."

His tone contains a warning—I'm testing his patience.

"I-I'm listening," I say.

"I suggest you do," he warns. "This is the only shot you'll get to understand a small piece of the mess you've found yourself in. Carlos ran the *Guarida*. He operated on both sides of the border, using his clubs as a front for his true trade in cocaine. Jaguar's continued his tradition, but in a lesser capacity. Thanks to Roy Pavalos, another man now claims most of the old Domingas territory. His name is Mateo Morello."

"Mateo..." I recognize that name though I'm not sure how. I think he said it once, referring to a passport. *Mateo is fucking me on the timeline—.*

"He and Jaguar have something of a truce now, but it's only a matter of time before one goes for the other's throat. The main territory in dispute sits along the border, the perfect spot to transfer goods from either side."

Could that be his intended route to reenter Terra Rodea? I start to ask, but Domino continues, even as my lips part.

"Jaguar's expanded his father's business well beyond what Carlos ever intended. The old man never dabbled in anything beyond the drug trade, and perhaps illegal weapons. Blinded by ambition, Jaguar's been taking on whatever business can get him the most money the fastest, morals aside. The only problem was the border. Without a stable crossing point, he found it hard to keep up a regular supply while avoiding the authorities. That's where Mateo comes into play. Both Jaguar and your father used him as a middleman. Ironically, I could communicate with him, even after I worked for your father, without drawing notice."

"How convenient," I interject.

He nods. "Unfortunately, Mateo has taken to transporting more of his own merchandise than Jaguar likes, but tipping the scales without an insurance policy would risk closing off his access to the border completely."

"So, what are you saying?"

"What I'm saying is that whoever can take out Mateo controls the flow of trade in and out of Terra. That puts us in the middle of a powder keg I'd rather not see blow up in my face."

I note the way he phrases that. Carefully. As if to disguise that one key player in this mix has every reason to crave the same outcome.

"What's your gain in all of this?"

He grabs the water bottle from me and takes a drink. Beads of liquid drip down his chin as he eyes the sky, letting the moonlight bathe his face completely.

"I never planned on making my move quite this early," he admits. Rarely have I heard him use this tone. Deep and rasping, devoid of any anger or rage. He's speaking unguardedly for once. "I knew I would leverage a strike against Pavalos and Jaguar, preferably at the same time. But once again you, Ada-Maria, seem determined to accelerate my timeline."

His eyes find mine, but I don't see anything remotely close to gratitude in them.

"What do you want from me?" I demand, hating how soft my voice sounds in comparison to his.

He shuffles to face me directly, his legs outstretched. "I want answers. Answers about Pia. You can start with the night she went missing."

A heavy knot of dread settles in my stomach. Perhaps I'm too much of an optimist, but I never imagined I'd have to relive those memories in the middle of the desert, seated beside a madman.

It's not fair. Pia is one of the few secrets that has always remained mine, ignored at my discretion—and I liked it that way. I relished the control that relegating Pia Inglecias to the past gave me, no matter how pathetic it was. And were I to provide Domino even a fragment of those memories, I'd want it to be on my terms.

Only mine.

"Why?" I ask, evading a direct answer for now. "What are you looking for? Besides, what makes you think I'd even tell you a damn thing? You've already established that I'm doomed either way."

"Ada..."

I brace for the rage I've come to expect. For his nostrils to flare and for his eyes to narrow. Instead, he merely steals another sip of water, wiping his mouth with the back of his hand.

"You aren't the least bit curious?" he asks, switching his tone from cold to cautious. "You claim you know exactly why Pia did what she did, but then I tell you that you're wrong. That your father killed her, and that it was over something far more valuable than money. And yet, you aren't curious as to the truth behind it all?"

"Why should I be?" I counter, but hell, he has a point. Maybe the answer is simple—I don't want to know. "Nothing changes the fact that I'm here with you now. You've already taken me from Jaguar, and I suspect that puts you in just as much danger. It seems like you're all out of threats, Domino."

He laughs before taking another long swig. "My Ada and her smart fucking mouth. So let's say I release you right now, and you manage to make it to Terra Rodea on your own–assuming Jaguar doesn't drag your sweet ass off to the *Guarida,* and you manage to become a free woman. A happy ending with sparkles and roses. But then what?"

I haven't dared to envision such a scenario. When I do, one glaring reality sucks any hope from the prospect.

"Oh, that's right," Domino softly remarks. "I'll tell you what happens—you go right back to being the daughter of Roy Pavalos. A man out for blood. You claimed to know your father better than anyone, so you do the honors and tell me what he might do to *you.* Especially after you've been in the hands of his enemies for so long?"

"Go to hell," I spit.

"I'll see you there," he snaps back. "Because we both know exactly what he'll do. He'll lock you inside that beautiful familial estate and beat that precious sense of loyalty back into you. Piece by piece. Then he'd bandage together whatever was left, package them neatly with a little pink bow and send you back out into the world under his discretion. There is no escape from him, no matter what you delude yourself into thinking."

Damn him. I never realized how a few short weeks without my father's presence might change me—and ironically, not for the better. Three weeks ago, I had a sense of direction, even if that direction led toward hell.

Now? My perception of the future is in pieces. And the reality I never wanted to face is staring at me—literally—impossible to ignore.

In a sick twist of fate, I went from having my father pull my puppet strings, to watching Domino Valenciaga dangle them directly in front of me.

"And," he continues, "are you really so sure he didn't try to have you killed? I know you don't trust me, but you aren't that stupid. What I've told you sounds plausible enough. Admit it."

I close my eyes, wishing more than anything that I had the strength to just ignore him and surrender to whatever fate this desert has in store.

But there is a possibility that fate could lead me straight to Jaguar, and it doesn't seem so tempting anymore.

"I want you to tell me the truth," I say, opening my eyes again to his silhouette bathed in silvery moonlight. He can seem so beautiful it hurts, his eyes a dangerous green. The sad part is, if he could offer even a hint of real kindness, I'd swallow anything he told me.

"No more lies," I rasp. "No more mind games. Tell me what you're really after. It's not like I'm a threat to you—"

"Ah, but that's where you're wrong." Without warning, he cups my cheek against a calloused palm. The intensity in his eyes sends a shudder through me. It's more predatory than smug. "You are the single biggest threat to me there is, Ada-Maria. With one word, you can destroy everything I've spent the past decade working toward. I can't risk you doing that. Not until you've proven yourself."

To *him*. It stings how easily he's managed to turn the tables, making me the enemy—when he's the one who dragged me into this mess.

"I'm starting to question if you really are a better option than Jaguar."

His hand slides down my jaw only to grasp my uninjured wrist instead. Possessively, he runs his thumb over the protruding bones. It's a chilling caress—and an unmistakable warning.

"I haven't broken your wrist the last time I checked," he softly reminds me. "I haven't whipped you until you were on the verge of death, either—"

"But you still whipped me," I hiss, ripping my hand from his grasp. "You took pleasure in hurting me, and you enjoy having me squirm for your amusement, so pardon me, Domino, if I'm not willing to place you on a pedestal."

"So, don't," he counters with that infuriating calm back on display. "Everything I've done has been for my own reasons; I don't deny that. But…"

I swallow at his hesitation. Any perceived weakness on his end is only a trap, meant to lower my guard. Still, I can't help myself by playing right into it.

Voice rasping, I ask, "But what?"

"I would be lying if I didn't tell you that there was another reason why I intervened when I did."

I suck in a breath. Could what he said before be the truth? God, I'm such a fool for even wanting to believe it…

"Then why?"

"Because your mother asked me to," he says. "And I can prove it."

So many emotions strike me all at once, I can't process them. I just breathe…

Within minutes I'm sobbing, feeling fresh tears mercilessly lash down my cheeks.

"How dare you?" Though, am I truly surprised by the depths he seems willing to sink to? I shouldn't be. "I can understand you hating me, but my mother was nothing but kind to you—"

"You don't even know the half of it." The worst part is that he seems to be agreeing with me. "Which is why I did what she asked. I intervened, though I would have done so regardless—but I can prove it, and more. So, what will you do? Continue to pout or listen to me for once, and take what I'm telling you at face value."

Listen to him. It's not like I have any other choice.

"What are you talking about? What did my mother tell you?"

"Not yet." He shoves the water bottle into my hand again. "I'll reveal that tidbit of information in my own time. But I will educate you on another topic—you. Keeping you away from Jaguar relies on getting you across the border in time. Every second you doubt me, risks that. So, if you want to stay alive, then keep moving. Now drink."

I've barely taken a sip when he snatches the bottle back, stowing it into his bag. I expect him to move on, leaving me to catch up. Abruptly, he snags my uninjured wrist instead, hauling me to my feet.

"We're almost there," he bites into my ear. "And whether you're ready to hear them or not, you'll get your answers soon enough."

CHAPTER FOUR

Morning comes with a scorching heat that sears my skin before the sun fully rises. Only sheer pride keeps me moving. If I stop, I doubt I could get up again.

Infuriatingly, Domino hasn't even broken a sweat. His speed remains steady over the uneven ground, and I suspect that I've only kept up with him because he's tailored his pace. If he wanted to, he could easily leave me behind to rot.

Would such an end be so bad, all things considered?

I'm starting to fantasize that very scenario when I spy something up ahead glaringly different from the reddish landscape surrounding it. The closer we come, the clearer it is to make out—a square structure of wood with a rusted metal roof. It looks like it could have been a gas station or a store at one point, though long since falling into disrepair.

"This is it?" I ask in between pants at Domino's back. "This is your way over the border?"

"Keep moving," he replies, hiking his bags higher on his shoulder. "The sooner you make it, the sooner you can sleep. We can't move again until evening, at least."

The veiled offer of rest spurs on my tired limbs, though I should have learned my lesson about trusting him by now. For all I know, beyond the walls of that decrepit shack, Jaguar lies in wait, ready to cart me off while Domino watches on with that blank, unreadable expression.

Even so, I can't ignore the way his words replay in my brain. *I wanted you. I stayed for you. I was always there for you…*

"Stay close," he warns.

I startle to awareness and realize that not only have I found the strength to keep moving, but I've surpassed him by a few feet. I wish I were brave enough to pull ahead entirely. Run. Get inside that shack and barricade it against him, or —better yet—breeze past it. Leave Domino and his twisted world behind and hope to come across anything better.

Though who am I kidding? The happiest ending I have to look forward to is dying before he or Jaguar can desecrate my body for their own means.

"Don't get any cute ideas," Domino remarks, and his relaxed façade cracks, revealing the tension lurking beneath.

Damn him. Teeth gritted, I slow enough for him to pull ahead.

Despite seeming so close, it feels like hours pass before we finally reach the crumbling shelter. With the sun beating down relentlessly, every second scrapes by. I'm standing only by pure muscle memory. Sweat soaks through my sweater, dripping down my forehead in rivulets.

Domino must sense my exhaustion because he appears by my side, grabbing my left arm the second I start to sway. "Don't look up," he commands. "Breathe in through your nose. It's just a little further."

I marvel at the concern. Then I remember that Domino Valenciaga always has a motive. Craning my neck, I eye him through a haze of stinging sweat, searching for whatever his aim might be.

All I find is the same handsome face that's haunted me for so damn long. Like always, I'm unable to discern an ounce of emotion from it.

With renewed determination, I focus on walking, forcing one foot in front of the other.

Domino releases me as we finally approach the door. Shrugging off his sack, he seems to inspect the area. Up close, abandoned seems too kind a term for this structure. More like… Lost. A small sliver of the world passed over by time, leaving behind a weathered husk liable to collapse should the wind blow hard enough.

"It's going to storm," Domino remarks, casting a wary glance at the sky. I copy him, skeptical. To me, it seems like an endless blue with nothing to shield the sun.

"The rain will help cover our tracks," he adds. "But it will make it harder if it doesn't stop by tonight. Get in. We don't have long to prepare."

It's strange to hear him speak so openly. I'm exhausted enough to chalk it up to my brain hearing what it wants to hear. Seeing what it wants to see.

Like the searching look he sends my way before he reaches for the door. Rather than test the handle or retrieve a key from somewhere, he wrenches on a loose plank of wood that seems barely attached to the structure overall. It gives way in a cloud of reddish dirt, and I do a double take at what lies beneath it.

A pristine electronic keypad affixed to the wall doesn't seem possible in an area so remote. Even more shocking is how it comes to life as Domino taps a series of keys. With a subtle beeping sound, a decisive metallic *thud* echoes somewhere behind the door.

Domino finally tugs on the rusted door handle, and it opens, but the interior doesn't seem worthy of the heightened security. The wooden walls are so decrepit in places, slivers of the reddish landscape outside are visible—and yet it's stuffy, the air thick. So much for Domino's promise of rest as well. There doesn't seem to be any furniture to "rest" on, let alone supply a supposed desperate trek across the border.

Even so, Domino only hesitates to grab his bags before urging me inside with a jerk of his chin. Then he slams the door behind us both, and I half-expect it to fall off its hinges entirely.

"What is this place?" I ask.

"Move." He pushes past me and crouches, smoothing his hand along the dust-coated floor. Without warning, he curls his fingers around one of the floorboards and tugs.

In a cloud of dust, part of the floor gives way entirely—a trap door. Coughing, I peer into the gaping square space cut directly into the earth itself. Wooden steps lead deep underground—too far to even see where they end from here.

"Come on." Once again, Domino hefts both bags and descends the staircase first. An unsettling rattle issues from the wood every time his foot lands against it, and I hesitate, noting that the trapdoor at least seems capable of standing on its own.

Still, I take another glance at the rickety door we entered through. My foot twitches against the wood before I remember there is no way in hell I could outrun him.

As if catching wind of my rebellious thoughts, Domino calls from below. "If you want to eat, shower, and sleep, I suggest you follow me. Or hell, take your chances with sunburn and the rattlesnakes."

His relaxed tone is back again, and I think that—more than any other factor—is what finally spurs me into inching after him.

It's a long descent, extending for several yards into the earth. Devoid of any railing, I'm forced to trail my left hand against the wooden planks lining the stairwell, each one gritty and coated in dust. The deeper I go, the more my eyes adjust. In the absence of sunlight, faint illumination comes from up ahead—a lightbulb hanging from the ceiling at the base of the staircase.

Naked wiring snakes from it, crudely nailed to the wall, eventually leading to a haphazard arrangement of black devices that must be part of a generator. Presumably, it's also powering the electronic keypad outside.

"You must not be so eager to rest after all," Domino taunts from up ahead.

"What is this place?" I ask as I descend the bottommost step.

Here, the floors are concrete, and the artificial lighting casts a grayish glow. Like a crypt. Domino, lurking on the other side of another doorway, looks ghoulish, more zombie than man. He's already dropped his bags, approaching me with both hands at his sides.

"Lie down on the bed and wait for me," he commands before brusquely mounting the steps. To secure the trap door, I assume.

I hesitate, frozen mid-step, even as my muscles ache with exhaustion. "Bed" carries two drastically different connotations where he is concerned. A place to sleep—but also a tortuous arena where he can tie me down, drug me, or inflict a far worse torment.

I toy with the potential outcomes as his footsteps resonate from above. Apparently, he's doing way more than closing the trap door, and I try not to let myself imagine what. Instead, I finally inch forward, peering beyond the doorway he came from.

Shock blinds me to any previous apprehension I may have felt. At first, I assume I'm hallucinating. There's no way that all of this could fit beneath such a seemingly dilapidated shack.

This being a square room, sparsely furnished, but with a queen-sized bed in the far corner, what looks like a mini fridge against one wall, and a wooden desk piled high with computer equipment. The sheer amount gives the stack of generators way more context. In fact, I doubt they're even enough to fully power the array of monitors—at least four —each one displaying a different view.

The footage on the first monitor is all too familiar—it's this shack. There must be a camera outside, positioned to capture the surrounding area. The second monitor features a grainy image of a small, wooden room. Upstairs? I can even make out Domino, prowling with his back to me.

The view on the third monitor, however, excites me the most—a web browser. Could a place this remote have internet access? Eager to find out, I surge forward, placing my fingers on the keys.

The previous user already had a webpage maximized. A news story, it seems, documenting the urgent case of a missing woman. I barely recognize the smiling image of the creature headlining the article, her smile blinding, her makeup immaculate, her hair perfectly styled in a fresh blowout.

God, I was so pretty—the way a doll is. Artificially beautiful. My father raised this woman to preen brightly before the camera no matter what hell she was experiencing internally.

And, damn, I excelled at it.

Thunk! Domino's footsteps continue to beat against the floor above, snapping me from my pity party. Tearing my gaze from the picture, I read the article itself for any relevant details.

It's sparsely written, mentioning the restaurant, and a shootout, but I scan the entire document twice before I realize one glaring omission—there is no mention of Tristan Lucas, dead or alive. Odd. There's barely any acknowledgment of my father, either. Other than the fact that my abduction is under investigation, this account seems suspiciously sparse. Too clean.

Either Domino's been lying to me about everything from the start, or someone else is pulling the media's strings, tightly controlling what they can and can't reveal. Law enforcement? Obviously, they wouldn't want vital details of an ongoing investigation to leak.

My gut, however, is warning that there's far more to it. Someone with influence is desperately trying to sway the public's perception.

The prime suspect? My father, of course.

Though how much influence he could wield supposedly from a hospital bed is anyone's guess. If he were ever in the hospital, that is.

Now is as good a time as any to find out for myself. With a wary glance at the ceiling, I lash at the keyboard one-handed, typing the most relevant term I can think of.

Roy Pavalos

The first headline to populate confirms his fate: **Local politician Roy Pavalos currently in critical condition.** With bated breath, I skim the opening paragraph only to find that the author included no details as to his status beyond the title.

But I do discover a tidbit of information that Domino never bothered to tell me.

According to sources, the Pavalos couple was ambushed by unknown assailants near the international airport. Though currently under investigation, a judge recently approved the politician's weekend travel plans...

Despite the writer's flare, I know that statement is pure bullshit. Why would—seemingly on the eve of his indictment—law enforcement suddenly grant my father permission to get on a plane?

More importantly, why wouldn't he tell me if that were the case? I was out with Tristan, but I never even got a text or a warning phone call. My father wouldn't leave without me.

Unless…

I suck in a breath as the room begins spinning. Helpless, I grapple for the edge of the desk to right myself. In the process, I knock a stack of loose documents to the floor.

Absently, I stoop to gather them, scanning the topmost pages as I do. Tucked among the pile is a handwritten list composed of words I vaguely recognize. Towns? There are roughly twenty entries, written beside various dates within the past few months.

All but four have been crossed out in black ink.

I don't have the mental capacity to question why that might be as my vision blurs with stinging tears.

Domino was right all along.

And he must be anxious to gloat. I didn't even see him come in. I just know that his hand is the force latching onto my forearm, steering me backward.

"So damn stubborn," he snarls against my ear. "I told you to lie down."

I'm too weak to resist his strength. The second I'm on my feet, he shoves me back, but I land on a surprisingly soft surface that isn't the floor.

The bed, I presume. The ceiling above is blindly white—fresh. My nostrils flare, picking up the stench of wet paint lingering beneath Domino's musk. Unfairly, he still manages to smell enticing while drenched with sweat and after spending hours in the sun.

"What is this place?" I ask, startled by how thready my voice sounds. My entire body aches in varying degrees of agony, bordering on excruciating.

And yet, somehow, it's easy to overlook it all in favor of waiting for his reply. As long as he speaks, nothing beyond this room matters. Just what he breathes into existence.

"This... Is one sliver of territory unclaimed by either Jaguar or Mateo."

He's moving. I can see his form flickering toward the foot of the bed though I don't have the strength to lift my head enough to see him clearly. He grips my ankle, yanking off my shoes one by one. When his palm grazes the sole of my foot, I stiffen.

"W-What are you doing?"

He doesn't respond, seemingly intent on his hands. Persistent, he rubs the sensitive flesh on my heels, and the pain gradually blossoms into something resembling pleasure more.

At the back of my mind, I realize what he's doing—massaging me. The shock of that alone lulls me into a daze so dizzying that keeping up with his words is more strenuous than the walk here.

Territory. Jaguar...

"This is where I've been storing five years of secrets," he continues. His voice floats through my ears as he continues his ministrations. "About your mother. Your father. You. What I have here should be enough to placate any doubts you have. You chose me once. You need to do that again, and again from here on out. Do you hear me, Ada-Maria?"

My eyelids are too heavy to keep open for longer than seconds at a time as my brain sluggishly churns through every word he's said. Something about information. Something...

"Do you hear me?"

"Huh?" My voice comes out too soft. A whisper.

My brain resists any commands I send its way, shutting down my body one sense at a time. Soon my eyes seem closed for good, and the only sensation I'm aware of is the steady pressure of his fingers rubbing both of my feet, gently manipulating the muscle. It kills what little part of me is still alert that he can give me this. A tiny fraction of mercy amid a sea of agony. If I expected to find that sympathy reflected in his voice, I'm sorely mistaken.

"I'll take any mystery out of what I want from you, Ada," he tells me. "I want you on my side, no need for threats, or lies, or deception. I want you to hear the truth for yourself. See it with your own eyes. And when this is all over, I want you to choose me. Only me."

I'm too far gone to process his request accurately. I just know that some part of me reacts to the heat in his tone. And for a second, I think…

I think I almost believe that he means it.

Every single word.

CHAPTER FIVE

It feels like I've barely closed my eyes by the time I reopen them to a pale ceiling and bare cement walls. A blissful confusion lasts for a few seconds before I remember where I am—in a shack in the middle of nowhere, with the very man who plunged my life into chaos…

Domino.

I toy with the possibility that he's locked me here, choosing this place as my new prison. Would that outcome even surprise me?

I don't have long to ponder it. A heavy sigh resonates from somewhere close by, containing a hint of a raspy baritone I'd know anywhere. He hasn't left me yet.

I turn toward the sound, wincing as my muscles ache in protest. This mattress is new, with a hard layer of crinkly plastic beneath the thin sheets that loudly betrays any movement. By the time I haul myself upright, I expect to be greeted with a smirking, smug Domino.

Instead, the room I find is empty, bathed in the glow of artificial light. He's here, though. I can sense it in the primal part of me that quivers, catching his scent in the air. Sure enough, another low sigh draws my attention, and I stand, swaying to find my balance. A few stumbling steps bring me to a section of this place I have yet to explore.

Whoever built this strange bunker managed to include a bathroom. It's smaller than the two at his estate, outfitted with a shower stall large enough for one person. Squeezed in beside a toilet and sink looms a tall figure, his jeans undone, one leg braced against the toilet seat.

I stop, swaying unsteadily as my gaze roves over him with a greedy interest I can't deny. Even his ass is beautiful, composed of rippling muscle trapped beneath tanned skin. Surprisingly, I'm more drawn to what he's holding, poised expertly in one hand. Any previous illusion of his drug use is finally confirmed. I've literally caught him one-handed.

He must sense I'm here before I even inch closer. Loose black hair shrouds his gaze as he cocks his head to find me. In the same smooth motion, he drives the tip of a syringe into his thigh, pressing the plunger down. I flinch in sympathy—though, to his credit, he doesn't even wince as the amber liquid floods his muscles.

Instead, he raises an eyebrow, more surprised by my appearance. "You're awake."

"I'm awake," I manage to croak.

He turns back to his thigh, withdrawing the syringe and capping the needle with the built-in safety cover. The way he manipulates the instrument conveys more confidence than some of the doctors and nurses I'd been subjected to during my stints in and out of the hospital.

He's done this before—many, many times. Still, he manages to project his trademark Domino Valenciaga coolness as he disposes of the syringe with some sleight of hand.

"I thought you'd sleep a little longer," he adds, eyeing me from over his shoulder. I've been out for a while. His appearance reinforces that suspicion; he's changed, switching the denim shirt for a loose black one.

"Don't tell me you were intending to give me a dose next," I counter. Would I welcome another unasked-for high? The sad part is I don't know. Some sick, degenerate part of me might even crave the offer.

Not that he makes one. He lowers his leg, standing at his full height. As he refastens his jeans, those dark eyes rake me over, his head cocked. "Not now," he says cryptically. "We need to talk."

An understatement if there ever was one. "T-Talk?" I don't know how to process that word coming from him. It could honestly mean a milieu of things, ranging from benign to terrifying. To soothe my unease, I just shrug and rattle off the first distraction I think of. "I'm thirsty."

As if prepared for the request, Domino approaches me, his arm outstretched. I jump, before I realize just what he has—a bottle of water.

I grab it, draining the entire thing within seconds. I've barely finished swallowing when he shoves something else toward me—a rag.

"You should clean up, first," he suggests. "Then, I'll explain my terms, and we can go from there."

Terms. It sounds so clinical, a polite explanation for what he really has in mind. Another test. A new mind game.

"You sure are taking your time revealing your evidence," I croak.

Though do I really want to know the truth behind whatever mysteries he has up his sleeve?

"Come here." He crooks a finger for emphasis. When I don't move, he stalks closer and snatches my uninjured wrist, hauling me deeper within this narrow space. The first thing I notice is a blurred, filthy mirror displaying my image over its cracked glass.

No wonder he's being so cautious around me. I look like hell. Admittedly, not as bad as I feel I should, all things considered. The makeshift brace on my right wrist remains intact, though the visible flesh looks mottled and bruised. The sight alone is enough to illustrate just how drastically my life has changed within the past few weeks.

Gone is the beautiful woman featured in that article. In her place is a broken creature composed of wounds and ruined flesh.

But someone did their best to treat me while I was out. The signs are subtle, at first. A Band-Aid here, another there… That same person cleaned the skin around my many scrapes and bruises, taking care to treat every single one.

I swallow hard, forced to admit that Ines isn't here to blame. That leaves only one other suspect…

My eyes dart toward him, but he's already staring back. I bite my lip, caught off guard by the fleeting expression crossing his face. It's pensive. Curiosity makes that elusive green of his irises more unreadable than ever.

"Hold still." Before I can resist, he's behind me, already tugging my jeans down my hips. I hiss as he peels the denim from my sore, sweat-soaked limbs. I've barely stepped out of the legs when he spins me to face him and turns his focus to my sweater.

"Why?" I croak, my gaze on his fingers.

"You stink." His tone is harsh enough to counter the gentleness with which he frees my injured arm from a sleeve. "Once you've showered, I can focus without having to smell you."

He shoves me back, and I stumble into a crudely made wall composed of plastic sheeting.

"What about the brace?" I inspect it again, noting it's sturdy exterior.

"It should be waterproof," Domino explains, still blocking the only exit. "Try not to submerge it though. It should hold long enough to get you to Terra."

"I think I prefer the villa oasis as my prison," I say, facing him again.

His amused grunt comes as a shock, and I miss the moment he turns a dial affixed to the wall, activating the faucet. The water comes out startlingly cold, stealing my breath away. Instinctively, I jump to avoid it—only to run directly into the body that comes to block my path.

I freeze, registering the hard planes of muscle pressed against me. He feels so firm. So goddamn solid. So hot. His heat is a barrier against any chill, and some greedy part of me craves every ounce. My body's needs are separate from my brain, and not even logic can serve as a big enough deterrent. I hate myself for the first coherent observation that comes to mind—I would have given anything to have him this close to me just weeks ago.

To have his hands on my bare back, the thick fingers possessively cupping my spine. I'm delirious enough to seek comfort in his touch, but some aspects of him can never be ignored. Like the roughened callouses that scrape at my skin when he draws me closer. As if realizing what he's done, he pushes me back, meeting my gaze.

The water pelting us gradually heats up, feeding wafts of steam that obscure our surroundings. He seems larger this way, looming above me, blocking any escape.

"God, you can be so fucking convincing." One of his hands nudges my chin disapprovingly, and whatever spell held me captive snaps.

I hate this man. Every inch of him should repulse me to the core of my being. It's sick to fixate on his mouth with sudden longing. Maybe the walk here exhausted me to the point of insanity? Or…

"Did you drug me?" I blurt out, recalling how many times we've shared the same water bottle. Maybe the needle was just for show, an act timed for me to witness.

Jaguar hinted that he had a high tolerance when it came to narcotics. It makes sense. All that wine and now the water. Apparently, he can drink it all and remain unaffected by whatever drug he laced it with—something strong enough to knock me under every time. What the hell has he been through to develop such a high tolerance?

"Would it matter if I *did* drug you?" He's closer, his lips brushing my cheek as he reaches past me, snatching something from a metal rack hung around the showerhead. "You're still alive and able to function—"

"So are you," I rasp. With every passing second, more information is coming back to me. Namely, his whispered conversation with Luis. "You mock me for my past, when you're no better than an addict yourself."

He doesn't deny it outright—and that's the unsettling part. Instead, he cocks his head as if surprised by the comeback. "Even drugged, you're still my mouthy Ada-Maria."

My belly flips at his gritted tone, and another confession rips from my lips. "I used to wonder what it would feel like to be yours."

God, I couldn't fake the genuine pain in my voice if I wanted to.

His eyes narrow, but he recovers quickly enough, reassembling his stoic mask. "You *are* mine," he corrects, smoothing his palm along my lower back for emphasis.

His tone makes it sound far from romantic. To be owned by him is a punishment, a position no woman should desire.

Before I can reply, he palms my shoulder, guiding me beneath the spray, rag in hand. He's soaked within seconds, his damp hair clinging to his forehead, threatening to obscure those haunting eyes.

This twisted intimacy does something to my brain, melting what little common sense remains.

"I wanted you to love me." I'm not sure where the confession comes from. Maybe I was drugged after all, and I'm ascending another high.

I hope so. It would explain the frown tilting his beautiful mouth downward—I'm hallucinating, of course.

"Love," he echoes while dragging the rag across my chest. "I'm curious. What does that term even mean to Ada-Maria Pavalos?"

The dangerously low cadence of his voice, paired with his steady ministrations, lulls me into a daze. I *must* be drugged. It's the only explanation for why I'd find anything but pain lurking within his touch. I almost forget that he posed a question at all.

Until he nips my earlobe.

"Love," he bites out. "Does someone like you measure it in terms of wealth? How much money a man can throw your way? How expensive a car he drives?"

I choke back a laugh. Ironically, the Domino Valenciaga I knew, was none of those things, just a humble man who drove a battered blue truck. Yet, he seemed more appealing than a million Tristan Lucases.

"I never cared that you didn't have money," I admit, closing my eyes to block out his face.

It stings to admit just how little I do know about him. Where his newfound wealth has come from, for instance? An estate like his couldn't be bought overnight. For years, he must have maintained it from a distance, all while working for my family in Terra Rodea.

Not to mention this place. An underground hideout in the desert, powered by a mass of electric generators, isn't a cheap expense, I'm guessing.

"Money means secrets," I tell him, sucking in a breath as his fingers graze my ribcage instead of the cloth. Slowly, he traces a path up between my breasts. When he stops, I realize that he's roughly in the vicinity of my heart.

"Secrets mean lies… I thought you were above it all. That's one of the reasons why I was so drawn to you."

"One of the reasons?" he prompts.

"I thought you were different," I admit. "Not perfect. No knight in shining armor, but someone I could trust. A man who didn't give a damn about money or power. Someone normal. Someone—"

"A fantasy," he warns against my ear. "Can I blame you, though? For being so damn naïve? For a woman who grew up as you did, you sure have an inflated sense of morality."

He's right. All this time, I desired a man more skilled at lying and mind games than my father ever was.

"Don't mock me." I sound like a petulant child, but maybe I am.

He can joke about it now, but in retrospect, my naivety serves to highlight how little access I had to good men in general. I took any hint of kindness and ran with it, despite knowing full well the kind of work Domino did.

He was never a saint.

"At least now I know better," I tell him, squaring my chin. "You hate my father because you want to be him. You sneer at his methods, but you wouldn't mind being in his place, is that it? Money. Women. Influence. You're no better than the rest. A selfish bastard—"

"Selfish..." He mulls over the word choice. Then he cocks his head and... He laughs. The sound raises goosebumps despite the sweltering heat. "Ada, if I were being *selfish*, I would have ripped you to pieces and gladly washed my hands of you to the first monster who came calling next. Anything after—" He inhales, taking his time to decipher my scent. Then he sighs as if the flavor eludes him. "I've done to protect you. Speaking of Don Roy, as horrible as you think I am, I'm sure you've tasted his wrath for yourself. More than once. Tell me something—" His voice deepens in a way that triggers a wave of unease. It's too soft. "He whipped you. Why?"

I bite back the insult that immediately comes to mind. Attacking him won't get me anywhere. If he's offering answers, I'd be a fool to spurn him now.

"He whipped me for the same reasons you did. Because I dared to question him."

I hate this memory. It unfolds swiftly, sucking me under. I can recall the smell of the office he kept on the second floor of the house—a long, narrow room that overlooked the tennis courts and gardens. Bookshelves lined each wall, containing everything from works of Shakespeare to Chinese philosophers. I think he considered himself a great thinker. For a man like him to rise from nothing to a seat of power, I suppose he was.

He could see beyond the limits most men heeded. Kindness. Empathy. Fear.

Ruthlessness was a weapon he honed to perfection, and he wielded it against everyone. My mother, it seemed, had already been drained of everything by him. So he turned to me.

“I asked him one question,” I say, seeing that very moment replay like some horror movie—one I don’t even recognize the star of. “Why. That’s it. Why.”

And because of that “insolence,” I deserved to be punished. In the world of Roy Pavalos, violence trumped all other forms of communication. Words could be misconstrued, and mercy was a weakness. That wasn’t the first time he whipped me—nor was it the last.

But I distinctly remember the shift in him that I never noted before. His eyes had been colder, his upper lip curled from his teeth, his anger unbridled. In his gaze, I saw a darkness that haunts me still—a callous disregard.

As though he could have killed me easily and dumped my body beneath the tennis courts.

It’s that man who could have killed Pia Inglecias. It’s that man who Domino served so diligently. It’s that man I’ve devoted my adult life to—and not entirely out of fear, either.

Mainly…

I never wanted to see him look at me that way again. His approval was preferable, no matter how I had to debase myself. No matter the cost. I gladly paid it just to feel like I mattered to someone.

Despite the hell my father put me through, I couldn't face his rejection.

I still can't.

Domino exhales sharply, snapping me back to the present. "I didn't have the upbringing you did. My family wasn't rich, and I didn't have the luxury of being shipped off to a boarding school."

He exits the stall completely, and I assume he'll leave, which seems to be his mode of operation whenever the conversation turns to him. Instead, he settles both of his hands on my shoulders, spinning me so that my back is to him.

"I would have given anything for a mundane experience like that. To have a life, even under the purview of an overbearing father. I might have preferred that…"

The pain in his voice is so tangible I can feel it like a noose around my throat, every bit as restricting as his collar was. If I still doubted that he truly is Navid Inglecias, his hoarse retelling offers ironclad proof.

"The pity was one thing," he adds, while dragging the rag down my thighs. All this time, he's continued washing me. "I could handle that. The sympathetic looks. The concern from strangers my mother endured whenever she shuffled me to and from the hospital. It was the pain I found unbearable. Men like your father, they boast about overcoming adversity and hardship to get to where they are. Poverty. Neglect. But they never mention the agony that comes with physical weakness. Tell me, how did Pia describe my condition?"

I stiffen as his hands still against my spine. One by one, he flexes each digit as if testing his strength against me. How easy would it be for him to snap bone the way Jaguar did?

He rakes both hands down to my hips as if to answer my question. *Very* easy.

And I'm powerless against him.

"I want an answer, Ada-Maria."

"That… That you had a heart defect," I say, utilizing the term Pia herself used. She rarely spoke of her brother, but always referred to him with respect. I don't think she ever resented him. Not once.

"Defect," he echoes. "That's one way to put it. My cardiac output was a fraction of what it should have been for a boy my age. I could barely walk a few steps without getting winded. No running for me, and certainly no boarding school. As one of my doctors once remarked, it was a miracle that I functioned to the extent that I did."

His hands settle against my hips as I try to imagine him too weak to walk unassisted. It's almost unthinkable. Was his temper just as volatile then? Or maybe this rage is his way of making up for lost time.

"How did you get your heart?" I ask.

He sighs. "I'm getting there."

A wave of warmth sears my back, and I assume he's stepped forward, filling the mouth of the stall, and blocking out what little light reaches this corner. I'm in my own parallel world of shadow, ruled solely by him.

"I need you to understand what it felt like," he continues, his mouth grazing my earlobe as he speaks. At the same time, his fingers creep up my shoulders, inching toward my throat. "Beyond the weakness. That was just one aspect of it, but the other? It was the *pain*. Though my heart was beating, my organs felt constantly deprived of oxygen. Do you know what that does to your muscles? Your bones? I couldn't take a breath without feeling like I was suffocating."

His thumb nudges my windpipe for chilling emphasis.

"My body was in a perpetual state of agony," he continues. "You are no stranger to pain, Ada-Maria. I want you to picture the worst agony you've ever felt, and multiply that tenfold."

My broken wrist should be the paramount experience—but it isn't. Ironically, only one agony fits that description—*him*. Hearing him claim I meant nothing.

"Not a day went by that I didn't wish for death," he adds. "So I found an escape in whatever I could."

His voice paints a grim picture, and my chest tightens in understanding.

"Tell me," I prod.

"Morphine. Codeine. You name it, and they pumped it into my veins just to give me some semblance of peace—" His fingers leave my skin, only to sink through my hair. As if from miles away, I hear the slap of the rag hitting the floor. Then his breath drowns out everything but the steady spray of the water.

He's closer, entering the stall fully until I'm forced against the far wall. The air in my lungs escapes in a gasp. Helpless, I brace my good hand against the slick plastic shrouding us, painfully aware of every inch of him. From the wet fabric of his shirt against my back to the harshness of his jeans on my thighs. Every scrape rouses an ache inside I can't deny.

"I can't put into words what that feels like. To crave oblivion just to keep your fucking sanity. When even breathing hurts too much. It's an affliction that I always believed you'd need a small fucking heart to understand. So imagine my surprise when, almost a decade later, I looked at the face of a woman and saw that exact same pain."

It's pathetic to be ravaged by jealousy for a woman I've never met. Especially now, alone in his grasp, close enough to feel his heartbeat hammering through flesh and bone. My pulse surges to match his, each beat thundering like a hammer blow.

"This woman," he continues so hoarsely my own throat contracts in sympathy. "I saw myself reflected in her sad, gray eyes…"

He cups my chin, guiding me to look back at him. I don't know what unsettles me more—the heat in his tone? Or the way his free hand comes to graze my belly, palm first.

"You were so damn beautiful. So lost. In so much pain—the kind of agony few can understand. I knew then that I wasn't wrong for seeing you as more than Roy Pavalos' daughter. That you were worthy of…"

He trails off without finishing, and I can barely find the air to speak. "Worthy of what?"

He laughs darkly before confessing, "Of everything. But nothing could ever erase who you are at your core. The daughter of Roy Pavalos, a man who turned deception into an art form. You have no idea as to the depths of his cruelty, do you?"

He wrenches me to face him, swiping my hair back. From this angle, I have a clear view directly into those endless, greenish eyes. They're as unfathomable as ever.

Though wait…

A rare emotion peeks through for an instant—one that stirs painful recognition. I saw it the night I hurt my nose, and again when Ines informed him that Jaguar was on his way.

Of course, the first time was years ago, the night I hit rock bottom, and he came to save me.

"I'll show you if I have to," he warns, his voice low. Enhancing the ominous anticipation building in my belly. "So, you know exactly what you've been up against without even realizing it. Roy Pavalos never gave a damn about you. But I have. From the very start, I've always been focused on little Ada-Maria. I want you by my side willingly. I want you to help me finish what my sister started. And I want you to know why."

He's even closer, his body pressed against mine, his hands sliding downward…in between my thighs. I groan through clenched teeth as fire rips through me, unexpectedly hot. I'll never get over how my body reacts to him. As though he's electric and I'm a live wire greedily leeching from him whatever I can take. Anything to feel pulsing and sensitive.

Alive.

The feeling must be mutual because his mouth greedily feathers over my parted lips, searing them with the heat of his breath.

"I want you to know why I've spent five fucking years at your father's feet. I need you to understand the truth, and I need you to realize that trusting in me is your only choice."

"Why?" I whisper.

His mouth is so close I feel every twitch of his lips as he speaks. "Because, even at my own fucking detriment, I can't seem to stop trying to save you."

His next kiss robs my breath, my senses. All I can do is arch into him, letting him nudge my legs apart, all while taking care not to jar my injured arm. I marvel at the gentleness, though the look in his eyes is anything but. They glow hungrily, as if he wants nothing more than to devour me whole.

Body and soul.

"The things I've thought about doing to you…" He draws in a ragged inhale as what feels like the rugged tip of a nail continues to trace the delicate flesh at his mercy. I gasp, my head spinning.

Somehow, I still manage to choke out, "Like what?"

He uses his fingers to spread me apart, arousing sparks with every harsh brush. I'm on tiptoe, arching into him.

"*Like*, pinning you against the wall until you know who you belong to."

Eyes blazing, he inspects the brace—a glaring reminder of another man who dared to claim ownership of me. My attention, however, drifts beyond it, to the front of his pants, reduced to a bulging mass of strained denim.

My throat dampens, lips parting around a plea I'm not brave enough to voice.

But he knows me too well. One of his hands withdraws, leaving a chill behind as he grasps for the zipper of his fly. Slowly, he lowers it, as if intentionally ratcheting up the tension.

I'm dizzy when he finally wrestles himself free, letting the water christen the taut, angry flesh beneath. I've never seen someone so aroused.

I reach for him, brushing the tip of him with a trembling finger. The sound he makes guts me.

When I meet his gaze, I swear I hear something snap. I'm in his arms within a heartbeat, his body in between my legs. There is no warning, before he slams into me. To the hilt.

It burns. It aches. It's incredible. No man should feel this good, and this violent. His next thrust wrings a cry from my lips that he swallows with a brutal kiss before trailing his lips down to my shoulder.

"I thought I knew what pain was, before you," he murmurs against my throat. There is a coarseness in his voice I'm not used to hearing. My breathing hitches as I contemplate what it might be. Honesty? "But nothing compares to the agony of Ada-Maria Pavalos."

Pointed, his tongue traces the path of my pulse. Then lower, lathing my breast. The heat of his breath paired with the steady sensation of falling water is…

Maddening. It's all I can do to keep breathing as my thoughts scatter. I've had so many men in my lifetime. Too many.

But none have ever felt like this. Touched me like this. Spoken like this.

"You drive me mad; do you realize that?" His heavy lids reduce his eyes to blazing slits. Intense doesn't even begin to describe the feelings he arouses. "Mad—" He punctuates the grated admission with a hard thrust.

And another.

Another...

My orgasm hits like a freight train at full speed. No mercy. No concern for my injuries.

It's painful, drawn out by his still thrusting cock until all noise is wrung from me. Helpless, I sink my teeth into his shoulder and ride out the final, brutal climax.

Wave after wave.

CHAPTER SIX

My descent to earth is swift and brutal. In some ways, it confirms my worst suspicion—Domino Valenciaga is a drug, capable of packing a devastating withdrawal. Rehab won't be enough to escape him.

Perhaps I never will…

It doesn't help that this time feels different. Harsher. Probably because the shower isn't connected to a seemingly endless water supply like those at his estate. At some point, the spray becomes ice-cold before slowing to a mere trickle. Then sensation is a shock, clashing with the fire still burning within my skin. As my awareness of the rest of the room returns, I'm freezing—everywhere but the parts of me engulfed by a consuming heat.

At least, this is one high we both seem susceptible to. His breath scrapes my throat, each exhale ragged, though no such unsteadiness is reflected in his body. Firm, his weight pins me to the wall, his hands on my waist.

I lift my head, finding him staring down at me. Something flits across his gaze, too dangerous to inspect in full. Whatever it is, vanishes as he sighs, withdrawing from me.

"We should get ready to move," he says, shutting off the water before leaving the stall. By the time I follow him out, he's already readjusting his sodden jeans.

Watching him brings back the full brunt of what we've done—what I've been doing with him from the start. Telling myself I hate him, only to be swept under the second he shows a hint of vulnerability. Again, I've proven how easily I fall prey to his manipulation.

Shame floods my cheeks, warring with a fragile hope that the concern I saw in him was real—this time, anyway. To distract from it, I do the only thing I can—focus on the present.

"What is this place?" I ask, paying the bathroom closer attention. The door to the main space has been left open all this time, letting out what little steam managed to accumulate.

At a second glance, the layout is cramped, most likely designed for just one person. Everything, from the mattress to the bathroom, seems less than five years old. Not to mention the faint smell of fresh paint and the electronic equipment.

"This?" He leaves my line of sight only to return seconds later with a handful of fabric he tosses my way—the bedsheets. "Think of it as a safe house. Jaguar and Mateo have dozens between the two of them, on both sides of the border. This one, however, was claimed by Carlos Domingas right before he died. I'm one of a small few who even know its location."

"You've been busy despite role-playing as a bodyguard," I point out, struggling to wrap the makeshift towel around myself one-handed. "Buying an estate in the middle of nowhere. Doing business with Jaguar and Mateo on the side. It's a wonder you even had time to do my father's bidding."

He heads into the main room without giving me a reply. I follow him, noticing the various items strewn throughout the small space. One is a square black case that he stoops to open. After a moment of rummaging, he offers a handful of items to me. The first is a black long-sleeved shirt and another pair of jeans in my size.

I struggle to dress while biting back my questions. By the time I wrestle one foot into a pantleg, I can't hold them back anymore.

"I'm tired of being in the dark."

He goes rigid, still fixated on whatever is inside that case.

"Please…" Blinking rapidly, I eye the ceiling, trying to make sense of the tumult of emotions running through me. Confusion. Fear. Shame. Hope, maybe, mixed in among the rest, dinged and tarnished by everything he's put me through.

"You want my trust?" he asks, shifting to face me. In his hands is a small box and a metal instrument I recognize with a pinch of fear. Scissors. "Then trust *me.*"

He stands, prying the scissor blades apart. From this angle, I have a clearer view of the words printed on the box—brown hair dye.

Something Luis said comes back to me. *You think I didn't recognize the face that's plastered all over the news reports? If you want to buy yourself more time, I suggest you cut her hair, at least.*

When Domino reaches toward my face, I have a chilling suspicion as to what he intends.

Maybe I'm just too damn tired to resist.

I DON'T KNOW HOW MUCH TIME IT TAKES HIM TO finish. When he does, my hair is still wet, though utterly transformed by the whims of the man behind me. He steers me before the bathroom mirror, and I do a double take.

This woman is a stranger, her hair no longer than her shoulders and several shades darker. My eyes look enormous in contrast, filled with fear.

"Is this part of your plan?" I ask, observing his expression in the mirror. "Do you really think a haircut and dye job is a good enough disguise?"

"Look up." He curls his fingers beneath my chin, tilting it himself. Apparently satisfied by the result, he releases me, turning his attention to the clumps of shorn hair coating the floor.

"How many times do I need to tell you to trust me before you seriously consider it?" he asks.

I don't think he realizes how those words resonate.

"So I'm just supposed to quietly accept everything you've said like a good girl? Question nothing?"

My breathing hitches, heralding the tears that slip free. I swipe at them angrily with my good hand, hating myself for showing weakness in front of him.

Though, for once, he doesn't seem willing to gloat. His heat penetrates my skin like a knife, conveying patience I can't deny. In his shadow, I look so small. Helpless.

"I… I want to trust you," I admit.

Does that make me a fool? If so, it's too late to deny it now when my body still burns with the remnants of him, and his taste lingers on the tip of my tongue.

"I want to know the truth. About Pia. My father. Everything. If you really want my loyalty, then just… Just be the man I thought you were, because looking back? I don't think he was entirely a figment of my imagination, and if there's even a small hope of that, then tell me now. Give me something to cling to."

"Something to cling to." He laughs, and I brace myself for the reality that this is the choice he's made. To lie and obscure. To push me away.

Then he turns, fixing those searching eyes on me. In them, I can see him wrestling with both halves of himself, coming to some grudging agreement. "Fine. Ask away."

There's no mocking in his voice. He means it, and I don't dare hesitate. "Who is Luis? Where are you taking me? What is this place? And what do you want with Pia's body?"

His lip twitches into a shocking cross between a frown and a smirk. Then he sighs. "Like I said before, consider Luis an old family friend. He was your mother's doctor. For a few years before Roy turned against him."

"My mother?" I blink, trying to recall seeing that man before. Then I remember that I rarely accompanied her to those grim medical appointments.

Domino did.

It doesn't slip past me how hard this must be for him to finally lay some of his cards on the table. To let me in, even a fraction. Despite every instinct warning me to remain guarded, I sense some part of me soften anyway.

"Why is he helping you?" I ask.

"Mutual interests. As for where we're going? Back to Terra. I need whatever information Pia stole to use as an insurance policy against your father. But he was never the real reason why I was in Terra Rodea in the first place. Roy Pavalos was the target, but trust me when I say that I could have lived out the rest of my life without thinking of that bastard once."

"So fine," I say, licking my lips. "I'll play along. What was the catalyst, then? You just magically found Pia's diary and decided to go on a revenge crusade?"

"No." He looks down, his jaw clenched. "It's not quite that simple. The 'catalyst' was a person. Someone you know well, actually."

This, I assume, is the revelation he's been preparing me for since the start of the conversation. Am I ready for it? I don't know. An impending sense of dread urges me to reenter the main room. I cross to the bed, perching myself on the edge of it. When I do, he appears before me, and the dread solidifies into terror.

"Your mother," he says, casually confirming my suspicion in the most unexpected of ways. "Years ago, she contacted me out of the blue."

"You're lying," I blurt, but he isn't smirking for once. His expression is too damn stern, revealing a hint of something I don't trust at first. As the seconds tick by, it doesn't vanish—vulnerability?

"I thought it was a trap at first." He starts to pace, raking his hands through his wet hair. "Somehow, she figured out my identity and was doing her husband's dirty work. Roy has a habit of annually tracking down anyone he sees as a loose end and dispatching them before they have the chance to strike. Maybe he learned I was alive and my connection to Carlos Domingas?"

"How do you even know it was her?"

"Because she sent me this." He crosses over to the burlap sack I recognize from our trek here. From it, he takes a small object that he holds up for my inspection.

Pia's diary.

"H-How…" But it makes sense, after all. Who else could retrieve that journal, but someone close to my father?

"I didn't trust her motives," Domino admits, as if reading my mind. "So, I ignored her. I assume she felt desperate enough that she called me directly, and I recorded her. Do you want to hear it?"

"I…"

It's as if someone decided to tell me that the planet I've been living on my entire life isn't earth. In fact, I think I'd believe that over *this*.

That my mother invited a viper into our family, with the hopes of what?

I'm staring into space, but he must take my silence as an answer because when I blink, he's before me again, this time holding a black device in the palm of his hand. Its shape roughly resembles a toy I used to play with as a child—a tape recorder. Grainy and distorted, a soft voice issues from it, filling the room.

"...I know you have no reason to trust me." I recognize that beautiful cadence—and yet, it sounds so different from the soft murmur I know so well. That explains it, though. Domino was tricked. This woman wasn't Lia Pavalos.

But then she sighs, and recognition lances through my gut like a knife.

"I don't even want your trust," she continued. *"I want you to gain Roy's. The only way to stop him is from the inside, and I'm sure that you know firsthand exactly what he's capable of, Navid."*

Domino hits a button, halting the recording mid-stream. He's made his point.

"How... How did she even find you?" I choke out in a rasp.

For what seems like an eternity, he eyes the device in his grasp. Then he shrugs, raising his gaze to mine. "Because she was the one who arranged my heart transplant."

"How?"

He holds my stare for so long that I'm numb by the time he finally speaks. "By sending my mother to Carlos Domingas." He continues to pace, stroking the dark stubble on his chin with one hand, still holding the recorder in the other. "I still don't know the depths of her connection to him. She never told me, even after all this time, and I can't exactly ask him. What I'm sure is that Julian had no idea, which only furthers the mystery."

"Juan." The name springs to my lips before I fully recall how I know it. Juan Domingas, Jaguar's younger brother who supposedly died years ago. Horrified, I remember the taunt Jaguar liked to repeat toward Domino—*Little brother.*

"You have his heart," I croak. At least I've finally stumbled upon the missing piece of that mysterious puzzle.

"Kindly donated by the Domingas family," Domino says darkly. I don't glean much gratitude from his voice. Instead, I distinctly catch a raspy note of something that might be…pain?

"That story is beside the point. I found out later that my mother was sent to Carlos by none other than Lia Pavalos. But as far as I knew, she hated that bitch," he adds bluntly, his gaze fixed somewhere in the distance. After a long while, he shakes his head, eyeing the recorder again. "So I didn't believe Lia at face value. Not until I heard her speak." He raises the device higher and strikes play.

"I know you have no reason to trust me," my mother said. *"But to be frank, you're the only person I have left to turn to, so imagine how I feel."*

A man answered her, his deep baritone unmistakable. *"You have five seconds before I hang up."*

I gape at the current Domino. Hearing his past self when paired with the present, it's obvious how much colder he's become over the years. Back then, his voice still held a flicker of emotion. Anger—more than when he speaks to me.

"Fine, how about learning the truth about what happened to your little sister?" my mother suggested. *"Don't tell me that you believed a fifteen-year-old girl could disappear overnight without a trace?"*

"I mourned my sister a long time ago," the past Domino said. *"And I refuse to let anyone use her name to dredge up the past, especially not a Pavalos. We're done here—"*

"She's dead," my mother said, so quickly that static almost consumed her words. *"Did you come to that realization by now? She's dead. I don't know if Roy is directly responsible, but I'm sure he had a hand in it."*

Domino's silence reveals his answer better than words could.

"Why are you telling me this?"

"Because she was just one in a long line of victims. Victims of my husband and his blind ambition. But I'll spare you the false sympathy. I didn't contact you out of some misplaced sense of guilt, but I need someone with as much of a stake in this race as I have."

Watching Domino's expression now, I think I have a decent mirror into how he must have looked back then, grappling with the revelations my mother told him. Obviously, he came to the decision to trust her, at least within his five-second deadline, because he finally speaks.

"Why the hell would I trust anything you have to say?"

"Because at the end of this, we can both get what we want. An end to the empire of Roy Pavalos. Did you read the diary?"

"You mean the recollections of a schoolgirl you now claim was murdered?"

A pang of guilt shoots through me at the grit in his voice. I can't imagine the pain he must have felt having someone dangle the past over his head.

Though petty vengeance smothers the pity. My mother merely played him the same way he's been playing me—doling out information in snippets at a time.

But this isn't the woman I knew for the past twenty-five years of my life. I don't even recognize her.

"Do you want to know why I'm really calling you?" she asked Domino as the recording continues. *"I'm afraid. I've seen the damage my husband can leave in his wake. No longer can I watch him wreak havoc and pretend I don't see it."*

"Let me guess. You've had an epiphany?" Domino asked.

"Something like that," Lia replied just as coldly.

"You really want me to believe that you would turn against your own husband?"

"No," my mother said. *"I want you to believe that what I've learned is horrifying enough that I can't be a part of this anymore. I can't stay silent, and I can't watch my daughter be roped into this darkness without knowing that I did something to stop it."*

"What the hell are you talking about?" That irritated note is a trademark of the Domino I know, but my mother wasn't intimated by him.

"I'm talking about women—young girls—being sold to the highest bidder. I'm talking about a criminal enterprise in which my husband can kill, beat, or destroy anyone to cross his path simply because he feels like it. I'm talking about his henchmen who do things that would curl your toes—"

"Why would she ask you for help?" I interject.

Domino merely raises a finger to silence me, letting the recording play on.

"Again, why contact me?" he asked.

"Can you honestly tell me that you aren't the least bit curious as to what really happened to your sister?" Lia replied. *"What she might have found on Roy Pavalos to warrant murder? Have you really been able to live in peace all this time without knowing why? I certainly haven't been able to."*

"So then tell me what happened."

"I don't expect you to listen to me without evidence. For now, just know that I have the answers," Lia continued. *"This was the first call. I'll let you think over what I've said before I contact you again."*

"And what if I were to tell your husband about this?"

Her laughter was a shadow of the charming giggle I grew up hearing echo off the walls of our estate. *"He wouldn't believe you, even if you played this recording for him. I assume you were smart enough to capture this conversation, yes? Keep it for your records. I have nothing to hide."*

"Except your evidence," Domino pointed out.

The line must go dead because the next few seconds only contain a staticky silence.

"What evidence did she give you?" I croak, my mind racing.

He tosses the recorder back into the sack, but I can't resist the thought that there might be more on it that he didn't play.

My mind keeps circling back to how my mother phrased my relationship with my father—*I can't watch my daughter be roped into this darkness.* I've never heard that note of horror in her voice before. In fact, I've never heard her speak so openly to anyone. Envy colors my view as I cycle through every interaction I've witnessed between her and Domino Valenciaga. I mistook his concern for her out of kindness, but was there more to it?

"What was the nature of your relationship with her?" I demand outright.

He raises an eyebrow, shifting from guarded to amused in a heartbeat. "She gave me what I needed to join a reckless crusade against Roy Pavalos, if that's what you mean."

"And what was that?"

His eyes take on a faraway look as he says, "I don't know if you're ready to hear it."

"So you lie and obscure." I haul myself upright, aiming for the doorway. "Maybe I should take my chances with rattlesnakes and heat stroke—"

"Wait." His voice…

The rawness in it stops me in my tracks. Regardless, he grips my forearm, but there's no real force in the touch.

"Your mother told me that only one person held the answers. About what happened to Pia. What she stole and why. Everything."

"My father?" I ask, meeting his probing stare.

But the look on his face is anything but smug.

"No," he says carefully. "*You*."

CHAPTER SEVEN

"M-Me?" Every ounce of air leaves my lungs. I somehow manage to croak just two words. "You're lying."

Though why would he? My mother is dead so there's no point in trying to turn me against her. A smarter move would be to convince me to join his crusade against my father by painting him as a murderer. It's what he's done all along, after all.

But did he ever believe that?

Or all this time, was I the one he truly plotted against? I think back to the collar. The whip. Everything he's done since.

Those weren't random acts of violence.

It was retribution.

"You believed her…" I stagger, grasping for anything to keep me upright. I find it in a wall of strength that nearly knocks me off-balance, sturdy and impenetrable. At the same time, I cringe away from him. "Don't—"

"She loved you."

I flinch at his tone. He sounds so damn angry, as if he cares more about my perception of her than of himself.

"You killed her." Angrily, I push against his chest. Unsurprisingly, he doesn't budge.

"She only ever went against your father for *you*, but I'm not here to rehash some family drama. For the longest fucking time, I tried to hate you. I spent every waking moment trying to square the woman I saw with the creature I've had described to me. By Pia. By your mother…"

"And what kind of woman was that?" I ask, even though I already know the answer.

He seems to take his time compiling one, anyway, his lips pursed in concentration. Finally, he meets my gaze again. "The kind of woman who betrays her friends, does her father's dirty work, and sleeps with any man who flashes a bit of money her way."

It's a fair enough impression—but admitting that doesn't make hearing it sting any less.

Especially when I contrast his opinion of me with the one I'd always held of him. This supposed stranger who entered my life, was a blank slate. Someone with a fresh, untainted view of Terra Rodea. How stupid I'd been.

"So you believed them?"

"No," he says, catching me off guard. "But I don't think you can blame them, either."

"Oh really?"

"No. Because of *him*. Roy Pavalos taints everything he touches. You've lived in blissful ignorance of who he really is for twenty-five years. As cruel as you think I've been to you, I haven't even told you the half of it—but maybe I should pull the wool from your eyes—"

"I know exactly who my father is!" I succeed in wrenching from his grasp and continue to back away until my shoulders strike the wall beside the bed. But then I turn around, fumbling with the hem of my shirt, exposing my back to him. "I have the scars, remember? I know who he is..."

But I think I've always stopped myself from understanding just what he's capable of. No more.

"Stop stringing me along and tell me. If you want my trust, then this is your only chance to earn it. So spit it out." I turn to face him, but the look of disgust on his face is the last sight I expect.

"Let's start with your father," he says. "I've seen the cruelty he is capable of firsthand, and I'm telling you now—you don't know the half of it."

I swallow hard at the confidence in his tone. It's a dangerous emotion where he is concerned, typically displayed before he reveals some trick hidden up his sleeve. Like a collar, a whip, or the cruel, cold truth.

"I do know one thing," I admit. "That you killed for him."

"You do?" he counters, cocking an eyebrow. "Because you saw the bodies for yourself? Or because it was simply in my job description?"

Ironically, his "job description" was one of the many things about him that seemed so damn conflicting. As sick as that makes me, I used to obsess over the work he supposedly did for my father. It was puzzling. How could a man, seemingly noble enough to attend to a sick woman, be capable of all manner of horrific acts at my father's behest?

"I never cared," I lie. "But that just puts into perspective how much of a hypocrite you seem to be."

He raises an eyebrow, those lips set quizzically. He isn't angry. More… Curious. "Oh really? Think. Why would your mother seek me out in the first place? Why would she want me so damn close to him?"

I feel my brows furrow. "What are you saying? You deserve brownie points for faking your loyalty to him?"

"Not quite." His voice takes on that low, grated quality that wrings a shiver from me. "I couldn't put a wrench into all of his plans, mind you. But where I could, I carried out Don Roy's orders, just in ways he wouldn't expect."

"Are you claiming you never killed after all?"

"No, I did," he admits, and the look in his eye confirms that grim insinuation. "In self-defense mostly. Typically, I arranged for slightly different fates for his intended targets. I made a note of them all. Meticulously. That was what your mother tasked me with."

My eyes narrow as I recall the list I found earlier. The one that seemed coded with various names and locations. Did he leave that document there specifically for me to stumble upon?

I wouldn't put it past him. God, the man is infuriating. Groaning, I dig at my temple with my trembling left hand, trying to see through the maze of lies and half-truths he's been spinning all this time. In the end, I can't make sense of a damn one.

"He would have found out sooner or later," I counter, exasperated. "Especially if there were no bodies to show for those executions—"

"Oh, there were bodies. All mutilated beyond true recognition—but dental records and DNA could, of course, be faked. After all, I convinced you with a clever arrangement of barbeque and a few persuasive words, didn't I?"

And perhaps I can feel less like a fool for falling for his trick in the first place.

"So you've spent half a decade lying to me and everyone else. What an achievement. And to think, I used to admire you."

What I intend as an insult has a vastly different effect—he smiles in a beautiful display of white teeth. It doesn't reach his eyes, however. They gleam, containing the fragments of his signature fearsome rage. "Do you even know what it is a woman *should* admire in a man? You talk about loyalty, but what about patience? I've wanted the same woman for the past five years."

The intensity in his voice steals the breath from my lungs. Tortuously, he lets the silence linger as if to prove how little power I have when he's like this. Starkly honest, his gaze taking on that distant, impassive shade of green.

"I've studied this woman in and out," he adds, crossing his arms. "I gave her the benefit of the doubt despite every fucking thing pointing to the same conclusion. I don't live in a fantasy land, Ada. I trust only what I can see. What I can taste. What I can feel."

"And what did you feel?" My voice sounds so fragile in comparison to his. "It must not have been strong, because you were still able to hurt this woman. Abuse her in the worst way. Make her doubt everything. Unless you're speaking of Alexi."

"Then you haven't been paying attention." His voice takes on that low, grated quality again, raising goosebumps with every strained syllable. "I've tried to deny it. Believe when I say that I wish more than anything that I didn't give a damn about you."

"So why hurt me? Why lie to me? That's not caring. That's not respect. That's not..."

I shy from voicing this particular word. It sounds so melodramatic to say, all things considered. And yet, I wind up blurting it out anyway. "That's not love."

"I think it's been well established that we both don't know a damn thing about what that word truly means."

As if that makes it any better. As if that excuses what he's done to me and erases the painful past lingering between us. Like hell it does.

"Besides, if hurting someone isn't 'love,' then what does that say for your father?"

The bastard. I hate the way he can do this—how he takes joy in twisting my perceptions and corrupting the world around me.

"Don't bring him into this—"

"Why not?" He uncrosses his arms, keen to take on the challenge—but the look in his eye doesn't inspire the dread I'm used to feeling. It's different, a softer hue of greenish-brown. "My own father was a drunk who ran out on my mother when I was too young to even tie my shoes. He left her pregnant, with a job that could barely pay half of the bills. She was too busy trying to keep a roof over our heads to do much else. I grew up believing that love was expressed in smothered tears and fake smiles. You wallow in your misery as the daughter of a wealthy politician, but I can assure you that growing up in poverty isn't much better. My mother never whipped me, at least." He sighs, his lips pursed. "I might have preferred if she could. If she had some outlet."

"I don't think any parent should look to their child as an outlet of any kind." Horror seeps into my voice, too real to disguise.

The hard line of his jaw softens a fraction—but even that slight change is enough to transform him. For a second, he resembles the man I used to pine over—stoic and unreachable.

"You have a point," he says thickly. His eyes lose their guarded nature for a heartbeat—and I'm frozen, holding my breath. "And a man shouldn't look to the one woman he claims to love as a symbol of everything he hates—*son of a bitch*!"

His tone is whiplash, and I recoil as if struck. Then I realize that his gaze isn't aimed my way, but on the nearby computer screen. One look, and I see exactly what has him on edge.

A sleek black truck pulls into the frame, presumably from one of the cameras tracking movement toward the shack. It skids to a stop in a cloud of dust, and two men climb out, moving swiftly in our direction.

CHAPTER EIGHT

"God damn it, Luis," Domino snaps.

I picture the gray-haired man. Did he betray our location?

"What's going on?" I ask.

Turning to me, Domino jerks his chin toward the floor. "Finish getting dressed. Then stay here and stay quiet. Don't even breathe unless I tell you to."

I stare as he mounts the steps, slamming the trap door behind him. Swallowing hard, I look back at the computer monitor in time to catch the men approaching the door. In the same instant, Domino opens it to greet them.

"Ralph, Mick. This is an unexpected visit." His voice easily reaches through the earth and wood down to me.

"Mateo had a feeling you snuck into his territory unannounced," a male replies, his voice unfamiliar. "He'd like to have a word with you. Clear the air, so to speak."

"Oh, is that so?" Domino's voice deepens to the raspy baritone I know all too well. "Is he keeping tabs on me now?"

"What's a little surveillance, all in the name of friendship, Dom? He would like to 'rehash' the terms of your agreement. Considering that Jaguar's raising hell from here to the border, it's not like you have plenty of places to go. Speaking of Jaguar…are you alone?"

"Why wouldn't I be?"

"Because Jaguar seems to think that you went on the run with someone that you weren't supposed to. How did he put it? His 'merchandise'? Mateo was very interested in that aspect."

"If Mateo is so interested," Domino replies, "why didn't he come here himself?"

"What would the fun in that be?" the second man replies.

I can't make out much of them from the grainy camera footage, but one man is nearly as tall as Domino, while the other looks to be a foot shorter. Both wear loose-fitting shirts and jeans, with the shorter man sporting a backward baseball cap.

As they barge inside, I can't tell from Domino's posture whether he believes them to be friends or foes, but I notice that he stands protectively near the trap door leading to the lower level.

"Mateo doesn't want a fight here, Dom," the first man states. "Why not come quietly?"

"Come quietly," Domino murmurs. "That doesn't sound very 'friendly.'"

"Well, I don't think you have much of a choice, considering that Mateo isn't in the mood to take no for an answer, and Jaguar is out for blood. You think Mateo is the only one who figured out you'd be here? The bastard's crazy as fuck, but he sure ain't stupid. Now… Let's be *friends*."

Silence extends for seconds before Domino's shape flickers in the footage. A heartbeat later, his voice rings out.

"Ada-Maria." I hear the rattle of the trap door opening and the staircase creaking beneath his weight. I stiffen as he appears in the doorway, his expression shadowed.

"Get ready to head out." It seems like he's speaking to me, but I'm already dressed, my boots firmly tied.

When I start toward him, he raises a hand in a silent command. Then he approaches the sack, grabbing something that he slips into his pocket. When he returns to my side, he immediately presses an item against my palm.

"Keep this on you—" Warm, his lips nudge my ear as he whispers, "don't let them see it. Anyone so much as looks at you wrong, be ready to use it."

I swallow hard, registering the weight of the object he's given me. My only reference source is the much smaller utensil that I'd use to slice cucumbers—a knife.

"Hide it." Domino guides the blade into the pocket of my jeans. It's thin, conforming to my hip. I can't even see its shape through the denim.

"Come on." Impatient, he leads the way toward the staircase.

I hesitate, unable to tear my gaze from the computer monitor. Those men hoover near the trap door, and it hits me all at once that, yet again, I'm on another dangerous precipice. With Jaguar, I had at least some small level of buildup to go on.

"Ada Maria—"

"Coming." I step forward, keeping my injured arm to my chest as I mount each step. Days of isolation have made me overly sensitive. I smell these men before I even see them—musk and sweat and the spicy hint of tobacco.

"So this is the little missy causing all of the trouble," one of them growls as I reach the mouth of the trapdoor. For a second, Domino's bulk blocks my view, but when he moves, I'm faced with the two figures I witnessed on the camera footage in stark detail.

The shorter one is blond, his smile crooked, his brown eyes beady. Beside him stands the taller man, his hair a cropped black, his skin tan, and his eyes a rich, unreadable brown.

The taller man inclines his head. "Shall we?" He's the owner of the first voice I heard while down below.

"Lead the way," Domino commands, but he draws even closer to me.

I follow him outside, relieved to find that the setting sun robs the heat of its intensity. A rich, orange slashes the sky just above the horizon, tinging everything in a bloody scarlet.

The truck the men drove is parked just a few feet away, coated in a layer of reddish earth. Apparently, they weren't in the mood to take the scenic walk Domino and I did.

"Looks like you'll have to ride in the ass end, Dom," the shorter man says while the other claims the driver's side. "Though, we could make an exception for your friend. I'm sure I could find a seat for her." His gaze travels up and down my body.

"Not necessary," Domino says, possession radiating through his voice. "She stays with me. Unless Mateo gave you alternative instructions..."

The taller man laughs him off. "Easy, Dom. Have it your way."

Leveraging his weight against me, Domino easily steers me toward the back bed. It's covered in dust, with only a low guardrail and a hatch to keep us from falling out. As we near it, the engine roars to life, revving menacingly.

"Here—" Domino grips my waist, giving me enough of a boost to climb up one-handed.

Swiftly, he settles beside me. At the same moment, the truck lurches over the uneven ground. Somehow, Domino manages to wrench the tailgate shut as the vehicle picks up speed. The only reason I don't go flying is because he slings his arm over my shoulders next, riveting me to his side.

"Buckle up!" one of the men shouts from the front seat.

Domino's expression is rigid, his eyes fixed on the rapidly receding shack.

"Don't trust them." His voice invades my ear, resonating deeper than the roar of the engine. In this case, I'm inclined to take him up on that advice.

We're moving recklessly across the landscape, seemingly with no clear direction. Up ahead, the moon is a faint circle of silver against a darkening sky while the sun still makes its final stand in a vibrant display of color.

In this moment, the inhospitable environment seems beautiful—a lovely contrast to the urgency Domino barely manages to suppress. His pulse is surging, spurring mine on.

Holding his stare, I ask, "Where are they taking us?"

He frowns, processing the question. When he finally lowers his mouth near my jaw, the wooden shack is no longer in sight.

"To Mateo. He controls the drug trade in this region. In terms of temperament, he's cut from the same cloth as Julian, though slightly more reasonable."

I recognize the note of caution in his voice. He speaks of my father the same way.

"What does he want?"

"He'll want to assert himself if he thinks he has my balls in a vice," he adds gruffly. "Just follow my lead and keep a clear head. He feeds off making people squirm."

"How did he find us?"

"Luis," Domino says grimly. "The bastard must have made a deal."

It's addictive, hearing him speak so freely. Amid the uncertainty, I'm reckless enough to push this brief window as far as I can.

"How did you meet him?"

Whether I mean Jaguar or Mateo, I'm not sure. Perhaps both, and I wait anxiously for whatever reply he's willing to offer. He claimed my mother played a role. I need to know more.

Suddenly, the truck picks up speed, sending the wind rushing past my head, whipping my hair into a frenzy. The chaotic noise provides cover for Domino to find my ear again and speak without the risk of being overheard.

"You already know part of the story," he points out. "Your mother meddled in my life to arrange a life-saving transplant. Maybe you should think from *that* perspective. How would she know men like Carlos Domingas?"

He's bringing this up for a reason. Perhaps not just to taunt me.

"You love to speak in riddles. Don't tell me my mother taught you that as well?"

"No." He adjusts his position, spreading out one leg over the dusty flatbed while keeping the other braced against the sidewall.

"As it turns out, you get a taste for various hobbies when you've spent the first half of your life on mandatory bed rest."

A chill washes over me. There's something so murky about his past, even though I knew everything there was to know about his sister.

Almost everything.

To think that there was a whole part of her life—a whole person—that I barely had knowledge of. Someone who, a decade later, has dominated my world in various ways. The shift is karmic in a sense, everything coming full circle.

But where will it finally end?

"Tell me more," I plead. "About your life with the Domingas family."

If it bothers him to continue this tale in the back of a truck, he doesn't show it.

"From what I've heard, Juan wasn't quite as charismatic as Jaguar. Supposedly, he was Carlos' favorite, the one he never believed was cut out to fit in his world. Too soft-hearted. Too weak. He was only nineteen when he died, but the circumstances were cloudy at best. I just know that they found him collapsed one day, and he never regained consciousness."

"So Carlos offered you his heart?"

It sounds odd to me, though I come from a world where men hoard everything from money to women selfishly. If one of my brothers were in the same position, I'm positive my father would rather let him die than relinquish a part of his precious Pavalos bloodline to anyone.

Would my mother do the same?

My memories of Lia feel as fragile as broken glass, far too sharp and numerous to ever put back together.

I picture her, beautiful with a delicate face, wide blue eyes, and gently curling hair in the same blond shade as mine. We were never similar in appearance or personality. I was curvy and cripplingly shy as a teenager, while she seemed born thin, and tall with a breathtaking beauty that didn't require a surgeon and makeup to achieve.

All in all, she was the shining example of my father's warped version of what family should be—meek, quiet fealty.

I always believed her innocent of my father's machinations, the humbling factor to his brash public persona—but I was dead wrong. All along, she was just as cunning.

"Carlos Domingas never offered a damn thing to anyone," Domino says, snapping me back to the present.

This area seems even dustier, and I'm coughing, jerking with every jolting lurch of the truck. From inside the cabin, I can hear the faint pulse of rock music, adding a strange contrast to the intimacy of this conversation.

"Then why?" I ask.

"You need to understand how the Domingases see the world. How they view their family and what it means to them. For Juan and Julian, there was no other reality than their father's empire. No talk of college or getting a job outside of the family business. The Domingas realm was their beginning and their end. Close-knit doesn't even begin to describe it. So, no, Carlos didn't just give me his son's heart. In effect… I merely took Juan's place. I became him."

CHAPTER NINE

He makes it sound more macabre than a symbolic acceptance, but I choke back my horror and listen.

"My mother had no idea what she signed me up for. Not that it would have changed her mind knowing the alternative."

His eyes are stormier than ever, fixed on the darkening horizon. What little sunlight remains is quickly snuffed out by threads of indigo and violet. Darkness rapidly consumes, and the car's taillights ignite the earth with a reddish tint that resembles hellfire.

"What happened?" I ask him.

He inclines his head, gripping me tighter as the truck lurches at an even higher speed.

"What happened is that I made a deal to stay alive. But at what cost? I didn't just accept a donation from Juan Domingas—for all intents and purposes, I became him, with all the same expectations as if I had been born into the Domingas clan. My past identity didn't matter to them. Carlos stripped me of everything I used to be and molded me into who he wanted. Looking back, I can't blame him, not fully. Who would want to lose a son if you could gain another? The only problem was that I was not Juan, not that it mattered to him. Julian, on the other hand…"

He tenses in the way he does only when he speaks of Jaguar. I once suspected that the animosity between them went beyond their little game with me in the middle—and I was right. It's far more personal than that.

"Julian couldn't accept that his brother was dead. To hear him tell it, Juan was a saint, a perfect soul. Innocent. Not a threat to him. But me? I was the opposite of that."

He laughs darkly.

"How?" I ask.

"Let's just say that Julian wasn't used to fighting for his spot. Suddenly, he wasn't the heir apparent, destined to rule after his father. But jealousy is only part of it. That bastard loves owning people, literally and figuratively. And if he thought I wanted you? Not only would you be a useful tool to destroy Roy Pavalos—the bastard he believes killed his father—but you would double as a convenient means through which he could control *me*."

I nearly choke as I remember something Jaguar said.

"If I were to fuck you here and now, plant my seed in that sexy little body. My child would make you mine in a way you could

never escape. Both of you would be my family. Forever and always..."

At the time, I told myself that it was his way of trying to unnerve me. But what if it wasn't a taunt, but a promise.

One big happy family.

"I never planned on selling you to him," Domino adds. "Not once." I feel his arm tense around me as if he expects me to pull away. Maybe I should.

Despite everything he's done, it still stings to hear him discuss my fate so casually. I can't reconcile that with the man who lurked within my line of sight for five years. The stoic figure I used to watch in the dark. The one constant I used as a crutch to get through the hell my life had become.

I can't see him as the monster who pledged me to a future no different than the one I escaped at my father's beck and call. I could glorify that past if I wanted to. Tell myself that I was only doing what any dutiful daughter would. That selling myself was *my* choice.

My mother thought so. The more time passes since hearing that recording, the more it stings, clashing with the part of me aching in mourning for her.

"How did my mother know Carlos Domingas?" I ask, returning to his original dare.

Domino sighs.

"Tell me!" Genuine desperation seeps into my voice. "She led you to a man you describe as a monster. How would she know him? How could she turn on my father like that? And—"

I break off, aware that I'm shouting, but I finish that statement internally anyway.

And how could she just abandon me?

"Your mother loved you."

"Did she?" This is the second time he's insisted that, taking up for her in a way he's never done for anyone else. Not my father. Not me. Not even Pia.

I don't know why it irritates me as much as it does. Doubt sneaks into my skull, arousing a million dangerous thoughts. Like the suspicion that his relationship with Lia Pavalos was far, far closer than he led me to believe.

How ironic would that be? Once my father's trusted right-hand man, he seduced not only his daughter, but his third wife, right under his nose.

"Did she know?" I ask him softly. There's no need to specify what I mean, and my heart tenses up in grim anticipation of the answer.

"Did she know about the plot your father hatched?"

Domino must take joy in spelling it out so clearly, but when I glance up at his expression, smugness isn't what I find. His eyes are narrowed, his jaw thoughtfully tilted. Every bit of the calculating bodyguard he pretended to be is on full display. No wonder my father was fooled by him.

"Yes," he admits, "she did."

My eyes burn. After all the pain I've been through during this nightmare, I would have thought that nothing could hurt more than his torment.

I was wrong.

"Which," Domino adds as my thoughts begin to spiral with betrayal, "is why she begged me to intervene and save your life. That's why she volunteered to lure your father into a trap despite knowing the risk."

A trap…

"The airport?" I ask. "She lured him there?"

"And she didn't hesitate. No matter how hard I tried to talk her out of it. So yes… Ada-Maria, she did love you. More than you will ever know."

The whiplash of these opposing emotions is enough to drive me insane. I think it does, actually. My perception of the universe shatters, and for a split second, I'm almost grateful to Domino Valenciaga.

But therein lies another harsh reality that his words lay bare.

"Why couldn't she tell me any of this herself?"

"Look at me." He brushes his thumb along my lip until I comply. "Put yourself in her shoes. She was married to a monster who corrupted her entire world in his image, even her own child. Don't deny that your father molded you under his thumb. You would have jumped off a cliff if he told you to."

I try to wrench out of his grasp, but he holds fast, forcing me to admit the truth that we both know.

If my father told me to jump in any context, I would only pause long enough to ask him how high. It feels so strange to reconcile that. These past few days alone, I've been able to convince myself that his hold over me wasn't as resolute as it was. That I always had some autonomy in the things I did and said. That I was the same Ada-Maria beneath the sex appeal and carefully cultivated image.

I was lying to myself, of course.

I squeeze my eyes shut against the threat of tears to no avail. They fall regardless as I recall the person I was leading up to my dinner with Tristan.

I wasn't the soulless monster my mother seemed to think I was.

It was worse than that. I was like a bird locked within a cage outfitted with barbed wire. I could tell myself that it wasn't my fault—that I never meant to cause the people around me pain.

Another lie.

After Pia went missing, I was the one who climbed into the prison my father built and gladly locked the door. It wasn't hard molding myself to his influence and becoming the perfect soldier used to further his aims.

It was easy, and his praise outweighed any doubt, comparable to whatever drug I happened to be on at the time. I never had to consciously take the blame for anything I'd done, because deep down, I always knew that I could blame him.

"How did you do it? How did you work for my father all this time? Did you use the drugs to dull your conscience?" I demand, scanning the planes of Domino's face. I want to see it—the same insecurities I feel, chewing at his sense of self-worth, making him feel hollow. I'm not the only one with a bad habit for pills—he's just far better at hiding it.

"Dom-Dom isn't like the rest of us," Jaguar told me on the balcony of Domino's estate. *"He has a much higher tolerance to most benzos, opiates, and the like. It would take a hefty amount to down someone like him. I'm sure he told you all about his tragic backstory."*

"One day, I'll tell you that story," he muses, and the ice in his tone feels like a door slamming shut. Our unfettered conversation is over, and the quiet, cold Domino has returned, glowering at the horizon with a vague expression I can't get a read on. Is it regretful? Or resigned.

"But now, I'll tell you what you need to know to survive. Keep that knife within reach always. Stay as close to me as you possibly can—Mateo will most likely try to separate us. See if you can keep that from happening. If not, the second you can, break away and head for the desert. Keep running no matter what. I'll find you. Do you understand?"

"You always change the subject when the topic turns to you." Rightfully, I'm irritated, but I have enough sense to still pick up on the warning in his tone. This isn't a mind game, I suspect.

Swallowing hard, I eye my injured arm and wonder what else Domino and his associates have in store.

"We're almost there," Domino warns before I can decide on an answer. "Get ready."

I follow the line of his gaze to a ridge jutting from the earth. Even in the semi-darkness, something about it draws attention. Perhaps it's the faint tendrils of light emanating from the base, slightly too bright to be moonlight. Kicking up a cloud of dust in its wake, the truck lurches suddenly to the left, veering toward the natural structure.

"Mateo is reasonable for the most part," Domino adds, continuing my haphazard history lesson on his enemies and allies. "But he's impulsive and prone to outbursts when he feels cornered. Jaguar must be bearing down hard on his ass for him to risk confronting me directly."

I can hear the irritation in his voice. He's on edge, but not for the reason I think I might assume at first glance. He's not afraid of Mateo, as much as he's worried about the lost time.

And he should be. A hospital can only hold a fully conscious and vindictive Roy Pavalos for so long. It's just a matter of time before he comes after any perceived enemy, guns blazing. Whenever I try to picture what he might do to someone like Domino who dared to betray him in such a way…

Domino might find himself being served on a plate, much in the same way he pretended to serve my father to me.

"Don't worry." His voice slips into my ear, and for a second, I wonder if he's truly read my mind. "This little hiccup will only delay my plans for you, nothing more. Whether or not it kills me, I will get you to Terra—"

"Get ready, Dommy Boy!" one of the men calls from upfront. "It looks like Daddy's home!" Raucous laughter gives the statement a sinister tilt.

Domino rises into a crouch, positioning himself near the exit. The closer we come, the easier it is to make out more details of this location. Tucked within the ridge's shadow is a square structure, much larger than the shack he brought me to.

I strain my eyes to make out a line of what looks like barbed wire fencing sealing off a narrow perimeter. Dark shapes flicker in the shadows, and I can finally identify the faint glimmers of light—flashlights.

For all their bravado, the men in the truck fall silent as we near the fortified barrier where a large metal gate bars access to an earthen road.

A man stands behind it, rattling a series of chains that clang menacingly.

"Looks like the boss is feeling feisty tonight," he calls, his voice gruff. "I suggest y'all don't keep him waiting."

"You hear that Dommy Boy?" one of the men upfront shouts. "I don't think Mateo's gonna be very forgiving of the fact that you've left him high and dry after all."

If the taunts affect Domino, I can't tell. He projects the same stoic calm, his eyes fixed on the gate and the figures moving beyond. I count at least six men roaming nearby.

From here, I can only make out the glint of what might be a square, one-story building—one with no windows. As the truck rolls along, we pass one of the men on patrol, flashlight in hand. The brief amount of illumination is more than enough to make out the massive gun slung across his back.

I suck in a breath, inching closer to Domino. I've never seen a weapon like that one up close. It looks military grade, and I suspect that most, if not all, of the men scattered throughout this fenced-in landscape, are carrying something similar.

Suddenly, the truck rolls to a complete stop.

"Well, Dommy, this is where we leave you." The tall man climbs from the driver's seat, leaving us parked in the middle of the fenced-in area.

Behind us, the gate slams shut, and a metallic clang makes me suspect the man we passed is using those chains to bolt it.

What is this place?

I remember what Domino said about his shack and wonder if the same method applies to this area. A stash house for the cartels before they smuggle their illegal goods over the border.

But what kind of smuggled goods would need this level of security or this much space?

I don't think I want to know.

When Domino places his hand on my shoulder, I let him guide me to the back of the truck. Grunting, he climbs out first in a fluid display of grace before reaching up for me. His hands land over my waist, slipping beneath the hem of my shirt to graze the flesh of my belly. I suck in a breath, too startled to resist as he easily lifts me down to him.

"Stay close." His lips nudge my ear as the two men circle around to meet us.

"Oh, one more thing, Dommy," the taller man says as his eyes slither in my direction. "Mateo would like to see you alone. No witnesses." His coarse laugh does little to soften the hostility lurking behind his thin smile. "Don't worry, though. Mick and I will be more than happy to entertain your little friend while you're busy—"

"She stays with me." Domino doesn't even raise his voice, but I feel goosebumps come to life over every inch of my exposed skin.

His stance is electric, his eyes gleaming in the glow of a passing flashlight. The second it darts away, he's a monster composed entirely of shadow, and—despite everything he's done—I never realized how intimidating he can be, based on his sheer size alone. The man is all bulk, and Mick, the shorter of the two, has the sense to take a hasty step back.

"Let's not cause a scene here, Dommy," the taller man warns, still grinning. I don't miss how his right hand falls to the front pocket of his pants though, and I can clearly envision him concealing some kind of weapon there. "Play nice. Boss' rules—no toys inside."

"She stays with me. I suggest you make an exception to the rule, Ralph."

The man's eyes narrow, his smile falling flat. "Listen here, you little bitch—"

"Enough!" A louder voice rings out across the clearing, and I whip my head toward it, finding a man standing in a rectangular doorway cut into the building. Orange light spills out behind him, illuminating his slender build and the rich ebony hue of his skin.

"Let them in," he demands, whirling on his heel to venture deeper inside. Booming, his voice easily reaches us. "I don't have time to clean up a mess, and I'd rather see her for myself. The little bitch who has Julian Domingas breathing down my fucking neck. But I'll tell you this, Domino—you so much as blink in a way I don't like, and I'll give my men the order to shoot you *and* your whore. Understood?"

"Damn," Ralph mutters under his breath. Hissing, he spits onto the earth, inches from Domino's feet. "Looks like you were just saved by the bell, boy."

"Likewise," Domino replies coldly. His grip on me tightens as he heads toward the doorway, and I scramble to catch up.

"We'll be here waiting, just in case Mateo changes his mind," the man with the raspier voice, Mick, calls out. "Or in case we need to clean up a mess after all."

CHAPTER TEN

I suppress a shudder while taking in as much of the building as I can.

Cut into the metal siding is a rigid door swung open to reveal a narrow room with an alarmingly low ceiling. Domino has to bow his head just to clear the doorframe, and he only has a few inches of space remaining once he stands upright.

The floor is dirt-streaked concrete that I highly doubt has ever seen a mop in its lifetime. Naked metal forms the walls, and the slightest noises echo, amplified times a million. I'm mocked by the frantic cadence of my own breathing, along with the steadier, deeper exhalations of the man beside me.

A long folding table cuts the room in half, flanked by an array of rusted metal chairs. At the far end of the table stands a man nowhere near as tall as Domino, but with a slender frame and confident build that gives him a similar allure. He's beautiful too, with large brown eyes set into a face composed of stern features and a chiseled jaw.

I think back to the days my mother would drag me to mass with her, and I'd eye the frescos on the walls out of sheer boredom. Some of them displayed breathtaking images of cherubs with soulless eyes, so real I expected them to blink.

This man looks like he stepped out of one of those paintings, leaving his wings behind.

"Mateo," Domino says, dashing any mystery of his identity. "I can't say I was expecting to pop in for a visit."

"Domino." Mateo smiles. "That's because I didn't expect to have Jaguar up my ass accusing me of betrayal, now did I?"

Whereas Jaguar gave off rough, unpredictable energy much like his feline namesake, Mateo is far harder to read. An animal comparison for him might be a serpentine creature. A sly, cunning snake.

"You weren't supposed to make your move for another three damn days. Should I inform you what that means?" He extends his hand, all five fingers erect. "It means that I didn't have the fucking time to get my men into place—" he lowers a finger, leaving four remaining. "*And,* I didn't finish the fucking passports you asked for. No wonder your little doctor friend came crawling to me, begging for my protection."

His upper lip twitches as if fighting a smile. It's as if he expects Domino to react. When he doesn't, he shrugs, three fingers held high.

"I've lost three days of running my operation in peace. And, finally, Domino? I've lost my patience dealing with you and that psycho at your back. You've caused quite the shitstorm, and my only question now is..."

He palms the table with both hands, leaning over it. The metal squeals in protest of his weight, shifting back and forth on wobbling legs.

"How the hell do you plan to make it up to me?"

Before Domino can even open his mouth, he raises an admonishing finger.

"Trick question—you can't. It's over, Domino. It's all gone to fucking shit. Jaguar is less than twelve hours behind you; did you know that? You'll be lucky if he doesn't send his little gang crashing through the gates any minute. How the hell could you fuck this up?"

"Julian is impulsive," Domino explains, his voice level. "You know that. You also knew that trying to predict him at all was a losing game. I warned you—"

"And I warned you that what you wanted wasn't easy to come by," Mateo spits back. "I can't just conjure false credentials and safe passage overnight, Domino."

"No. But you could have your contacts draft fake papers in less than an hour if you wanted to. You purposefully drew this out in a bid to play the long game and milk Julian before you made your move against him. That was your mistake."

Mateo scoffs, his brows drawn together. "No. I think my *mistake* was getting in the middle of your sibling rivalry in the first fucking place. I had a shipment planned for tonight—a big one. Thanks to you, Jaguar won't let anything leave my compound that isn't your head on a bloody stake. I miss this delivery, I miss my money, and I'm sure you wouldn't want that, would you? Of course not."

"Should I hazard a guess as to what you're transporting that could be that time sensitive?"

"Don't play coy with me." Mateo's voice loses the polished edge. "Don't pretend like you didn't know the nature of my business before you roped me into your plan to circumvent Pavalos."

"And I warned you that I won't ever come near your 'business.' We had an agreement between us, and that didn't include being your errand boy."

Mateo's smile widens. "Ah, I see you've already jumped to a conclusion about how you can graciously solve the problem you created for me. There is another solution, of course—" He turns his eyes on me, and the allegory of devil and angel is starker than ever. "Everyone from the Feds, to Pavalos' proxies, are pissing themselves to get their hands on her, should she happen to be alive. Ada-Maria. Last I heard, the bounty for any information surpassed half a million, and I'm sure it will climb by the day. That's a lovely, tidy sum to more than clear up this misunderstanding between us."

My breath catches at the implication. My father is looking for me.

If he's willing to pay that much money even for information, then there's no way he would throw me to the wolves the way Domino claimed. Right?

I eye the figure in question, but I can't gauge a read on him —though his motives take a back seat to the predatory greed in Mateo's gaze.

"What's stopping me from putting a bullet in your brain and taking her for myself?" Mateo asks.

"I can think of several reasons," Domino replies. "I'll settle with just one, though—within the time it takes me to bleed out, Jaguar will already be at your throat, ready to take over your entire little enterprise. You know it as well, which is why you didn't have Mick and Ralph do your dirty work the second they found me. To go against Jaguar, you need tact, which you frankly don't have."

"You think you're the only one who knows how little Jagger's brain works?" Mateo counters. "Give the bastard a pretty woman to stick his dick into, and he'll be too distracted to give a damn about anything, at least for a few hours. I've been dealing with him long before you came along, Domino. And while you were up Roy Pavalos' ass for the past five years, who do you think had to wrangle Julian's ego on a daily basis?"

"And who do you think still kept him on a leash, despite being up Roy Pavalos' ass for the past five years? Convince yourself that you can take him on alone if you want to. Leave me out of it. As for her…" Domino's upper lip coils back from his teeth for a heartbeat before he reassembles his mask. "Threaten her in front of me again, and you won't have only Jaguar to contend with."

"Brava!" Mateo throws his head back and claps as he circles toward our end of the table. He moves with easy grace, lighter on his feet than Domino could ever be.

Up close, he reminds me of the models I mingled with at social events, beautiful and lithe, bred to be ogled rather than fight.

Most wouldn't consider my father intimidating at first glance, either. He isn't beefy like my uncle Rodrigo, and his charming grin softened the planes of his face. If I didn't know him, I'd see the same fatherly figure most in the city did.

They never witnessed his temper unbridled like wildfire, burning anything within its reach. Or heard the low baritone that could make the insane seem convincing. Doable.

I just need you to get close to him, Ada-Maria. That's it. Close enough to teach the lying bastard a lesson. Prove your loyalty to me. To this family. Don't you give a damn about anything beyond yourself?

My father's unassuming demeanor shielded the monster lurking beneath, capable of any and everything. This Mateo must be cut from the same cloth, just as dangerous.

"Ada-Maria Pavalos in the flesh." I startle from my thoughts as a warm hand captures my chin, lifting it.

My nostrils wrinkle at his scent. I'd expected something delicate, like perfume. Not the acrid stench of cigarettes and beer.

"She's sexy; I will give you that. *Despite* your shitty attempt at a makeover," Mateo adds, raising an eyebrow. "But I've known you long enough to sense that pussy isn't what gets your heart pumping. No, Dom, I don't think it is." He strokes along my jaw and shrugs. "Who knows what secrets lurk inside this pretty skull. That's the real draw for you, I'm sure. Rumor has it Roy kept her close and fed her dirt on allies and enemies alike. Why, Ada-Maria here is a literal fucking encyclopedia on the political intrigue of Terra Rodea. Some men would pay a pretty penny to discover just what those secrets might be."

"And you won't ever get the chance to find out." Domino grips my shoulder, drawing me closer to his side.

Mateo, however, doesn't relinquish his grasp, and I'm trapped between them both.

"You want my help, then you play by my rules," Domino warns. "She isn't even on the fucking table. Understood?"

Smirking, Mateo releases me, raising his hands in a gesture of surrender. "Understood. *Claro*. But I want you to ask yourself who would be a better ally if your chances of getting her into the city turn out to be a pipe dream? Me? I'll just sell her, you know that. Take my money and run. But Jaguar?—especially if the greedy bastard thinks he can get a rise out of you by dangling her body before you in pieces? Oh, Domino. You and I both know that by the time he *does* sell her, there won't be much left. Think about that while you fix the mess you've made."

Domino hisses through clenched teeth. "Where is the drop and when?"

Mateo chuckles, beaming once more. "I'll save the details until you're already in too deep to pull a fast one and decide to make up with Jaguar out of spite. I'm no fool, Domino. Everyone knows that all little Julian Domingas wants is his happy family intact—which is why you have the balls to go against him in the first place. We all can't be so lucky."

I look at Domino, watching how he processes that statement. His eyes narrow imperceptibly, but his expression is otherwise blank.

"I will say, that my little detour isn't too far out of your way," Mateo continues, shrugging. "Two birds with one stone."

"Where?"

A petty realization comes to me—Domino isn't the only one prone to speaking in riddles. I thought he learned it from my mother, but what if it's merely the way Carlos Domingas and his associates interact—via mind games and subtle manipulation.

Mateo must be an expert at this tactic because his eyes gleam with barely concealed excitement. He's enjoying this. "Do you take me for a fool? I know how you operate,

Domino. I'll tell you in good damn time. But first... You can explain what it is you want from little Ada Pavalos, here. As I've stated, the pussy can't be *that* good—" his gaze slithers over my body. "What are you up to?"

"Keep her out of this," Domino snaps. "That's your second warning."

Mateo chuckles. "You think you're far smarter than you are, Dom. Lucky for you, we're on a time crunch. You best get on the road now—" he reaches into his pocket, withdrawing a set of keys that he tosses to Domino, who catches them in a fist. "The job is simple on its face. Nice and clean. You drive to one location. Wait for the goods to be loaded. From there, it's an easy drive to the second checkpoint where you will receive the final cargo. Then you drive it over the border and drop it off at the end destination. Sound easy enough?"

A muscle in Domino's jaw twitches. "It sounds simple," he says softly. "Too simple. What the fuck am I transporting?"

"Ah, but that's the thing." Mateo winks, stroking his chin. "I think it's best if you don't know that little detail. You drive. You leave the truck where you're told, and that's all you have to know. The trip overall will take two days, but I think you can spare the delay given the alternative."

"And if I fulfill your role as an errand boy, what do I get? A participation ribbon and a pat on the head?"

"Yes." All traces of humor leave Mateo's gaze. "And you get my blessing to cross the border. Unless you want to take your chances with Jaguar's men instead?"

He waits for a reply that doesn't come.

"Good," he says with another dazzling grin. "Give my men time to get the truck ready, and you'll leave within the hour. Until then, make yourself right at home, and be sure to play nice. Unlike Jaguar, I don't keep my men on leashes."

Still smiling, he strolls from the room. "Oh, and Domino?" his voice drifts in through the doorway. "You aren't to look at the cargo. Do that, and you forfeit any protection I might otherwise provide you. Just do your job like a good boy, and there won't be any problems."

As he retreats, Domino faces forward, glowering at the far wall. "Stay close to me," he warns. "Something's off."

His hand tightens over my wrist, and I can feel the tension vibrating through his very bones.

"What do you mean?" I croak.

He cocks his head as if listening for something. I do the same, scanning the activity taking place outside. The men are patrolling in the darkness like before, and I don't spy anything abnormal.

Then again, I've never been in a camp of criminals preparing to smuggle something over the border. The tension infects my entire body, leaving me trembling and on edge.

"What do we do?" I whisper to Domino.

"Nothing for now." The words have barely left his mouth when approaching footsteps near our direction.

"Looks like it's your lucky day," Mateo declares with a booming laugh. "We're ready. Remember, you drive to the first checkpoint—and no peeking. You might be in for a surprise if you do. The truck has a tracker embedded in it, of course, along with an *explosive* little surprise should you decide to be naughty and break my one, teensy rule. This way." He beckons us with a curt nod, and I follow Domino out into the darkness.

"There is just one other thing," Mateo says as I pass him. Suddenly, he lunges, snatching my arm.

I barely choke out a scream before Domino is spinning on his heel, tensed to fight. At the same time, Mateo snags a fistful of my hair, wrenching my head back as something jarringly firm encircles my neck. His hand? No, it's too thin, the shape horrifyingly familiar.

Domino's expression only cements the suspicion. "You son of a bitch—"

"A *smart* son of a bitch," Mateo says, releasing me. "Did you really think I'd let you go off with my merchandise and trust that you'd play nice? Think again. These are my terms—a nonnegotiable deadline."

I stagger forward, nearly colliding with Domino—but I'm too focused on my neck to care. With trembling fingers, I trace the contours of the strange, metal device constricting every breath I take.

"A shock collar," Mateo declares. "A brand-new device my boys devised, specifically outfitted with enough juice to kill the wearer instantly, should they step out of line, of course. And don't think of doing something stupid, Dom," he warns as the other man advances, his hands clenching into fists. "I'd be a fool not to have a backup detonator—" He reaches into his pocket and withdraws a small black device that I assume is a remote. "Luckily for you, and your lady friend, you can keep her skull intact as long as you do as I asked. Keep your word, and I'll keep mine. Any questions?"

"You bastard," Domino growls, but he pivots, coming to my side instead. His eyes scan the collar, and I catch that rare glint of emotion I've come to dread—fear.

"Now, we can get down to business. This way." Mateo stalks forward, heading out.

A nudge from Domino is my only cue to follow.

With every step, I'm reminded of the restrictive, constricting pressure on my windpipe. Something Mateo said won't stop replaying in my mind. *You can keep her skull intact…* What the hell did that mean?

"Keep moving," Domino warns grimly, pulling ahead of me.

I can't find enough breath to reply. Instead, I focus on putting one step in front of the other, exiting the structure last. Up above, the sky is a deeper, rich blue that enhances the glimmering moonlight. I can make out the moving shapes of the other men, and as we round the metal building, I finally get a better sense of the scope of this camp.

It's massive, with the barbed fence surrounding the entire perimeter. Yellow floodlights provide an orangish glow that illuminates a walkway beaten into the earth itself, leading to a makeshift parking lot where two massive vehicles sit side by side. One has its headlights on, throwing off a blinding glow.

"This is your baby," Mateo says, gesturing to the truck in question. "The other is a decoy. Mick and Ralph will deploy on a similar route to draw off any suspicion. Your pickup point is a location north of here. That will put you within a day's travel of Terra Rodea. The drop-off is a terminal just outside the city's entrance. You'll go through my route and use the false documents in the glove compartment to escape any unwanted notice. Once you finish the job, you'll be free to go, and we can maintain our friendly relationship. Any questions?"

"The collar?" Domino demands.

"Oh, that comes off at the final checkpoint. As long as you reach it in time with no little hiccups. Mick and Ralph will be my eyes and ears until then."

Without another word, Domino starts for the truck, pulling me behind him.

"Oh, there is one other thing," Mateo adds as we near the passenger's side door. "Since you're filling in for a trip that was already scheduled, the expectation is that you're a driver, returning an empty vehicle after completing a shipment. A female passenger doesn't exactly fit with that cover story, does it?"

"That sounds like your problem," Domino says smoothly. "She stays with me."

"So you say," Mateo replies with a grunt. "But if it comes between you blowing my operation and winding up in federal prison or being a good boy, I think you know which option is preferable. After the pickup, the girl goes with Mick and Ralph, who will cover your rear, and then you can reunite once you cross the border and secure my goods. Everyone is happy." He laughs again, eyeing Domino as if he's preparing for an outburst—a fight I suspect he's itching to have. "Let's keep our *heads* about this, shall we?"

"Fine." Domino nods with a casualness that shocks even me. "Have it your way."

He wrenches open the door and grips my waist, hauling me inside. I scramble onto the seat as he slams the door and circles the truck.

I can't hear whatever words pass between him and Mateo before he opens the driver's side door, but his eyes blaze in a way I can only compare to a handful of moments.

Namely, when I first woke up in his estate and realized the man I'd come to trust only saw me as an enemy.

As the driver's side door closes behind him, he grips the steering wheel before jabbing the key into the ignition.

I open my mouth, prepared with a million different questions—but he shakes his head. "Wait."

I follow his gaze and find Mateo looking on from the edge of the field. Devoid of the spotlight, his real expressions break through his confident façade. He's angry, his teeth gritted. I'm not sure if he can see us through the glass, but I sense his gaze is firmly fixed in Domino's direction.

A hostility that Domino more than reciprocates.

Quiet rage emanates from him as we wait, presumably for a signal to move. In a crackle of static, noise emanates from the console in between Domino's seat and mine. A radio? Another barrage of noise provides a clearer idea of what it is. Voices?

"We'll take the lead, and you follow," a man declares. Judging from the tone, it's Ralph. The other truck revs its engine and then pulls off as two men wrench open another gate on this end of the encampment. "We'll head west, around the main highway for now. First checkpoint in five hours. I assume you won't attempt any unnecessary detours. Until then, we'll be in touch. Safe travels!"

Their laughter echoes ominously before the noise cuts out altogether.

In silence, Domino starts to drive, maneuvering the truck through the gate. The second we clear it, the semblance of civilization once again gives way to the seemingly uninhabitable desert.

"Son of a bitch," Domino hisses through clenched teeth. "I was wrong."

I whip my attention toward him, feeling my heart in my throat. "What? You mean you *didn't* expect him to outfit me with a shock collar?" Despite my terror, my voice comes out barely louder than a whisper.

"Loud noise won't set it off," Domino explains, though that reassurance lessens my unease only a fraction. "I suspect Mateo has it rigged to his discretion. Given that he mentioned the bounty on your head, I doubt he'll be in a rush to detonate it—"

"You don't sound very confident of that," I snap.

But he sighs, almost as if in defeat. "There's something else. Mateo is rarely this reckless. Whatever he wants transported must be hot if he's scrambling to rush it over the border now. The bastard's set us up on a suicide mission."

"So, what now?" I keep dragging the tip of my finger along the edge of my collar, barely touching the cool metal.

Domino takes his eyes from the road long enough to shoot a searching glance my way. "Mateo's hedged his bets, but I am no one's patsy."

"So, what are you planning?"

I'm not familiar with this side of him up close. The calculating man with the intelligence to supposedly outsmart even Roy Pavalos. Someone who could go undetected in the heart of my family for five years. A man that even my mother trusted, though to what aim?

I still don't know.

There's no better time than now to ask, but when I lick my lips in preparation, he sighs.

"Tell me about the night my sister went missing. All of it. Whatever you remember."

"Why?" I blurt out, completely thrown off by the change in subject. "It's hard to remember much with an explosive collar around my neck—"

"Just tell me," he insists. "Call it curiosity, but I need to know."

If possible, I'm even more on edge, my stomach in knots. One reason why he's mentioning this now is driven by pure paranoia. I voice it anyway. "So that you can confirm whatever hate bias you have against me?"

Rather than argue, he faces the road, dead silent.

But I'm not finished. "Was that your plan all along? Toss me to those men and walk away, knowing that you achieved at least one of your aims. You've destroyed another Pavalos—"

"No. I want you to confirm my suspicion that I'm not a fool for risking my neck to keep your ass safe. That I'm not craving a woman who could be a fucking murderer. Don't play coy with me—" he adds before the shock fully sets in.

Murderer. When paired with the topic of Pia, I don't think he'd use that term flippantly. What the hell did my mother tell him?

"Whether it insults you or not, I need to know," Domino insists. "Tell me... Please."

He keeps his gaze on the road as he speaks, and the only indication of emotion is how his eyes blaze.

"I would never hurt Pia." Even I can hear the lie in my own voice.

I may not have hurt her directly, but I played a role. I did my duty as the good daughter, and I didn't let myself think of the consequences. But I never thought those consequences could go beyond a few hurt feelings.

I still can't believe that she's dead. Not really. Domino will take me to Terra Rodea, dig up the lawn of his old home, and we will both realize that he was played for a fool. Pia is still out there. Because…

The alternative is too terrifying to consider.

"Ada…" His voice is so gritty I imagine him shoving each word through clenched teeth. "Please—"

"All I remember is screaming at her," I admit. It's strange to hear him in this role, pleading for answers. "I took her diary, and she confronted me outside our old dorm building. Did my mother tell you that part?" I force a hollow laugh. "She loved me so much that she had me shipped away to a boarding school just twenty minutes from the house. What kind of mother allows that?"

A mother who surrendered her child to the machinations of Roy Pavalos.

"Pia was my friend," I reiterate. "I never wanted to hurt her. She started screaming at me that I was a traitor and a horrible person, and I told her to go to hell." It all unfolds so clearly in my mind, nearing the point in the nightmare where I usually wake up. "I tried to leave. She grabbed my arm. And I pushed her—"

Those words stick in my throat, and I can't find the space to say anything else. In my head, I shoved her away, determined to leave.

The memories after that are a blur. I just remember getting home. Breaking down. Crying so hard it felt like my ribs might break.

"I never saw her again after that." My voice cracks, and for the first time, I let myself fully acknowledge the pain lurking behind the mental wall I've locked all thoughts of Pia behind. I miss her. God, I miss her so much. "I did love her, and I wish I knew what happened to her—"

"You think you don't?" His voice is so cold I jump and peer in the side-view mirror, half-expecting to find Mateo and his men in hot pursuit. But no. Now, at least, I can identify the source of his animosity toward me.

Pia. It's always been Pia.

"I don't think," I rasp, licking my lips to find traction to keep speaking. "I *know* I don't know what happened—"

"Really? Because your mother seemed to think that you did."

It hurts, like a rusty knife sinking deep, to hear him speak of my mother so freely. So intimately. I cringe from imagining how they must have interacted, trading secret glances, and whispered lies. It's so hard to process the idea of her actively working against my father, but Domino's confidence undermines any lingering doubts I may have. He is a man who trusts few and claims to understand only a handful of people. Jaguar. My mother. My father.

He's studied them like a book.

And he wouldn't make a claim like that if he didn't think he could prove it. Knowledge of that suffocates me, and I reach for the handle of the door even though I know jumping out now would be futile. I entertain the thought anyway.

But then I picture the humiliation of having him be the one to rescue me. Again.

All with that hate shining in his eyes.

"What are you saying?" I ask, facing him directly.

"Ada…" He sighs in exasperation, gripping the steering wheel so tightly that his knuckles strain against the skin. "You asked me why your mother would believe you were too much like your father? Think back to the events surrounding Pia's disappearance and honestly ask yourself why that may be."

"Stop speaking in riddles and just tell me!"

"No," he says darkly. "I'll show you." He reaches into his pocket, withdrawing an object that he tosses onto my lap.

I barely manage to catch it, preventing the small device from falling—the recorder.

"Press play," he demands, coldly eyeing the road. "And after this, no more lies."

CHAPTER ELEVEN

I suck in a breath, registering the feel of the device against my palm. It's so light despite containing something so weighty—my mother's voice. The last words I'll ever hear her speak.

Am I ready to listen?

"Press play," Domino commands, making the decision for me.

I stall for a few more seconds, cycling through the potential explanations. Did my mother learn about my father and Pia? Or perhaps she told Domino some trivial story about me as a teenager, and *that's* what's fueled his hate.

I hope he truly is that petty. There is only one way to find out. Finally, I press play.

"...I love my daughter," my mother said, her voice a shadow of the soft murmur I always knew.

"I do. But I never protected her the way a real mother should. I let her be swayed to sin, and I stood by as Roy corrupted her soul. You ask why I would come to you? Because Navid Inglecias died years ago, far too weak to ever prove a threat to him. You are one enemy he will never see coming. I used to be content to wait for God to take action upon Roy, but I'm afraid I can't wait any longer. After what he's done to Ada…"

"What has he done?" Domino's voice is a jarring reminder. I'd been so lost in hearing my mother speak, I'd forgotten this conversation was from the past. *"Frankly, I don't have the time to listen to your heartfelt regrets."*

"I know you don't," Lia insisted. *"I'll cut right to the point, then. Unwittingly, your sister took something she didn't understand the significance of. Something that, even revealed after all these years, will paint him out to be the monster he's always hidden from the world. It's all part of a web more twisted than you can imagine. All this time, the bastard thought I didn't know. That he was that damn good at hiding everything from me. He even kept a file on your family after all these years. I didn't understand why at first. He's afraid."*

"Cut to the point," Domino snapped. *"You said Pia's dead. How do you know that? Prove it, or we're done—"*

"Wait!" Lia inhaled raggedly, her anxiety so palpable I can feel it, tightening my chest with every breath. *"All I know is the morning after your sister went missing, Ada-Maria was so distraught I couldn't get a word out of her. Hysterical. There was blood…"*

My heart pangs. *No.* This is too much—obviously another mind game. My thumb twitches over the stop button.

"Don't." Domino grabs my wrist, taking one hand off the wheel. "Just listen."

"She was covered in it," my mother said matter-of-factly. *"Her back looked like it had been torn to pieces. Shredded… Roy wouldn't tell me what happened, and Ada… It was like she became another person overnight—not that I can blame anyone but myself."*

"What are you saying?" Domino demanded, his anger as electric then as it is now.

Lia sighed. *"I'm saying that you have every right to revenge, but the only reason I'm contacting you at all is Ada. I want my daughter protected when Roy's lies inevitably catch up to him. He has far too many enemies. I can't protect her."*

"Why would I give a damn about your family?"

"Because if you protect my daughter, I will ensure that you have access to resources you could only dream of, and plenty of connections to topple Roy Pavalos from the inside out. It could take years to achieve, but I think if your ordeal has taught you anything, it's that patience can be rewarded."

"But at what cost?" Domino bit back. *"I don't think your 'resources' are quite the gift you believe them to be."*

"Perhaps not, but you don't have any better options. To take down Roy, the most vital piece will be finding your sister's body. Only one person in the world can help you do that."

"Your daughter? I hope you don't think I'm stupid enough not to pick up on what you've been alluding to."

"No, you're not," my mother admitted. *"And I won't insult your intelligence by denying it. I think my daughter might have played a role in your sister's death, but even if she did... She isn't evil—"*

"Stop the car."

I lunge for the door, gasping as pain lances up and down my injured arm. But I don't care. I ram against it until it flies open.

I only catch a glimpse of the dark, uneven landscape below before I jump, throwing myself onto the ground. The collar jolts with the movement, biting into the tender flesh of my throat—but by some miracle, I don't black out instantly, instead landing heavily on my knees, tasting dirt. Belatedly I realize why—he's already stopped the truck.

"Damn it!" I hear the driver's side door fly open, and I scramble to my knees as Domino races to my side. I've only gone a few feet from the vehicle itself, but the earth is jagged and rocky beneath me. Domino almost slips as he comes to a stop.

"Are you fucking insane? You want to break your legs next—"

"Get away from me!" I lash out, one-handed, but the anger toward him is irrational. The real source is already dead and gone. I can't scream at her. I can't slap her. Can I even hate her?

Yes. A sob rips from my throat, and tears fall as everything I thought I knew finally crumbles down around me.

All these years… She knew. Long after I told myself that I was just *that* good at hiding it. The abuse. The pain. The fear. I never went to her directly. No, like the good daughter I strived to be, I merely swallowed it all and smiled through the discomfort.

Meanwhile, she twiddled her thumbs and begged for help from a stranger rather than come to her own daughter and…

What? Apologize?

The wounded little girl in me demands more than that. She should have used whatever resources she promised Domino to cover her own escape. She should have divorced my father like his previous wives did and never looked back. She should have intervened the first night he reached for a belt or a whip.

She should have protected me.

But that would have been too easy, I guess. Instead, she primed a stranger to destroy her own family rather than do the job of a real mother.

I hate her. I hate her so much it hurts, like my chest might explode from the sheer intensity of it all. Ironically, my father never inspired this kind of seething rage despite everything he's done. I never made the excuses for him that I did for her, perfect, precious Lia who always stood faithfully by his side.

"I need you to listen to me." Domino's voice seeps into my skull, inescapable no matter how hard I shout to drown him out.

Because I *am* shouting. Screaming.

"How could she? How?" My throat aches, but I can't stop. "How could she just leave me there if she cared so damn much? How could she ignore what was happening in front of her own goddamn eyes? She should have never reached out to you in the first place. She only had to come to *me*!"

I would have listened. I spent so damn long convincing myself that a good daughter obeyed her parents' demands no matter how demeaning, how cruel, or senseless.

Or how twisted.

I'd been taught that being a Pavalos trumped any other loyalty or moral—but not only by my father. My mother's devotion served as a living example of his twisted standard. God, I used to seethe at how she could stand beside him and smile. If she could do it, then how could I ever dream of breaking away?

Domino should have known that better than anyone. My burning eyes latch onto him, standing paces away without an ounce of visible emotion. He should be smiling. Laughing. Gloating.

This is what he wanted all along, wasn't it? To hurt me.

"You… You believed her. You never even asked me. Had no proof. Nothing. You just took her word, and you think I'm the sick one?"

More tears fall as I recall just how oblivious I was to them both. The times I would pine after him like a cat in heat, or when I took pity on my mother for what her life had become.

"I never did anything to you," I croak as my vision blurs. "I only admired you. You think you've done all of this to destroy my father, but you haven't. You've become worse than he is. You're the same kind of monster! …Say something!"

I'm unnerved by his silence. It stretches on and on. When I wipe away my tears and see his face clearly, his frown is unexpected.

"Your father was only one of my targets," he admits, sinking into a crouch.

I steel myself against the part of me that lurches at the concern in his voice. The genuine Domino is so elusive that I'm never sure when he's merely putting on an act at my expense. Though…he's rarely composed himself like this, speaking freely on my level, no hands around my throat, no blood spilling between us.

"A mere stepping-stone on a much larger goal. Your mother had her flaws," he tells me. "She was self-righteous to a fault, and prone to underestimating those around her. She used the Bible as a litmus test and refused to acknowledge when it fell short. She loved you more than I think you will ever know."

"And she turned you against me from the very start," I surmise.

"No." He cocks his head, surprising me. "In fact, I think she went through great lengths to ensure I couldn't kill you, even if I wanted to."

Does that upset him? His eyes darken, as unreadable as ever. Desperately, I try to decipher something, but he reaches out, smoothing a stray piece of hair from my face.

The gesture disarms me, and my rage sputters and dies. "What do you mean?"

His mouth tilts into a grim smile. "Think back to what you told me about Pia. Something only you would know—and information conveniently missing from her diary."

His tone conjures one episode in particular—Pia's affair with my father, and her possession of my mother's ring. He's right. Only one person could have deliberately hidden that detail. "My mother… She ripped out the missing pages?"

He nods, removing his hand from me to stroke his chin instead. "I assume she felt that only you could fill in the blanks."

"So you're blaming her for holding me captive? For whipping me?"

"Give me more credit than that, Ada-Maria. I had more voices than your mother's in my ear."

I start to deny that assertion, but then I remember that he had Pia's diary all this time. And there was one other "voice" who had every reason to poison him against me.

"Alexi."

He smiles in a far-off way, devoid of any warmth. "She has no love for you, that's for sure. But even petty gossip isn't enough. I saw what you would do for him without asking any questions. No hesitation. Seemingly no regret. You don't realize the kind of woman you come off as. So goddamn vulnerable one minute..." He extends his hand again, stroking his thumb along my cheek. "And heartless the next. You fuck with men and women for the sheer hell of it. And yet I am supposed to ignore the countless voices telling me the same thing?"

"Yes." I shrug off his touch. "If you ever want to claim that you cared for me in some way, you would have. You wouldn't trust the word of a woman who fucks a man like Jaguar either. Did she help you spy on him too? Or is she just drawn to anyone who sees themselves as an enemy of my family?"

Domino chuckles, inclining his head, his gaze shrouded by shadow. Only the planes of his face, highlighted by moonlight, have any definition, rendering him as impassive as the landscape surrounding us. "Not that it's any of your business, but Alexi's reasons for working with Jaguar have nothing to do with you, though I doubt you can believe that. In your world, everything revolves around Ada Pavalos."

"So what are her reasons, then?"

He shakes his head. "That is for her to tell. Just know that her rationale for supporting Jaguar is no different than yours for supporting your father. Loyalty, however misplaced it may be."

I stiffen at the comparison. "Then why not protect her from him the way you have me?"

Though, has he really? When I think through his actions, they could be merely characterized as him selfishly protecting his asset. My life matters to him until the second I deliver whatever information he's after.

His expression, however, doesn't portray the cold cruelty I expect.

"Do you think what I've done has been to protect you?" Again, he fingers a lock of my hair—only he tugs, triggering a stab of sharp, brief pain. The second I gasp, he relents. "No… Everything I've done has been entirely selfish. When all of this is over, you might find yourself envying Alexi."

I slap his hand away and relish the brief surprise that crosses his face. As much as he claims to know me inside and out, he didn't predict that.

"You always try to distract when I get too close," I croak. "Just tell me the truth. Please."

"The truth…" He appears to mull over the question. Hell, I have to wonder if he even knows why himself. "The truth is that Mateo isn't planning to uphold his little plan. My guess is this 'checkpoint' is really an ambush, and his men will strike at the first opportunity. The bastard knew better than to risk close combat with me. When he strikes, it'll be out in the open or with no warning. Usually, I'd let him play his little game and turn the tables when he least expects it."

"But this time?" I prod, sensing an unspoken *but*.

His mask wavers before finally cracking to reveal the unease lurking beneath. "Things will get messy from here on out. What I need is your trust—"

"Then tell me what you're really after. No more games. No more lies."

"Fine." He moves too quickly to track.

Before I realize it, I'm on my feet as well, pinned to the side of the truck. His breath nuzzles my cheek, his eyes so intense it hurts to meet them head-on—a dazzling green rivaling the moon itself.

"What am I after?" he murmurs, lethally soft. "Everything. All of it. I've waited long enough. I didn't spend five years at your father's beck and call for the hell of it. No one—not Mateo, not Jaguar, and certainly not Ada-Pavalos… No one will stand in my way."

His shoulder jerks—my only warning before he captures a fistful of my hair, twisting the strands through his fingers.

The motion draws my mouth more readily within his reach, and he takes advantage, pressing his lips against mine.

But only *just*.

It's torturous intimacy. Every breath we take is shared despite the pressure on my throat. His scent poisons the air entering my lungs, reinforcing his presence in every way imaginable. Even the threat of my skull exploding any second on a madman's whim can't distract me from him.

"I once believed that I'd be content with destroying everything Roy Pavalos has built with my bare hands. Then taking whatever remains from Jaguar and seeking out the peace those motherfuckers denied me. I thought that was enough…"

He's so angry. I can feel every movement of his lips to punctuate each word. He means this, all of it.

"Along the way, I've changed my mind. I've set my sights beyond the downfall of my enemies. I'm going to take Ada-Maria Pavalos for myself—" His free hand captures the back of my throat.

"W-What?" I inhale greedily just to find the strength to question. "What do you mean?"

"I *mean* that, when this is all over, you'll be begging for me—and it won't be as a ploy to save your life, either. No, I'm adding you to my tally, Ada-Maria, in more ways than you can even begin to comprehend. First, I'll pry loose every secret Roy Pavalos instilled inside that pretty little head. Then, I'll come for your body. Your soul."

His possession is a physical entity I can actually feel settle around my throat, every bit as oppressive as this collar.

"And if I refuse?" My voice shakes so badly in comparison to his. It's laughable that I could ever stand a chance against his might.

And yet, he seems to take pity on me, removing his hand from my neck to stroke my cheek. Roughly. His fingers shake, revealing the sheer level of restraint he's utilizing.

It's like he's constantly battling himself when it comes to me —an unending war between lust.

And hate.

"You won't have a choice," he tells me. "You were mine the second I tasted you. Ever since that first day in your father's office when you strolled up to me in that tight fucking skirt. Mine then. Mine now."

"But for how long?" It's dangerous to provoke him, but it's the only card I have left to play. "If Mateo—"

"You leave Mateo to me."

"Why should I?" I counter, voicing the argument that's been circling my brain, impossible to ignore completely. "I don't owe you a damn thing. If anything, I should be looking for a chance to escape. Who's to say what you'll do with me after you get what you want?"

I've never asserted myself like this to him. I want him to react with shock.

Instead, he looks thoughtful. "I already told you that your mother ensured your safety," he says. "Do you want to know how?"

He raises the recorder he must have had at the ready and presses play. My mother's voice fills the void, and I'm not prepared for the pain I feel all over again.

"I will help you, but know this. My daughter has the answers you're looking for. You keep her alive. No matter what happens, you protect Ada. Do you understand?"

My eyes burn, surprisingly dry. I must have cried every tear I had left.

"Is that why you tortured me?" I ask him. "You knew you couldn't kill me. But I hate to break it to you, Domino. I don't know a damn thing about any of this."

He levels me with a searching gaze. The longer he looks, the more his expression hardens. "I'll make you an offer," he suggests. "One we can mark now in blood to cement in every way that matters. You trust in me, and I will never forsake you. I swear on my life."

He cuts his gaze down to my chest, peering at the spot where my heart frantically beats.

"You stand beside me, and I will always protect you."

"So you keep saying." But my arm, let alone the various scrapes and bruises all along my body, betray that.

"And words mean nothing," he replies in agreement, sliding his thumb beneath my chin, lifting it. "You keep forgetting that I am not your father. I won't rely on threats to get my way. I have my reasons for wanting your help, but if you see this through to the end, you stand to gain your own resources to work with. Your own power. You do realize that should anything happen to your father, everything he owns goes to you."

Shock has me gritting my teeth. It's pathetic that I *didn't* realize it. Of course, my father's possessions would be divided among me and my two brothers, Demelio and Pablo. Not that an inheritance changes a damn thing. I stand to end this nightmare with my family in tatters.

"Lucky me," I hiss. "I might get a few dollars out of it."

"Don't play coy," Domino warns. "You know damn well the difference between being under your family's shadow and the chance at autonomy. You think Jaguar or Mateo will allow you to claim that for yourself? Hell no. I'm offering you more than a chance to stay alive. I am offering you a new life."

"Just under *you* instead of Roy Pavalos?" I snipe.

"Under me." I shiver at his guttural tone. "That is exactly the future I foresee for you."

I recoil, scrambling to brace my good hand against his chest. I'm proud of myself for doing that much—for pushing against him despite his strength. He overpowers me, anyway, brushing his mouth across my lips a second time.

Only he lingers.

Lunges.

Claims.

This kiss is fiery—more dangerous than anything Mateo or Jaguar could offer. I must resist. Otherwise, he'll believe he's won this round.

My first impulse is to bite, clamping down over the tip of his probing tongue. I savor his pained groan, triumphant. Until he growls. *Oh no.* That sound is sharper. Grittier. Excited.

Rather than retreat, he surges, grinding my body against the unyielding metal. He's so big, capable of brutalizing me with little effort—but he doesn't. The gentleness with which he imparts every slow, searching kiss terrifies me more than if he bit me in return. I'm helpless against this form of attack, letting him in further than I should…

Working my jaw to keep up, I kiss him back. Harder. More.

Of all the comparisons for my brain to jump to, Jaguar comes to mind, his cruel intensity and need to devour. For what it's worth, Domino is a different kind of predator. One adept at luring his prey into a false sense of security. Pretending as though, for a second, his aim isn't to kill—he wants something more. Something too vast and elusive to convey in just one kiss. It's evident in the groan that catches in his throat as our chests collide. The way he avoids putting any pressure on my right side.

His touch is invasive, easing between my legs to stroke along my inner thigh. Possession radiates through his fingertips, wringing a shiver from me.

God, I hate him the most when he's like this—so close to the ideal I've built up inside my head. My fantasy Domino would kiss me like this. Hold me like this. Exhale harshly against my skin as though the scent of me mattered more to him than fresh air. Like I mattered.

To someone.

But I was burned by that lie once.

"S-Stop." I rip away, panting.

To my shock, he steps back, swiping his hand over his mouth.

"You're right. We need to move before Mateo decides to show off his new toy." He's cold in an instant, all trace of passion gone.

The ease with which he can change so drastically should be a warning sign. A smart woman would take it as a clear contradiction against whatever he says. Actions speak louder than words.

And right now, he has his back to me, retreating toward the driver's side of the truck. "Come on. Get in."

I follow him warily, but as I reach the passenger's side door, a noise catches my ears. Voices—but too faint to be Domino.

"…you better answer, you son of a bitch. What the fuck is your status?"

Domino sighs, reaching for a radio shoved into the console between his seat and mine. "Road trouble," he snarls into the receiver. "Meet you at the checkpoint. I wouldn't want you to slow your own progress by doubling back."

A reply comes quickly, garbled by more static. "You son of a bitch—"

"See you there, Ralph." Domino must switch off the radio because all noise from it dies completely. In the resulting silence, he sighs again.

"For now, we have no choice but to play along with Mateo's little scheme and look for an opening. I have a few contacts I can try to find more info about this collar—" He reaches out, running his thumb along the edge of it. "Once the truck has the first load of merchandise, I could use it for leverage. Then I'll come for you."

He meets my gaze, drilling in the promise. "Afterward, we get to Terra."

"And what if you can't?" I ask.

"There is no *what if*," he counters. "Failure isn't even an option."

CHAPTER TWELVE

Our destination isn't a random shack in the middle of nowhere this time. Instead, a small town unfolds, seemingly out of thin air, as the dirt road gives way to one more maintained. What few buildings we pass sport colorful exteriors, and stray dogs dart through the alleyways. The glimpse of normalcy is a stark reminder of everything I've lost during this hellish ordeal.

Far too soon, the small town flits by, yielding to more desert and endless road. Above, the sun begins to rise, painting the horizon in shades of pink and amber before igniting the landscape entirely in a soft golden glow. It hits me how beautiful this part of the world is, though ragged and inhospitable.

Much like the man beside me.

It's been hours since we last spoke, but I resist the urge to prod him for more information—like where the hell we're headed exactly. Soon, my questions are answered for me as an industrial complex appears on the horizon.

DELCORP DEPOT reads the black lettering on a rusted sign affixed to a barbed-wire fence lining the road. Three large brick warehouse-style buildings form a row, with an asphalt parking lot full of trucks visible behind them.

Even if Domino wasn't tense beside me, I'd sense something was off with this place. A sinister aura emanates from the property. Every muscle in my body stiffens—especially when I glimpse a familiar vehicle parked alongside the gate.

"Get ready," Domino warns. "Remember what I told you and follow my lead. Trust me."

Trust him. I don't know whether to laugh or take those words at face value, now that the time to put them to the test has come. It isn't like I have much of a choice.

If this really is an ambush, the key players are already in place. Mick and Ralph stand beside another man who motions for us to stop. As Domino complies, rolling down the window, the third man calls, "Bring it around the back for loading."

"As for the little Missy, she can step out and join us," Ralph adds, his smile revealing several missing teeth. "Then we can both get right on our way."

Domino doesn't move for so long that I start to question if he'll drive off entirely. Then, without a word, he leans over me, and shoves open the door on my end.

"Get out." His tone is low, his gaze averted. My belly quivers. Am I pathetic for wanting reassurance? A look. A glance. Anything.

"Can we get a move on?" Mick snaps, his impatience palpable.

I jolt to awareness and realize that all eyes are on me. Cautiously, I descend from my seat. On shaking legs, I approach the three men, feeling the back of my neck prickle with awareness.

I turn to find Domino watching me, and I swear something unspoken passes between us.

Encouragement?

If so, he hides it well. Outwardly, his expression is stone. When the unfamiliar man gestures him onward, he drives, and my stomach sinks. If the worst comes to pass, this might be the last time I ever see him.

"We should get going," Mick warns as the truck rounds the corner. "Before they finish loading."

That must be what the third man intends to oversee as he heads in the same direction, though on foot.

"Relax," Ralph counters, smoothing his hand over the stubble coating his chin. "We have time. More than enough for us all to get acquainted on the road—" he winks at me. "There are about another five hours until the next checkpoint. Go take a piss while we wait."

Frowning, Mick saunters off, leaving Ralph and me alone. Their truck is smaller than the one Domino took, resembling an RV.

"You nervous?" Ralph wonders, coming to stand beside me.

I look over and flinch as his eyes blaze with open lust.

As strange as it feels to admit, Domino inspired a different set of emotions from the start. Hate, yes, and some fear as well, but there was also a familiarity I couldn't deny. I knew him. Sometimes, I could even read him, but this man is a new animal, and it strikes me just how rusty I am.

Less than a month ago, I could smirk coyly and converse with someone like him, all without breaking a sweat. I would relish the glimpses he snuck at my breasts and plot a plan of attack to get what I wanted.

This time should be no different.

Squaring my shoulders, I crane my neck to take him in, utilizing the skills my father taught me. He's tall, holding himself in a cocky way that conveys he's the leader of his little duo. I can't overpower him outright, his bulk evident in muscles that strain his arms.

Licking my lips, I weigh my approach. For now, friendliness seems like the best option.

"Where are we going?" I ask, making my voice soft.

He smiles, stepping even closer. "Just a simple little road trip. A nice long drive through the desert and the back roads. We'll be safe and sound back in Terra Rodea before you know it."

"Are you from there?" Inferring from what little information Domino gave, Mateo must regularly import his "goods" over the border. As a result, these men probably know this landscape in and out, and won't be easy to outrun even if I could.

"No," he admits, his eyes narrowing. "But I've dabbled in the city here and there. I know your daddy from his reputation. And I've certainly heard of you." His tone deepens with double meaning, and my cheeks flame.

Desperate to get my bearings again, I ask a more pointed question. "What kind of stuff are you carrying? These trucks are, um…big."

A hint of suspicion flits across his gaze. "Nothing that you need to concern yourself with."

Damn it. I force a smile and think of parties and alcohol, and the drug-fueled ways I used to spend my time. It wasn't so hard to play dumb back then.

"They look hard to drive," I stammer. "I just hope the stuff isn't too heavy. It could make us slower."

His gaze loses that hard edge. "Don't worry yourself about that—" he fingers a lock of my hair without warning, and I bite my lip, determined not to flinch.

"We'll drive pretty fast, but we'll still have plenty of time to get to know each other better. Let's head out."

Right on cue, the truck we drove in rounds the corner, Domino visible in the driver's seat. If this really is a setup, he excels at disguising any tension.

For now.

"Looks like we're all ready to go," Ralph says, slapping the side of his van. "Mick, hurry up, you son of a bitch. It's time to get on the road." To me, he extends his hand. "You'll ride in the back. We've made it nice and comfortable for you."

Dread builds ominously in my belly, but—despite their obviously predatory intentions—Ralph and Mick aren't the source.

It's *him*. The man who claimed to watch me from the shadows, always. Unaware of his attention, I'd been able to suppress my own emotions time after time. I never had to contend with those dark, watchful eyes on me in the moment. I never had to sense the anger emanating from him.

God, it literally feels like I'm balancing on a wire, trusting Domino Valenciaga not to let me fall.

But I'm past being afraid. Inhaling deeply, I extend my hand toward Ralph and follow him into the truck.

This time, I don't look back.

CHAPTER THIRTEEN

It's one thing to humor Domino Valenciaga. The true test of my insanity comes in just how far I am willing to actually put his plea to the test. *Trust him.*

The sad part is that I've spent five years doing so implicitly, if only believing that he'd save my life out of loyalty to my father. Now, I'm not sure what is driving him. His heated confessions?

Or the blatant fact that my mother made sure he needed me alive to reach his aims?

Neither reason should matter. He may need me, but what if I don't need him? I've manipulated my fair share of men long before Domino Valenciaga came into my life, and something tells me I'll have to do the same long after.

Still, those weeks of isolation have left me woefully unprepared for just how jarring it is to face the full brunt of one man who sees me as only an object, let alone two.

"Welcome to your palace for the time being," Ralph says as he leads me through the narrow space. It looks like an RV, though one modified to have a single exit near the front and the driver's seat partitioned off from the back section we're in now. Overall, it's relatively clean, consisting of a small kitchenette, a booth with most of the leather seating worn away, and across from it is a raised ledge with a mattress on it and a stained set of white sheets. My stomach crawls at the sight, but I never let my smile so much as flinch.

From the corner of my eye, I sense Ralph in between me and the exit.

"We should get on the road," the other man, Mick, calls, approaching the open doorway. "Mateo will skin us alive if we show up late to the next…*checkpoint*."

I stiffen at his shift in inflection.

Ralph, however, continues to smile, though it doesn't reach his eyes. "Alright. We'll both take the front for now. You just sit tight, little Missy."

I swallow hard, weighing my question carefully before voicing it. "When will we meet up with Domino again?"

Ralph's grin stretches a little wider. "Don't worry your pretty little head. We'll meet up with him at the final checkpoint once we're in Terra and he's completed his job. Then you can get rid of your little necklace and be on your merry way."

His laugh turns the statement into a joke more than an earnest promise. Regardless, he leaves, closing the door behind him, and I'm sure I hear a lock engage.

Heart racing, I perch myself on the edge of the booth, contemplating a million different options. The first, and the one I'm hoping for the most, is that both Mick and Ralph don't have nefarious motives at all, and I make it back into Terra unscathed.

The more likely option is that Domino was right, and we've sprung their trap. So now what?

I inch closer to the front of the truck, where a wooden partition separates it from the back. I can barely hear the scuffle of the two men settling into their seats before the engine roars to life and the vehicle lurches into motion.

I press myself against the panel, straining my ears for any hint of conversation. I only catch grunted snippets before a barrage of deafening rock music drowns out everything else.

Damn it.

Alone, I'm left to dwell on the inevitable. I turn to one of the small, filthy windows near the bed that offers a view outside. I can't get a good glimpse of the road behind us—or if anyone is on our tail.

Stop. I shake my head to banish the doubt. My sole concern should be keeping myself alive. Should Mick and Ralph deviate from their supposed plan, I can't overpower them physically. Not without the aid of a weapon. Ironically, I still have Domino's knife, and I slide my hand over my pocket, feeling its shape beneath the denim.

Not that I know how to use it. My methods always relied more on manipulation than violence.

Liar, a part of me whispers. The last time I ever saw Pia replays in my mind over and over again. I cursed at her. Shoved her. Then ran.

I tell myself that Domino—or anyone for that matter—is jumping to conclusions by assuming that I had a bigger role to play in her disappearance. I loved her. I would never hurt her.

So then who did?

Could a fifteen-year-old girl really learn information on a man like Roy Pavalos salacious enough to kill her over? It sounds too sordid, even for my family.

The twisted part is I think I'd sooner get a straight response from Domino than my father. The thought of seeing him again makes the air stick to the inside of my chest. It's a cruel form of whiplash to go from believing he was gone for good, to now having to accept that he isn't dead after all. Across the border, in Terra Rodea, Roy Pavalos is alive and well, and maybe I truly am as pathetic as Domino claims I am for hoping that everything he told me was a lie.

No one could blame any woman for being unwilling to accept that both of her parents may have loathed her all along. My mother was one thing, with her lofty ideas and pious catholic upbringing. But my father…

While St. Margaritas was barely a twenty-minute drive from my family's estate, we rarely spent time together in those days. He had his political events to attend, and my mother had her many charity organizations and parties. Even before everything went to hell, I was an afterthought to them of both.

That all changed not long before Pia went missing. Suddenly, my father displayed an interest in my life that he never had. Little did I know that, like always, it wasn't me he was interested in. Just what he could have me do *for* him.

A sudden noise jars me from the memory. I startle to awareness, blinking as the vehicle skids to a stop.

Hope rises in my chest. Is Domino here after all?

My heart pounds as I ease myself to my feet and inch toward one of the windows. The sun blazes, illuminating a landscape that doesn't remotely resemble a checkpoint. Instead, the ruthless desert extends seemingly for miles. From the front of the truck, I hear a door open and close, followed by footsteps approaching this side.

They're too slow to allude to an unwelcome visitor. As the figure appears in the window built into the door, my heart sinks. Mick, his teeth bared in an expression far too gruesome to be considered a grin. He takes his time, toying with the latch before finally opening the door.

"Hey there," he calls to me. "Ralph is gonna take over for a while so that you and I can get better acquainted."

He mounts the steps one by one as an alarm goes off inside my skull.

Regardless, I have enough sense not to let my unease show. I force my tried-and-true smile, keeping my back close to the partition. He's barely closed the door behind him when the truck lurches into motion, and the familiar rift of rock music seeps through the wood again.

I'm painfully aware of how enclosed this space is. The door is the only realistic exit, but he positions himself in front of it and gestures toward the mattress with a wave of his hand. "Have a seat. Let's have a nice talk for a bit."

I follow him woodenly, perching beside him on the stained sheets. The second I do, his hand lands over my thigh, squeezing the flesh. "I'm sure you and Domino got up to plenty of fun."

Damn it. The last thing my brain should be focused on now is how foreign his touch feels. After days of being subjected primarily to just one man, the rough sensation of another's touch is grating on my frayed nerves.

I've forgotten how to preen and primp. How to endure. How to lie so well that I fooled even myself.

It's harder to tap into the muscle memory that made it so easy to submit to unwanted advances.

Snap out of it, Ada!

I smile back and force my hand to twitch toward him. "Are… Are we close to stopping?"

With his gaze on my leg, he begins to stroke up and down, bringing his fingers alarmingly close to my inner thigh with each pass.

"I ain't one to follow the tabloids and shit," he says against my ear. "But I heard of you. Prancing around, spending your daddy's money. Even as fucked up as you look, you're still pretty damn hot." He brings his other hand near my cheek, brushing the tangled hair from my face. "I'm sure Domino has had plenty of fun with you, the bastard. What about you and I have some fun as well? I think you might enjoy this far better."

His hand boldly dips between my legs, and any other time in the previous month, I think I would have spread them willingly—assuming I had a directive from my father. Maybe that's the twisted reason why it's so damn hard now. Why my entire skin threatens to crawl off my body as I register his touch. My thighs twitch before I even realize it, clamping his hand between them.

He laughs, undeterred. "Don't tell me you're a picky little bitch? I think you should play nice. It's a long drive back over the border, and Ralph plans to take a turn at the next rest stop. So let's have our fun while we can—"

He's too fast, shoving me onto my back, easily maneuvering on top of me. Pain lances up my injured arm, and my mind goes blank as blood rushes to my ears. I register the moist heat on my neck first below the collar—his mouth.

Both of his hands claw at my chest, trying to wrench up my shirt, heedless of the brace on my wrist.

I inhale through my nose, biting back the agony to fixate on an immediate course of action. I can't panic. He's too strong, his wiry body seemingly composed of solid muscle. The second I even acknowledge his strength, I feel his knee jab into my hip, blocking the knife from my reach. All I can do is rely on instinct. So I blindly lean in the direction of his mouth.

The bastard doesn't even stop to question my supposed change of heart. His lips lash at mine sloppily as he fights to shove his tongue down my throat. The taste of him is ten times worse than the smell—like licking an ashtray.

Still, he rolls onto his side to give me better access, wrenching me on top of him. In the same course of time, he manages to draw the hem of my shirt up over my breasts, struggling to pull it off completely.

My thoughts are a scattered mess, overpowered by the need to escape. Run. It takes everything I have just to swat the fear aside and think.

With him on his back, I have a clearer view of the window straight ahead. Should I manage to escape from the RV, I wouldn't make it far without being seen over the relatively flat terrain. There's nowhere to hide.

But, if I somehow manage to catch both men off guard, could I even drive the truck?

As if my thoughts were the cue, the entire vehicle suddenly pitches sharply to the right.

"Shit!" Mick shoves me off. Panting, he glowers in the direction of the driver's seat. "Fucking bastard. What the fuck Ralph? Playing around when—"

"No fucking game!" The rock music cuts off, allowing the other man's voice to reach us clearly. "Someone's on our tail!" He grunts, and we're thrown so hard against the side of the truck I taste copper. My ears won't stop ringing as I blink to regain my bearings and find myself sprawled over the far end of the mattress while Mick scrambles to his feet.

"What the fuck?"

Again, the vehicle pitches sideways, but the entire floor vibrates this time, the windows rattling in their frames. It's as if the road switched from asphalt to uneven earth, and we're going fast. Too fast.

Panic surges up my throat—a flavor composed of blood and salty sweat—but I still have the sense of mind to recognize a way out when I hear one. Someone is behind them.

Domino.

My heart swells with a mixture of hope and disbelief. He's here—and I have no better chance to assist in my rescue than now.

I'm already crawling to the edge of the mattress, but Mick doesn't react. He's at the partition, bellowing at the wood.

"What the fuck is going on? Ralph?"

Suddenly, amid the crunch of the tires skidding over earth and gravel, the truck comes to an abrupt stop. My stomach lurches as I lose my balance and nearly careen into him. I barely manage to brace myself against a countertop bordering the kitchenette—but for the first time, I have a clear shot to the door.

At the back of my mind, a part of me warns that there's no way I can outrun these men. But it's not like I have any better options.

I bolt onto my toes and throw myself down the small set of steps. Fumbling for the door, I manage to grip the latch, but the second I try to open it, my hair is tugged viciously from behind.

"What the hell? You little bitch!"

He wrenches so hard I fly back, landing on my hip, feeling the middle step bite into my side. Pain washes over me as my wrist is jarred in its brace, but there isn't time to indulge in the agony. A flicker in my peripheral vision betrays the moment he reaches for me again, clawing at my arm. Frantic, I kick out at the door with both feet, utilizing every ounce of strength I can muster. With a violent pop, it flies fully open.

"Fuck!" Mick succeeds in yanking me back, and I slam into the wooden partition, gasping out as my vision goes black.

It returns in snippets at first. I just see Mick standing over me. His hand curling into a fist. That fist flying through the air.

Then bright spots dance across my vision.

I'm lying on the floor when I can see clearly again, feeling the gritty linoleum against my cheek.

"You stupid bitch!" Mick steps over me, pounding on the partition. "Ralph, what the fuck? How many are on our ass? You don't think it's him? Mateo swore they made a deal—"

"Just get the fuck up here!"

"Shit."

I feel a hand latch onto my ankle, dragging me down the hall. A door opens, and I'm shoved inside a narrow space, too dark to make out clearly.

"You stay here, you fucking bitch!"

The door slams trapping me alone as heavy footsteps rattle the floor. He must leave the vehicle entirely because I hear a far-off shout. Then a louder, sharper noise draws a scream from my throat.

I recognize it, despite only having heard it once before in far more morbid detail.

A gunshot.

CHAPTER FOURTEEN

Two loud pops rip through the air. Then silence falls, one so heavy only the sound of my breathing disrupts it. Scrambling to my knees, I fumble in my surroundings, straining my eyes to get a better view of where exactly I am.

An acrid, putrid stench gives me a grim idea. As I feel out, my hand lands over a firm, round surface that confirms that horrific suspicion. It's a bathroom, barely larger than a closet, consisting of a small toilet and a minuscule sink. I blink as my eyes adjust to a faint sliver of light. It comes from one direction in particular—a small window with a wooden shade partially drawn over it. I lunge to my feet and push it higher, but a thick layer of dust and grime obscures any view.

Shit.

Desperate, I strain my ears for any sign of Domino, hoping against the worst. The sound of those gunshots keeps echoing in my mind, but I can't let myself consider any scenario in which he isn't alive.

Think, Ada! My heart is pounding so fiercely it feels like it might crash out of my chest. A cold sweat coats my back, and my teeth won't stop chattering. I think I'm at the point where my brain has learned to block out the pain, but only for as long as the adrenaline remains high.

Luckily, there seems to be plenty to keep my nerves on red alert. Someone's coming. I can hear their steps approaching from outside, along this end of the RV. They move slowly. Cautiously.

Not Mick or Ralph. The cadence is different, more graceful, and not heavy with bravado. Someone unfazed even by gunshots.

My heart swells with recognition, and I pound on the door as hard as I can. "I'm in here! Domino!"

A sound echoes that I assume is the main door rattling on its hinges. Those slow, steady footsteps continue—belonging to the figure cautiously mounting the stairs one by one until, finally, they slow near my hiding place. The latch jiggles as it's tested, rattling the entire frame.

"It's locked," I call, pushing against the flimsy panel. "Can you open it?"

He's silent—but a subtle click sounds as the door finally gives way. I scramble to push it open…

Only to recoil in the same motion, putting as much distance between myself and the figure on the other end as I can.

“Hello there, little minx,” my rescuer growls.

I go cold, registering all the ways this isn’t right. His voice is far too deep for one. The cadence alone cements my instinctive fear, but I’m pathetic enough to hope I’m wrong. Pray.

In a swift, controlled motion, he steps forward into the light, and reality grossly contradicts the sight I expect to see. Domino isn’t the one standing here, panting with the effort of taking on two armed men alone.

This figure is too broad. His eyes are darker, his smile predatory.

Jaguar.

Alarm belatedly surges through my veins to replace the shock. My free hand is in my pocket before I know it, grasping for the knife.

“Easy,” he purrs, raising both hands in a gesture of surrender. They’re empty—he’s unarmed. Or so he wants me to believe.

His dark pants could certainly disguise the outline of a weapon. As I inspect both pockets, he chuckles.

“Is that any way to show your *gratitude*?” His guttural tone transforms the word into something violent, even as his smile remains intact.

I can't stop myself from scanning the sliver of hallway behind him, hunting for someone. Anyone. The RV itself is empty apart from us. I can't hear the signs of another person.

Did he really come here alone?

"I didn't believe it," he murmurs, shifting to block my view. A whiff of his scent hits me full in the face, heightening the dread building in my stomach. I step back, pressing myself flat against the wall.

It's no use. His widening smile confirms what my own logic tells me—I'm trapped.

"Dom-Dom *really* left you all alone, and in a state such as this—" his eyes trace the contours of my collar, but he doesn't seem alarmed by the sight. "That's a damn shame, darlin'."

Left you. I ignore the word choice, for now, desperate to keep my breathing in check. He leans against the doorframe, his bulk apparent as muscle ripples through his shoulders, down his arms.

"You're lucky I came to rescue you when that bastard didn't." He extends his hand, and a closer view reveals the calloused surface is streaked with reddish dirt. "Come on. Let's get you out of here."

Any other day I wouldn't hesitate. Survival would be my paramount concern, and I wouldn't feel this irrational pang in my throat at the thought of Domino leaving. Some pathetic part of me wouldn't keep wishing for him to show up. Now.

Please...

"Did you hear me?" The shift in Jaguar's tone is so chilling I jump. Sweat slicks my palms, threatening my grip on the knife—and his gaze cuts to it instantly.

"Don't tell me you were hoping for *Domino*," he chuckles out the name, and yet the broken cadence is more unsettling than his previous growl. It's enough to shatter his gallant hero façade. This is no rescue.

"Choosing him has only gotten you that shiny new accessory around your neck to complement that pretty black eye," he adds.

I wince, self-conscious despite everything else demanding my focus. He's too big to overpower. Too heavy to outrun. My only hope at all is to find a way past him and hide.

But how?

The sight of his outstretched hand carries the same damning inevitability as a death sentence. I leave with him now, and I'll never see Domino—let alone Terra—again.

So fight, a tiny voice in my head insists. *Do something!* The plan forming in my mind is desperate. Insane. The Ada Pavalos from a few weeks ago would never consider it.

But she hadn't been beaten and maimed and betrayed twice over.

"Don't tell me you'd rather stay here. We don't have long before Mateo catches wind of this little party. I bet the first thing he'll do is try to set off that pretty little necklace of yours. The bastard never could share his toys."

The threat strengthens what little resolve I feel building within me. Tightening my grip over the leather handle, I look up.

"Where are we going?" I ask, my voice hollow and trembling.

Jaguar's gallant grin twitches, and I recall a lesson I once learned the hard way—he doesn't like to be questioned. "Somewhere safe." He extends his hand again, flexing the fingers impatiently. "Let's go."

I step toward him—only the knife is still in my grasp. Even as I reach out, I seem unable to let go of it. So I don't, twisting my hand so the blade-side faces down. In slow-motion, I watch as the metal bites at the calloused palm in its path with a ferocity I shouldn't even be capable of.

"Shit!" He instinctively rocks back on his heels, snatching his hand away.

A tiny sliver of space opens beside him, and I lunge. There isn't time for shock or horror. I just pivot, sprinting over the peeling linoleum.

Rather than shout, Jaguar just…

Laughs. Slow and leisurely, his chuckles meld with my hammering pulse, creating a twisted melody.

"Oh darlin', if you wanted to play, you only needed to ask."

This narrow hallway is unending. It feels like an eternity before I reach the steps near the door and stagger down them. My ears pick up the sound of footsteps in my wake—but they're too soft.

Too slow.

Too patient.

"I'm going to have so much fun breaking you..."

The taunt chases me out beneath the cripplingly hot sun. My eyes stream, glazed with sweat as I try to find an exit. Something. By chance, I spot the driver-side door of the cab left ajar, and I lunge for it, wrenching on the handle.

I've barely widened the gap when an arm swings out to slam against my chest. Ralph? Choking back a scream, I grapple with the knife, swinging it senselessly before I realize there's no use in fighting.

Ralph isn't attacking me. He's too still. For the first time, my nostrils register the spicy, overwhelming stench of copper as my eyes note the scarlet substance painting nearly every surface. Blood. Puddles of it flood the seat, adding a gruesome backdrop to where this man's head should be.

"Oh God—" Nausea crawls up my throat. Frantic, I stagger back, running straight into another body.

Only this one is standing, pulsing with dangerous virility.

"We'll chalk this little outburst up to shock," Jaguar murmurs against my ear. He snatches my chin in the same instant, easily fighting off my attempts to break free. I can't see him from this position—only feel his unyielding strength easily wrestle me into submission. "A little nap should help you feel all better."

A shadow rushes at me from the corner of my eye, too quickly to dodge. A sickening thud resonates through my skull next.

And the world goes black.

CHAPTER FIFTEEN

I wake up dazed. For a few precious seconds, I float in blissful ignorance, relishing the peace...

Then the pain sets in. Fear comes next, flooding my veins with each frantic beat of my heart. Soon, every nerve in my body burns with desperate energy—it's electric. The air itself contains a warning—a masculine scent infecting my lungs with every breath. *Move. Danger.*

Rustling noises heighten my anxiety before I even hear it—a voice piercing the silence like a knife. "Wakey, wakey, Ada-Maria." Though in a ghoulish singsong, that guttural baritone requires no introduction.

It's as if an invisible hand yanks away the veil of sleep shrouding me. I'm painfully awake. Heart racing, I spring into motion, scrambling to guard my head before I even get my eyes open. When I do, darkness is all that greets me. And pain. I'm lying flat on my stomach, but a pulsing ache stabs through my left side. Paired with the cold, grainy texture of the floor beneath me, I suspect I've been thrown here, unceremoniously.

Judging from the telltale weight on my throat, I'm still wearing the collar as well. That isn't the only unwelcome realization. A groan rips from my lips as I crane my neck back, taking in my surroundings via what little illumination there is. The room isn't entirely dark—a monstrous shadow is blocking most of the light, letting in only a trickle of orangish glow to see by.

"There we go." As the "shadow" looms larger, the scent in my nostrils turns cloying, betraying what it really is. Or who. Someone tall, with handsome features so perfect they could have been chiseled into stone. A name instantly comes to mind, inspiring a wave of terror that leaves me quaking.

Jaguar.

"I have to say," he murmurs, sliding his tongue across his lip. Those predatory brown eyes glitter with malicious intent—too real to be imagined. "Despite looking like hell, you're still damn fine."

Fear paralyzes me as he grips my chin, wrenching it back. The side of my face burns, and a fiery agony near my eye warns that once again, I've met the hard end of a fist. His?

"No wonder little Dom-Dom's chosen you as the star of our little pissing contest."

He leans forward, bringing his face into clearer focus—as well as the room behind him. It's narrow, with plain walls and a low, water-stained ceiling. My fear grows; I don't recognize it.

Confusion makes me dumb enough to speak. "What… Where—"

"Uh-uh." He tightens his grip with a force that mockingly contrasts the false gentleness in his voice. "Don't worry. You and I are going to have a nice little chat about everything. But first? Darlin'!" He gestures with his free hand, and a soft voice greets him, the speaker out of my view.

"Yes, sir?"

"Get little Ms. Ada here all cleaned up. Then show her around. She won't be our guest for long."

"Yes, sir."

He releases me, turning on his heel as a smaller figure appears by his side. She's thin and pale, wearing a black bra and a skirt barely longer than a pair of underwear. Her brown hair has been tied back from a delicate face, every feature accented by dark makeup.

"Bring her to the showroom when you're done," Jaguar calls. "See you then, Ada-Maria."

His chilling laugh echoes as he retreats through a doorway, shrouded by what looks like a curtain of hanging beads. Their sparkly nature contrasts sharply with his darker demeanor, giving our surroundings a more garish edge.

"Come on." The woman steps forward, reaching for my injured wrist before she changes tack, grabbing my other hand. "We don't have long. You don't want to make him angry. Trust me."

"Where are we?" I ask.

"That's not important," the woman whispers. Persistent, she tugs me to my feet, using her slender body to stabilize mine. "Just follow me, and keep your mouth shut."

I'm limping to keep up as she hurries me through the doorway. The hallway beyond is narrow, with no windows and only a naked hanging lightbulb to illuminate the way. With furtive glances, I inspect whatever I can to get my bearings. My feet are bare, scraping against a gritty linoleum flooring. I run my hand over my pocket, unsurprised to find my knife missing.

A few feet down from the room we exited, the woman guides me through another doorway. A small sink sits along the far wall, along with a shower stall.

Shit.

"Over here." Near a filthy mirror, the woman releases me, tugging at my shirt.

I look even worse than before, mirrored over the smeared glass. At least now, I have a clear view of the collar. It's about an inch wide, shiny enough to reflect what little light there is. If I wasn't aware of its sinister nature, I'd assume it was a choker-style necklace.

Just one with no way of opening it.

Intent on her task, the woman doesn't seem to notice my preoccupation with the device. She reaches for the clasp of my jeans next, but I back away, raising my hand defensively. "What are you doing?"

"Just do what I say." She keeps darting her gaze toward the door. "He can't be kept waiting. Please..."

With frantic movements, she continues to undress me. Given that I can barely keep my balance, I have no choice but to relent, craning my neck to take in the rest of the room. There are no windows in here. No indication of what or where this building might be. Apart from the overall grime, the air smells wet and moldy. Are we underground?

"We need to hurry," the woman insists. She scurries away with my clothing in her hands, pausing only to bark over her shoulder, "Wait here."

I follow her anyway, unable to shake the dread building in the pit of my stomach. It's as if an invisible clock is ticking down. When time runs out, who knows what will happen?

Nothing good for me.

Luckily, the woman seems too distracted to notice when I peer into the hall after her. She heads left, disappearing through another doorway. I can see someone moving just beyond the archway. Jaguar?

No, they're too thin. Another woman?

"Please! I told you not to move!" The brunette reappears, frantically ushering me back into the bathroom. In her hands is a strip of black material that catches the light. She unfurls it, revealing a dress only a fraction more conservative than her skimpy ensemble.

"Put this on—"

"Where are we?" I step back, heart in my throat. "Please. Just tell me something."

"P-Please." Her eyes cut fearfully toward the doorway before she steps forward, bringing her mouth near my ear. "You're in hell," she whispers. "And the man who brought you here? He's the devil."

With that admission, she grimly tugs the dress over my head. I'm numb as she tackles my hair next, revealing a pouch she must have carried here as well. Inside it is a brush and a tube of lipstick that she swipes across my lips.

Taken all together, I don't recognize myself. It's a change more drastic than just a haircut and a dye job. There's something in my eyes I don't ever recall seeing there before. A hard, frozen expression.

I shiver before I fully process why—I look like someone.

I look like Domino.

"Come on." The woman takes my uninjured arm, pulling me into the hall.

This time, we head right, venturing further. The hallway itself is plain, borderline decrepit. Any room we pass looks barely furnished. Most contain cots covered with thin blankets and a few chairs. Past them all is an archway opening onto a larger space that vaguely resembles some of the clubs I used to frequent—just not one in the upscale part of Terra Rodea.

The walls are bare concrete, sporting a row of what looks to be windows, each coated in a layer of black paint to block out any view. A bar looms at one end of the space, plastered with posters of half-naked women. Across from it is a round stage with a pole in the center, and seated in a booth beyond it, lurks the room's lone audience member.

He slowly claps as I approach, and my body comes alive with a mixture of pain and unease. There's a predatory quality in his gaze that even Domino lacks. Something violent and insidious.

It's hungry.

"Step right up." He crooks a beckoning finger at me while the woman by my side remains rooted in place.

He's wearing a similar outfit to the one he wore at Domino's estate. A black shirt and dark-wash jeans must be his preferred style. The tattoo on his arm remains bared, etched with such detail it seems to move, the jaguar prowling along his bicep.

When I'm only a few feet away, he leans back, appraising me with another searching glance. As I am about to take another step, he snaps his fingers, and I instinctively stop short. Satisfied, he nods, a smirk playing across his lips.

"Welcome to one small sliver of my domain." He gestures to our surroundings with a wave of his hand. "This lovely place here is a new acquisition. Within a few weeks, it will be the belle of the ball. A star attraction. Not that you'll be here to see it."

My stomach flips as I pick up on the dare he doesn't voice. *Ask me why.*

Licking my lips, I weigh the least dangerous response while simultaneously inspecting the rest of the space. Apart from the windows, I don't see a door—but there must be another entrance.

"Eyes up here," Jaguar snaps. Terrified, I whip my gaze to him, but he's still smiling. "Come closer."

Sucking in a breath, I take a step. His scent worms into my lungs, lethally potent. I swear, the pain in my arm intensifies with every inch gained as if heightened by his mere presence.

Only God knows how I manage to suppress the shiver ripping through me as he captures my uninjured wrist, pulling me the rest of the way—violently. With a startled grunt, I land on his lap. My knee digs into the seat cushion at his side, and his hand on my hip is the only thing to steady me.

Through a heavy-lidded gaze, he inspects me yet again, and I can't even begin to unravel the tumult of emotion lurking behind his eyes. An overarching theme can be assumed, however—rage. "I'm surprised Dom-Dom let you out of his sight, let alone with those two fuckers. Not that he had much of a choice, given your flashy new hardware—" he nods to the collar. "Who knows what naughty things they might have done to you if I didn't happen to swoop in? You're welcome."

He grips my chin, applying a subtle amount of pressure with his thumb. Then more…

Belatedly, I realize what he wants, and I rush to pry my lips apart. "T-Thank you."

"You're welcome." He grins, but his eyes remain flat, coolly observant. "What were you doing so far away from old Dom, anyway? Don't tell me he grew bored of his little Ada."

My cheeks flame at the insinuation, but his malicious tone triggers another concern. I don't see Mick lurking around this room. I contemplate the risks of questioning him again, but the curiosity is too great to smother. "The men I was with, are… Are they—"

"Dead?" He phrases it so casually. As though he's referring to the weather and nothing more. "Yes. It will send a nice warning to Mateo and clean up loose ends. I'm a big fan of neatness. Tidiness." His deepening tone makes my heart stutter, and his smile grows even wider.

"Domino did a bad, bad thing by taking you from me. It wasn't your fault, of course…" As he speaks, he trails his finger up along the curve of my brace, grazing the tender flesh of my shoulder beneath. With every dangerous caress, I jump. "But I think it's best if you learn sooner than later—"

Pain! I scream before I even fully register what he's done—dig his nails into my forearm, jarring the limb. Just as quickly, I choke off the cry, gritting my teeth against any sound. My eyes water at the fiery agony darting through my right arm, but I breathe through it, straining to hear every word he says next.

"Domino has no loyalty," he explains, loosening his grip. "The bastard is cocky enough to think he's always been one step ahead, but he isn't the only one with friends in high places. I know all about his little plan to stab me in the back, then take you and the Pavalos empire for himself. My question is, do *you* know what he's planning?"

He gently strokes the hair from my face, but I've learned my lesson. I don't say a damn thing.

"I'm sure he's filled your head with plenty of silly little lies," he says, unbothered. "You don't want me as an enemy, Ada-Maria. But don't take my word for it. I want us to be friends. I'll even give you a gift, to prove my sincerity."

I brace myself as he reaches into the pocket of his jeans and withdraws a silver, square item that I recognize instantly. It isn't a weapon, but no less dangerous. A remote, much like the one Mateo taunted me with.

"It wasn't hard to find who Mateo used to supply his little toys. I was even able to have this particular collar reprogramed to a different detonator—" Jaguar wiggles the remote while I scramble to keep up. Reprogramed? My puzzled expression must amuse him enough to enlighten me without prompting. "With this, you won't have to worry about Mateo getting trigger happy, as long as I block the signal every twenty-four hours. Removing it completely will take a bit of finesse, though."

He inspects the contraption in question, but disgust isn't what I see flash through his dark eyes. It's glee. Ironically, I once thought that Domino's familiarity with a whip was chilling, the hallmark of a true monster.

I was wrong.

"This baby is a unique design, used primarily by one man who likes to keep his girls under lock and key. Care to guess who?" he asks, an eyebrow raised.

I clamp my lips against replying, and he shrugs.

"No? I'm sure Domino would recognize it."

His tone is deliberately casual, daring me to question him. When I don't, he laughs, fingering the curved bit of metal resting directly over my windpipe.

"Lucky for you, I'm willing to help you remove it. Would you like that?"

His tone is more playful than earnest. He's lying.

I nod anyway, fighting to keep any skepticism from my face. "Y-Yes."

"Good." His smile falls in a way that heralds the sinister nature no doubt lurking behind this "offer." With a flick of his wrist, he returns the remote to its hiding place. "I'll let you be in control for once. Control of who lives and who dies. I bet Domino never gave you that privilege, huh?"

He narrows his eyes when I don't react. Jerkily, I shake my head, but I'm too terrified to question him. *Who lives and who dies…*

"Isn't that right?"

I nod, feeling my pulse hammer in my throat.

"So I'll tell you what your prize will be. I'll continue to jam that pretty little collar's receiver in exchange for a life. Don't worry," he adds as I flinch. "Not your own. In fact, darlin', I think this should be an easy choice to make. Domino or your father. Which one will get blown to pieces?"

His inflection never changes. I can't tell if he's serious, or merely spinning a game of wordplay.

"Pick," he warns, pressing his thumb against my lower lip. "I won't ask twice. Unless you aren't flattered by the honor."

"N-No." I shake my head emphatically, nearly falling off his lap in the process. "No… I-I'm grateful—"

"Then who," he demands, leveling me with a cold stare. Gone is the mocking semblance of warmth. He is all ice. "Who dies first?"

My heart lurches, recalling the last time I heard him utilize this low baritone—right before he broke my wrist with his bare hand.

"I don't understand what—"

"Should I tell you something, to make your choice easier?" His breath prickles over my skin, like the warning sparks before hot embers catch fire. "Let's start with Domino, first. The bastard stole from me, did you know that? He's nothing but a fucking thief. He promised you to me, practically used you as a fucking bargaining chip in his war against Roy Pavalos, and then decides that he doesn't want to share after all. He hasn't told you the real reason he hates the bastard, has he?"

His fingers flex against my thigh before withdrawing. Then he snaps them inches from my head.

"Yes, sir?" a woman calls from beyond my view.

"Whiskey on the rocks," he demands, cutting his gaze up to mine. "Make it two."

A commotion comes from the direction of the bar. I assume the other woman never left and is fulfilling his demand, but I don't dare take my eyes off him. Balancing on a highwire must feel like this—like the slightest twitch of a muscle in the wrong direction could lead to disaster.

"My father used to run with Roy Pavalos." He tilts his head in a seemingly casual motion, but I'm not fooled. His upper lip curls back, his eyes narrow. He's angry—much like Domino when he recounted his past. "He considered him like a brother at one point. Trusted him with his life. Until one day, the bastard decided he didn't want to share his empire anymore. Not that I could blame the motherfucker." He extends his hand again, making me flinch, but he reaches past me, grabbing a shot presumably from a tray. "Here."

He offers me one before draining his own glass. I rush to copy him—but he snatches my wrist before I can take a sip, sloshing liquid from the rim and down onto my fingers.

"A toast first," he grates, his voice low.

He lets the silence build as if daring me to propose a reason of my own to toast to. My lips twitch. I'm ready to blurt the first thing that comes to mind.

Raising his glass higher, he beats me to the punch. "To mercy," he murmurs, mutilating the word into something violent. "Now drink."

I immediately throw my head back, choking down the burning liquid as the collar's edge bites into my windpipe. I've barely swallowed when he takes my glass, handing both to a woman who scurries out of sight.

"Yes, Roy Pavalos wanted it all for himself," he says, continuing his tale. "What he didn't know, was that my father was one step ahead of him." He taps my chin with the tip of a calloused finger. "He thought he had someone on the inside, you see? Someone he could trust. Someone he revealed his whole plot to take down Roy Pavalos once and for all to. Care to take a guess?"

My mind goes blank. According to Domino, Carlos died long before he went to work for my father. Could he be referring to Pia?

No. Something flits across his expression, transforming it for a heartbeat—hatred. Hate so consuming it chills me to the core. If I didn't know better, I'd assume he was referring to *me.*

"You look like her," he murmurs, cupping my cheek while my heart pounds against my ribcage. "Just a little, around your mouth. That sly cunt. She played my father for a fool, but it was his own damn fault for trusting a Pavalos. What she stole from him, though? That I would like returned to me very, very much."

Something in his grated tone emboldens me to brave the risk and ask him outright. "What?"

I cringe in anticipation of a blow.

"A ring," he says simply, lowering his gaze to my twitching hands. "Silver. Ornate. Worth a massive fucking penny in more ways than one."

I can barely keep my expression blank. I knew someone who owned a ring like that…

"My father entrusted it to Lia Pavalos once upon a time," Jaguar explains, returning his attention to my face. "May she rot in hell."

He waits, displaying that predatory intensity once more. He wants a reaction—an opening to pounce.

Defiantly, I make my face blank, constricting every last muscle. My jaw is throbbing by the time he finally sighs in defeat, still stroking the side of my face.

"You have a lot to atone for, Ada-Maria. Dom-Dom's sins, as well as your bitch of a mother's. But first… You can accept your gift now. Who should be punished?"

His tone leaves no room to stall. "I…"

"Sir!"

I whip my head around just as a door opens near the stage. Painted the same color as the walls; I didn't notice it before. Another man stands behind it now, his face bathed in shadow. "You should come to see this—"

"You dare to fucking interrupt me." Jaguar's grated baritone is as startling as a bucket of ice water being dumped over my head. So chilling. Soulless.

But the other man is persistent. "I… Sir, there's something you should see."

Jaguar doesn't reply for a handful of seconds that feel like an eternity. Finally, he shrugs me off, and I barely manage to stand without falling, swaying to find my balance.

"Baby!" He snaps his fingers, and a woman appears in the doorway I came from—but she isn't the slender brunette. Shock rips through me, and I forget to school my expression.

"Take Ada-Maria to her room," Jaguar commands. "We'll continue this later."

"Yes, baby." Her voice a husky purr, the woman stalks forward, grabbing my arm only out of sheer obedience, I suspect. Disgust radiates from her—almost as much as the loathing I'm sure exudes from me.

We make it into the hall before she finally wrenches away, spinning to face me.

"What the hell are you doing here?" she hisses.

"I could ask you the same question," I counter, but disbelief robs some of the hostility from my voice.

She looks like hell, a shadow of the woman who pranced around Domino's estate days ago. Matted, blond hair hangs loosely down her shoulders. Her outfit—a skintight pink mini dress—is less revealing than mine, but it's rumpled, giving the impression that she's worn it multiple times without it being washed.

Stalking ahead, she turns into a room a few doors down from the bathroom. It's small, with a battered leather couch along one wall, two narrow cots, and little else. With a forced yawn, Alexi stretches out her arms and throws herself onto the sofa.

"Ada-Maria, here at last," she says, an eyebrow raised. "Frankly, I'm surprised Domino gave you up after all. He seemed determined to fight over you like a dog with a bone."

I hate the familiarity in her voice. It rouses those nagging suspicions as to her relationship with Domino all over again. Just how close were they?

No. I quash the thought, gritting my teeth. Now isn't the time for petty jealousy. That relentless sensation of seconds counting down returns. *Tick tock.* Paired with the looming threat of Jaguar's "gift," everything in my body is warning me that when time runs out…

This won't end well.

I need to escape.

Or wait for Domino, a tiny voice in my head whispers. God, I hate the part of me that longs for him. It's unexpected. Weak, not to mention just plain pathetic. For all I know, Domino is already at the border and hasn't looked back.

The truth is, he was right—he can find Pia on his own. I'm no longer necessary to his grand plan.

It's time to devise my own strategy for survival.

"Where are we?" I ask, ignoring the bait for now. "Near Terra?"

Any hope I have is dashed by her scoff. "Hell no. Far from it—" her eyes dart warily to the door before returning to me. Sitting upright, she leans forward, lowering her voice to a whisper. "Jaguar won't risk letting you out of his grasp. Not until he knows for sure what Domino wants you for. I bet he'll move out soon and bring you straight to his compound."

"The *Guarida*?" I ask.

If she's surprised by my use of the word, her scoff disguises it. Then she laughs. "That place is paradise in comparison. No, Ada. He's taking you *home*."

A feeling like falling washes over me. I can taste my own fear, welling on my tongue like fresh blood—then I realize it is blood. I've bitten my tongue hard enough to bleed.

"Why?"

Her eyes blaze, as if my perceived ignorance is an insult. "Don't be stupid. He won't let Domino take you anywhere. Not until he knows what he wants you for."

"Domino wants me to settle a score," I say. "Nothing more."

"Oh, bullshit! And you really believed that? God, you were always so goddamn gullible, Ada. This is about far more than revenge. I'm sure you could guess that by now. Though it's not like you could go far with that shit around your neck."

Weighing my options, I decide to play into the narrative. "So tell me what I don't know?"

She stands, coming toe-to-toe with me. Her beauty is as incredible as ever head-on—but undeniably frayed. Her makeup is smeared in places, her breath sweet with the faint hint of alcohol.

"Wake up, Ada. The world doesn't revolve around you. This is all much, much bigger than your surgically enhanced ass. God, I don't even know what would be better. Crushing your fragile worldview by telling you the truth? Or letting you find out the hard way."

Her smile is mean, her lips peeled back from her teeth—but in her eyes lurks an unstable, wild expression I recognize instantly. Fear.

"You can't tell me," I say, taking a shot in the dark. "Can you?"

Bullseye. She flinches, her lips pursed. "You always were too fucking dumb for your own good, pretending to be so sweet and innocent while your father ruined lives. No wonder Pia couldn't stand you."

I wince. I should have expected this line of attack—but that doesn't make the jab sting any less.

"I don't remember you being that close to her, either—"

"Closer than *you* were. You see, we both came from families that valued hard work. We didn't have the benefit of spending our daddies' money with no damn clue as to where it came from." Her confidence repaired, Alexi steps up to me, inclining her head. "She hated you. Little Ada-Maria with more money than brains, too fucking dumb to see that her daddy was a murderer."

"And yet, you always seemed to want my leftovers," I bite back.

"You make it sound like it was hard," she says, raising an eyebrow. "The truth is, Ada, the only reason men like Tristan gave a damn about you in the first place was because of your father. They wanted him, not you. Though hell, at least Roy Pavalos took pride in gloating over the lives he ruined. Did you even know, or are you still playing naïve after all this time?"

"Know what?" I say, genuinely confused.

"You would think the fact we were friends would have made a difference to him," she says coldly. "But it didn't. When he needed my father out of his way politically, he made sure he was ruined for life. That we *all* were. There wasn't even a penny left for me to inherit. Did you even notice? Or were you too busy trying to cover your ass after Pia went missing?"

I couldn't hide my surprise if I wanted to. I didn't know. From what I remember, Alexi's father was a prominent businessman who dabbled in politics, but a bad investment deal became public and ruined his prospects. I never even considered that my father might have been behind it.

In hindsight, I should have.

"I…" Words fail me, though I doubt she'd accept an apology. Something else she hinted at worms into the forefront of my mind, and I latch onto it like a shield against guilt. "What do you know about what happened to Pia?"

"As if you don't know," she spits back.

"It isn't often that you know something I don't," I say coldly. "Why not test your luck?"

Her eyes cut to slits. "You really think Domino gives a damn about you? Think again. In fact, you being here just proves it. The bastard must have been planning to ditch you all this time. Now it all makes sense…"

Her harsh laugh slips beneath my skin, irritating prickling insecurities. I can't resist playing right into her trap.

"What do you mean?"

She places her hands on her slender hips, and I find that the beautiful manicure she sported at Domino's estate is now chipping and cracked. "I mean, Domino told me all about his plans for you. I just didn't realize that he was serious."

Ice water—that's what this sensation is comparable to. Cold, grim fear drips over me in waves, each one more disarming than the last.

"What plans?" I demand.

Her smile tilts into a cruel grimace. "To leave you behind to rot."

Without another word, she saunters past me, slamming the door in her wake.

Chasing her down would be the smart thing to do. Demanding answers—dragging them out of her if I have to. By the time I can form a coherent thought again, I'm leaning against the wall, running over every damn detail of the past few days. Who honestly knows what Domino's true intentions have been at any given moment?

He lies with such chilling ease I can't even blame myself for falling for part of it. I believed him when he claimed he needed me to find Pia, at least. Though he hinted that wasn't the case either.

There isn't time to cry and dwell in despair.

The strange part is…

Despite how my eyes burn, no tears ever fall.

CHAPTER SIXTEEN

Alexi doesn't return after several minutes. By then, I've snapped out of my pity party. Fuck her. A few days ago, I might have played into her little mind game—not now. I don't need her help to find a way out of this. I just need to think.

Cautiously, I stand, taking in the room more carefully than before. It's small and narrow, with no other exit, and no window to peer from. Before I can fully weigh the risks, I creep to the door. It isn't locked, and the corridor beyond is empty, though voices and echoing footsteps betray a hive of activity.

Jaguar claimed this was a "new acquisition," apparently not the *Guarida* Domino threatened me with. Another club? Either way, there has to be an exit.

Cautiously, I reenter the hall, shivering as my bare feet contact the floor. The next room down isn't empty. Two women lounge on a pair of rickety cots. Their eyes rake over me before darting away, but they don't call out.

So, I keep walking, nearing the archway separating this section from the larger space Jaguar dominated. A glance through it reveals that the "showroom" is empty now, but that ominous tension feels heavier than ever. It doesn't help that Alexi's taunt keeps replaying in my mind. *The bastard must have been planning to ditch you all this time...*

I fight to ignore the pain of betrayal. All that matters now is finding a way out. With a glance over my shoulder, I inch forward, my eyes glued to the door beyond the stage. It's unguarded, but the second I take another step, someone grabs my forearm from behind.

"You idiot," that same person hisses against my ear. The soft cadence diminishes some of the fear washing over me—it's not Jaguar. "Risk your life if you want to but act reckless, and everyone will suffer. Then again, you never gave a fuck about anyone but yourself, did you?"

I spin to face Alexi, her eyes slits. "Go be a good girl and wait your turn—" she jerks her chin toward the room she first led me to.

"Don't touch me." I shrug her off, turning back to the door. "Like hell will I listen to you—"

"Fine. Then what about him? Domino left a message for you. Did I forget to mention that?" she taunts in a whisper. Could she be lying?

Possibly.

And yet, she smirks as I whip around to face her. "Even though he's probably back in Terra by now, I'm sure you're pathetic enough to want to hear it."

It hurts to acknowledge the fleeting desire. Shame forms a knot in my chest, making it harder to breathe.

"Good," Alexi hisses. "So, turn around, go back, and *wait*."

Open hatred is written all over her face, but something in her eyes makes me hesitate. That fear I caught a glimpse of is back—just ten times more obvious. A heartbeat later, it's gone, squashed behind a cold glare.

In the end, I don't know what finally makes me retreat. It isn't that I believe her. Maybe it's the gnawing acceptance that waltzing from the front door most likely won't be the way to leave this place.

When I return to the room, I sit on the nearest cot, facing the door. Unease is a blanket, threatening to suffocate me, but Alexi, for all her bravado, doesn't appear.

It wouldn't be the first time she ever failed to follow through. In school, bailing was practically her MO. I think it's one of the reasons Pia was so drawn to me in the first place—as a backup for shallow friends like Alexi who couldn't be counted upon to remain enamored of her twenty-four-seven.

For the first time, I regret that my captivity isn't more thrilling—no whips and chains to distract me. It's too quiet here. My thoughts run rampant, taunting me with a million different realities at once.

The first is Jaguar's cruel insinuation. Domino never intended to keep me safe. From the start, I was only ever a bargaining chip, used at his discretion—but I can't get his words out of my head. Or how he said them…

A man shouldn't look to the one woman he claims to love as a symbol of everything he hates…

But even his betrayal takes the back seat to a growing horror.

Pia. My own mother insinuated I might have something to do with her death. Did I?

God, I can't remember. Nausea constricts my throat, threatening to bring up what little remains in my stomach—but my gagging is a reminder of the discomfort I've ignored up until now. I'm starving, but that gnawing, persistent hunger isn't the comforting friend I've relied on all these years. It merely reinforces how many ways there are to truly suffer. Another method of torture Jaguar can employ.

I can't stay here.

Lurching to my feet, I head for the doorway. I've barely taken a step when a figure strides from the shadows, her hands on her slender hips. "You really don't know how to fucking listen, do you?" Alexi hisses. "No wonder Domino got bored. And Tristan, too, while we're on the subject."

Her cool smile gives no indicator of even a hint of grief.

"You seem heartbroken by the fact that he's dead," I snarl.

"Why would I be?" She waltzes past me, reclaiming her sprawled position on the couch. "Don't tell me you are? Funny, because I don't think Domino would keep this little secret—Tristan was planning to sell you out from day one. Though I doubt that would turn you off. It seems like you have a thing for men who don't give a shit about you."

I shouldn't be so surprised that she knows. After all, Domino named her as his coconspirator, helping him keep tabs on Tristan's whereabouts and motives.

"Apparently, you knew them both better than I did. Fine. But… You said Domino left a message for me?" My voice breaks, and I hate myself.

But Alexi doesn't seem pleased by my curiosity. "Domino must have a thing for damsels in distress, though I shouldn't be so surprised he fell under the spell of Ada Pavalos, like so many other fools."

"I guess that's why he entertained you, then," I snap.

She nods. "We don't all have rich, powerful daddies to clean up our messes and pay for our bad little habits." Her gaze turns distant. "Some of us have no choice but to make a deal with the devil."

Domino or Jaguar in this instance? She doesn't elaborate.

With an exaggerated sigh, she stretches her arms and rises to her feet. "I suggest you stay here," she warns on her way into the hall. "Jaguar doesn't take kindly to disobedience, and don't be fooled by the others. They'll sell your ass out in a heartbeat."

"Wait!" I start after her, seething with irritation. "What did he say?"

I nearly run into her as she stops short. "Apparently, he thinks you're a pathetic bitch who would be better off overdosing than letting Jaguar have you. I think I'm of a different mind, though. I hope you suffer."

She skips off, swaying her hips, but I've lost the urge to follow her. Instead, I sink back onto one of the cots, kicking myself for trusting her in the first place.

Seconds pass, but she doesn't return to gloat. In her absence, the noises of the others nearby take over again. Coughing. Whispering. Crying? The various sounds create a deafening murmur—until a sudden commotion shatters the hush.

"Girls!" a man shouts, but his voice isn't deep enough to be Jaguar. "Everyone out now. Line up! We need to clear out. Now!"

I rise to my feet and peer into the hall. At least ten other girls swarm from various directions, all heading toward the showroom. I join them without thinking, finding myself in the middle of the pack, being herded past the stage, through the door the other man came from.

My pathetic escape plan is revealed for the folly it was the second I cross the threshold. This isn't an exit, at least not outright. Instead, we're led into a small, bare room lit only by a single overhead light.

"You keep your mouths shut," a man demands, guarding a pair of metal doors. "Get into the truck."

He shoves open one of the doors, allowing in a rush of fresh air. I inhale it greedily, sensing the same dryness as the desert Domino and I traversed. So, Alexi was right—we aren't near Terra.

"Head out," the man commands.

One by one, the women hurry past him, onto what looks like a parking lot. Beneath their frantic breathing and the man's shouts, lurks the hum of what could be a truck engine. We're being moved, and dread suffocates me. What did Alexi say? *He's taking you home...*

"Hey!" Someone rams into me from behind, jarring my shoulder. "Get out of my way!"

The voice is Alexi's, and I assume her nails are what I feel digging into my forearm next. I recoil instinctively, only to feel something press against my palm, small and firm. The shape is too familiar to mistake.

"This is for *Domino*—not you," she snarls against my ear before what feels like a bony hand slams into my lower back. "He said you'd know when," she adds before raising her voice to loudly snap, "I said move!"

Head held high, she waltzes past the man and through the doors.

"Hurry up!" Impatient, the man practically shoves the woman ahead of me forward. When his eyes fall over my face, however, he raises his hand. "Not you. You stay with me."

He pulls me aside, and I panic, clenching the object in my grasp. This dress has no pockets. The only space I can think of to hide the syringe is beneath the edge of the brace, against the swollen palm of my right hand. Thank God. It's thin enough to fit, but even the slightest pressure against my wrist is excruciating. White spots speckle my vision as my pulse hammers through my eardrums. Desperate, I suck in air, fighting to breathe.

Focus, Ada! I blink until my vision clears. From this angle, I have a clearer view of the outside. A parking lot was a correct guess, but a narrow one, squeezed behind another brick building. Yellow headlights paint the asphalt, illuminating a slight sheen of rain.

"Next!"

The final three women scurry out, heading left, hugging this building, presumably to be loaded into the back of the truck.

Once they're out of sight, the man takes my arm. "Come with me."

He steers me through the doorway, and the rain is as bracing as a slap, the air heavy with tension. I can practically taste the unease emanating from those nearby. Even Jaguar?

I don't have to assume for long.

As my vision adjusts, I hear his voice first, rough and grated. "She rides with me."

Blinking, I make out a large truck, its headlights blinding, but the man doesn't pull me in that direction. Instead, we head past it, where a van waits. It's black and sleek, resembling one of the luxury vehicles paraded by rich politicians through the heart of Terra Rodea.

The door to the back seat is already open, and the man shoves me toward it. "Get in."

I scramble onto the leather as my spine stiffens with awareness of the predator nearby. His scent fills the space along with the spicy tinge of smoke. A cigarette? I look up to find him watching me, seated on a leather seat before a tinted-glass barrier. Presumably, the driver is behind it, responsible for the van lurching into motion. Overall, the interior has been custom designed, outfitted with leather seating on either end and a minibar placed in between.

"You and I need to finish our little chat," Jaguar says. In one hand, he sports a lit cigar, the burning embers igniting his gaze. "Have you decided yet?"

The rain patters off the windows, adding a chilling backdrop to his question.

"I..."

For whatever reason, something Alexi said comes back to me. *You were always so goddamn gullible.*

That might not be a bad thing? It just means the curiosity in my voice is genuine as I ask, "Who do you think I should pick?"

His eyes narrow, and I nearly choke—before I realize that his expression doesn't contain the volatile anger I'm used to. He's thoughtful. I can only pray that sentiment lasts.

"Your father is a bad man, baby," he says, tilting his head back against the headrest. "But Domino? He's dangerous. Roy Pavalos, from what I've seen, follows a creed. He has loyalty, if only for himself—" he chuckles, and I feel my cheeks flame, as though I'm the butt of his unspoken joke. "He has some honor, more than our little friend Dom, anyway. *That* bastard? He has no loyalty."

The sick part is that I can agree with him in that sense. Domino seems to pledge allegiance only to himself.

But I can't forget what he said to me in the shower. *Even at my own fucking detriment, I can't seem to stop trying to save you...*

"I'm sure you've realized that," Jaguar says, intruding upon the memory. "While you've been here, safe under my care, do you want to know where that bastard has been?" A deep laugh resonates in his chest. "He's at the border, attempting to cross as we speak. So much for his gallant hero streak."

He puffs on his cigar, igniting the end a deeper red. The glow reflects off his irises, mimicking flames.

"Do you even know why he wanted you in the first place? Politics. Our Dom is a very smart lad. He likes to play it safe, and for him to blow his cover as a Pavalos lackey, you must be very special to him. Do you know why?"

Danger. My spine tightens as I sense the double meaning behind his words—suspicion.

"I…"

"No!" He snaps his fingers, sitting forward. "Speak clearly. Do you know what he wanted you for?"

"He hates my father," I croak. "He wanted to hurt me, I guess."

"Hurt you…" Apparently satisfied by that answer, Jaguar sits back, stroking his chin with one hand while the other taps his cigar into an ashtray balanced on top of the bar. "And he did, didn't he? The bastard. I will only treat you how you deserve to be treated. Do you understand that?"

"Y-Yes," I say quickly.

"Good." His smile widens, his teeth glimmering in the dark. "Dom would never give you that kind of assurance. Promises mean nothing to him. Neither does upholding his word. *Loyalty*."

This time he gives the word a noticeable emphasis. The same way my mother might refer to her prayers and the religious figure they centered around. With utmost reverence.

"He made my family a promise once…" He turns his gaze to the window, scowling at the darkened landscape. I copy him, unable to make out anything definitive. It's pitch black. This road, however, is bumpy, jostling the van almost constantly.

Every movement jars my arm, forcing me to grit my teeth against the pain. Sweat drips down my neck, and I'm sure he'll notice I'm hiding something. Though hell, maybe I should use it now? Domino's "gift" could serve as more than a mocking joke.

It's the only chance I have to escape. Even as the plan unfurls, doubt undercuts any hope I feel. I'm not stupid enough to believe that I could catch Jaguar unguarded. Unless…

"A promise to honor the Domingas name," Jaguar continues. "To remain by my side, family in every way but blood. We gave that motherfucker everything we had to offer. And do you know what he did?" He extends his empty hand, curling the fingers over his palm one by one. "He fucking spit in my face."

His anger is chilling, resonating in my bones.

"I could have killed the bastard a million times over. Do you want to know something? I've offered him chance after chance to make things right. But for you… I'll make an exception. You ask for his head, I'll bring it to you. After I exact an apology from him, of course. Just say the word."

Fighting to keep my face blank, I think back to his twisted "offer." Of course, it was never a real choice at all.

And it should be an easy concession to make. Tell him I want Domino dead and keep myself alive for a while longer.

But with Jaguar, I suspect that nothing is just talk. Every word matters to him. Even a death threat wouldn't be uttered without a consequence to pay down the road.

"So what will it be?" he demands, flicking his cigar again. "I've been patient, but I'd like an answer. Now."

I drag my tongue across my dry lips. "I—"

"Come here." He crooks a finger, and every ounce of air leaves my lungs.

Shit. Even now, I can catch the glint of something peeking beneath the edge of my brace. I can't risk him seeing it as well.

"Ada-Maria." His tone takes on that lethal edge, and I have no choice but to jump out of my seat. By chance, my gaze happens to fall across the mini bar, and I angle myself toward it, keeping my right arm close to my chest.

"I… A toast?" I don't even know what exactly I'm asking for. Maybe I should take Domino's advice literally? For all I know, this could be a lethal dose.

One last high before the inevitable.

"A toast," Jaguar echoes in a tone that makes my entire body go cold. I force myself to keep breathing as the seconds tick by. Finally, he sighs.

"To your decision, I presume?" His laugh raises goosebumps, but I find a small shred of relief in the absence of that volatile anger. For now.

"Yes." I drop to my knees before he can change his mind, forced to stabilize my injured hand against the floor of the van.

As I reach for the bar, Jaguar chuckles again. "Make mine a whiskey."

"Okay." Shaken, I tug on a glossy handle, revealing a mini fridge, complete with multiple selections of liquor. Beside it, is a small cabinet containing an array of shot glasses.

Suddenly, the vehicle jolts, throwing me against the cabinet. I grit my teeth, using the momentum to angle myself away from Jaguar's gaze. At the same time, I wrestle the syringe free and tuck it against a corner of the fridge, out of his sight.

At a glance, I can tell it's full, the amber liquid impossible to identify. I'm reminded of the night I tried drugging Domino—and failed. Perhaps this time, I should take whatever it is myself, and hopefully pass out before Jaguar could make me answer a damn thing. Some pathetic part of me craves that easy exit.

"Is there a problem?" Jaguar asks.

"N-No." I grab the first bottle of whiskey I spy and attempt to open it one-handed, all while using my body to shield any glimpse he might have of the fridge's interior.

"Here—" A shadow comes for me out of the corner of my eye. I barely choke down a scream as I recognize it—his hand.

He easily wrenches off the lid before grabbing the base of the bottle from me. Holding my gaze, he jerks his chin toward the cabinet.

"A glass, baby."

I snatch one—belatedly realizing that the syringe is still in the fridge. If I move even an inch, he'll see it.

Impatient, Jaguar clears his throat. "You need a bit of *home training*, don't you?"

My belly quivers at the malicious emphasis he puts on those two words. I recall how Domino utilized his whip, and I suspect this man has a similar method of "training" in mind.

"H-Here." I nearly drop the cup in my rush to raise it—straining my arm as far as I can—and he delivers a generous shot, seemingly none the wiser.

"Now yours," he prompts.

I set the full shot on a tray built into the top of the cabinet. Shit. There isn't a feasible way I can think of to spike one drink, let alone his.

"I have to wonder if you're stalling," Jaguar says with another coarse laugh. He reaches for me again, raking his thick fingers through my hair. "Hurry up."

I jump into motion, grabbing a fresh glass, but I don't hold it out to him.

"I-I can pour this one," I say, forcing myself to meet his gaze.

He smiles, but I can't read his intentions as he sits forward, offering the bottle to me.

I set the shot on the bottom shelf of the fridge and grab the syringe, sticking it into the cup while praying my body shields the sight. When I reach for the bottle, Jaguar's face is expressionless.

By the grace of God or sheer luck, the van jolts again, throwing me forward a second time.

"God damn!" Jaguar shouts.

He turns his focus on the driver, and I balance the bottle between my knees, grab the syringe, and rip the cap off with my teeth. My fingers shake as I empty the contents into the glass. Just as I sense Jaguar turn back to me, I knock the syringe out of view and pour a generous serving of whisky.

"It's about damn time," he snaps as I add the fresh shot to the tray.

Then I return the bottle to the fridge, knocking the empty syringe further back.

"Good girl." Jaguar's slow smile returns, unfurling over his lips as I shift toward him.

"To Domino," he murmurs, grabbing a drink from the tray.

My heart sinks, and I scramble to disguise my disappointment. Only God knows which one he took.

Looking at the remaining shot, I can't tell if it's tainted or not.

And it's not like I can refuse.

Slowly, I take the glass, bringing it to my mouth.

Jaguar eyes me expectantly, and it's a frantic heartbeat before I realize what he wants.

"To Domino," I croak.

He throws his head back, downing the whiskey in one go. I follow him, only to sputter as the burning liquid sears a path down my throat.

"Damn," he hisses. "That's some good shit."

He slams his glass down onto the bar and sits back, threading his fingers together behind his head. "Now, where were we? Oh, I remember…"

From this angle, his tattoo seems alive, twitching in motion, ready to pounce.

"I'll be honest, it doesn't matter who you pick," he adds, inclining his head thoughtfully. "I just want to hear it from your sweet mouth. I don't think you realize just how special you are. Daughter of Roy Pavalos. Toy of Domino Valenciaga. Our little Dom-Dom rarely pledges his loyalty to anything, but he sure seemed determined to hold onto you."

I can hardly keep up with what he's saying—I'm too busy tuning into every inch of my body, waiting to sense the telltale signs of an impending high. My head feels light, my breathing unsteady. Though hell, it could be due to a drug, or a mere result of being so close to a man like this.

Even his smile seems sinister. "I didn't think anything could distract the bastard from his vendetta. Five years of his life thrown down the drain. And he hasn't even told you why?"

But I know why—because my mother roped him into her own personal war.

It's dangerous to play with him. Dangerous to risk asking him a damn thing.

Still…

"You can tell me," I rasp, steeling myself for violence in return.

Instead, he laughs. "Domino has his own damn ambitions. Don't be fooled by his rodeo cowboy act. He's no better than I am. He stood by your father's side for five years. That's plenty of time to pick up a few things. From the very beginning, the bastard has had his eyes on the top. Me? I don't pretend to be anything other than what I am." He removes his hands from behind his head, extending them on either side of me as if the calloused skin is proof of his words. "I want Domino to return to the fold like a good boy. If not…"

He frowns, his brows wrinkling. The expression casts him in a different light for a split second. Just as quickly, he recovers, wrestling his lips into a shadow of that sly grin.

"We'll see just how badly he wants you." He swipes his thumb along my jawline, lifting my chin for appraisal. "And how far he'll be willing to go—"

Alarm dances up my spine before I even realize why. Then I feel the subtle jolt rocking the vehicle—we've stopped.

"What the hell?" Jaguar reaches back, rapping his fingers on the glass partition. "Why the fuck have we stopped? Andre?"

No reply comes from the other end.

Hissing, Jaguar reaches for a control panel but misses. Only to swipe and miss again. "The hell?"

He shoves me away from him, and I go flying, knocking my shoulder off the paneled wood siding. Panting, I look back to find him sitting upright.

Or trying to. His hands grip the edge of the seat, the knuckles stark white. Suddenly, he slumps forward to his knees.

"Jaguar?" Paralyzed by uncertainty, I don't move, even as he pitches over onto his side. It could be a trick. Hell, is it even possible for a drug to work this fast? Still, when he doesn't so much as twitch, I inch forward, tapping his shoulder. "Jaguar?"

He groans, his head lolling. A pinch of hope grips my chest —but then I see his eyes.

Both remain alert, glowing with rage. I go still, tensing for the moment he'll recompose himself. When the seconds tick by, I risk reaching toward his hip, finding his pocket.

I swallow as I feel through the thick material. The collar suddenly feels heavier, threatening to cut off my breathing with every ragged inhale I manage to drag into my lungs. Then…

I spread out my fingers as far as I can, and despair washes over me. It's empty. Desperate, I lunge for the other, grunting as I struggle with his weight. At the same time, I keep glancing at the partition, expecting it to lower at any minute. By now, the driver must realize something isn't right.

When my fingers strike a cool, metallic object, all thoughts of caution leave my mind. I rip the remote loose and shove it into what little space there is in the brace. It hurts like hell, but I ignore it, focusing on the interior of the vehicle instead. As the adrenaline wears off, a frantic sense of impatience replaces it.

Now what?

The van hasn't moved despite the hum of the still-running engine. For all I know, we could be surrounded by his men.

Even so, I don't think I'll get a better chance than now. Teeth gritted in determination, I reach for the nearest door.

I've not even touched the handle when it's suddenly opened from the outside. The second I inhale, my pulse surges, my chest so tight I can't even breathe fully—but even while suffocating, I'd recognize this scent anywhere.

This man anywhere.

It feels as though the universe slows to a crawl as I turn my head, catching only a glimpse of the figure lurking beyond, his hand outstretched.

One word from him, jolts me back to awareness like an electric shock. "Run!"

CHAPTER SEVENTEEN

Everything is a blur of frantic movement and impenetrable darkness. By the time I regain my bearings, I'm panting, dripping wet, lying on the earth as a stronger force keeps me steady. Jaguar's van is a distant shadow, edged by blood-red taillights. Somehow, I've been transported outside it—but the how isn't a mystery for long. Presumably, it has everything to do with the heavy body pinning me flat.

Maybe I'm dreaming, but never in a million years could I envision this smell so perfectly.

Or this voice.

"Don't move. Not until I tell you to." The guttural baritone triggers a wave of conflicting emotions. Relief? Dread? Fear?

It feels like ages before he finally lessens the pressure, hauling me to my feet. "We need to run. Keep your head down."

I crane my neck instead, fighting to see his face. "How did you—"

"Come on!"

It's raining heavier than before, turning the earth into sludge. Through the chaos, I can still make out the ruby glow of the van's taillights. It's unmoving, the back seat door thrown open…

But Jaguar never appears.

"This way." Domino steers me in the opposite direction, deeper into the darkness. Soon, I can't see the road anymore. Just a turquoise sky and endless black. My only sense of where I am comes from the muddy earth at my feet and the few noises loud enough to break through the downpour.

Raised voices echo in our wake. Shouts. Then a louder, sharper blast rips through my eardrums.

"Get down!" Domino wrenches on my arm, dragging me to my knees, and his weight settles over me once more. Despite the danger, he's steely calm, his breathing steady. It seems like barely a few seconds have passed when he hauls me to my feet again.

"It isn't far," he warns. Is that concern in his voice? If so, he doesn't slow our pace any, dragging me after him. "We don't have long before Jaguar sends out the cavalry."

Blinking through the rain, I realize that we're down a ridge, where, hidden from the road, sits a hill just big enough to hide another truck behind, barely visible in the dark. It's smaller than the one he drove from Mateo's.

Domino hastens to it, wrenching open the door to the passenger's seat. Once I'm inside, he quickly claims the driver's side, starting the vehicle. As the overhead light clicks on, I'm not prepared for the man I'm faced with. If anything, he should appear stone-eyed and impassive, the way he has from the start.

Not now. He looks so…

Furious. Rage vastly different from the anger I'm used to seeing in him. He's not gloating. Hell, he's not even looking at me.

But my eyes are drawn to him, tracing the planes of that stern face. A streak of scarlet along his temple makes me stiffen.

"You're bleeding—"

"What?" He frowns, eyeing himself in the rearview mirror. Sighing, he swipes at the blood and shrugs. "It's nothing."

"I'm beginning to have a new appreciation for your planning," I croak.

He grips the wheel. "I suggest you put your seatbelt on."

I warily glance back, half expecting to see a whiz of flying bullets heading our way.

"He'll be down for a few hours, at least," Domino says, reading my mind. "But his men won't be. I'd rather put as much distance between us as possible."

"How did you know?" I still can't wrap my mind around every little variable he must have accounted for. It puts his entire scheme into a new perspective. "About Alexi, and the drug. How did you even know I would be able to poison him in time—"

"I didn't." His expression is constricted, his mouth tilted into a thoughtful grimace. His obvious confusion is the only reassurance that I didn't imagine his denial.

"What? But you gave Alexi the drug…"

He nods. "And I still had every intention of having to fight my way out of there, tooth and nail."

"Why? You thought I'd take the drug myself? Alexi hinted as much."

"Because I underestimated you," he rasps. "Again."

It's so strange to hear him admit as much out loud—let alone with genuine awe in his voice. If only the circumstances were different, and we weren't on the run for our lives. I think I'd have the energy to gloat. As it stands, all I can do is stare at him.

"One would think I'd have learned my lesson at least." His gaze darts in my direction, settling over my face with an intensity that makes my cheeks flame. Then his attention drifts downward, and his eyes cut back up to mine. I suck in my breath at the hint of relief I see in them.

"How did you get here?"

"I was right," he snarls, turning his attention back to the road. "Mateo set me up, but not how I expected—I wasn't his target, *you* were. The bastard made a deal with Jaguar to hand you over. Though, I'm guessing things didn't turn out how he planned—" he nods toward my neck. "But he left you with a fucking souvenir."

"Jaguar claimed he reprogramed it at least," I say weakly, lifting the detonator. Only God knows how I managed to hold onto it. For something so damn small, it feels incredibly heavy. "As long as I press it once a day, supposedly Mateo won't be able to set it off."

And hopefully, Jaguar didn't keep another remote for himself.

"That sounds like him," Domino says coldly. "What the hell happened back on the road. You were only out of my sight for five damn minutes."

"We were attacked. Mick and Ralph are dead."

"Shit. I knew something was off," Domino admits. "I was stupid enough to think that neither one would act before the next checkpoint. My mistake. Given that the truck hasn't blown up yet, I assume Mateo is hoping to reclaim his merchandise."

"How did you get here?" I demand. "How did you even know where I was?"

"Because I know Jaguar. There were only a handful of places he could head to. Luckily, I still have some friends in low places. One thing I don't understand, though, is that he wasn't moving you toward the border. If anything, he was bringing you deeper into his territory. It isn't like Jaguar to hide his toys."

"Alexi was there. She said he was bringing me 'home,'" I say, shuddering at the prospect.

Domino scowls, his knuckles white against the wheel.

"What's wrong?"

He risks taking his eyes off the road long enough to send a searching look my way. Then he sighs. "Rumor has it that your father is awake. Even on his deathbed, Roy Pavalos will have a plan B in mind. Jaguar must have been planning to use you as leverage to buy more time."

I'm in too much pain, and far too exhausted, to even process those words properly. I close my eyes instead, resting my forehead against the glass of the nearest window. If Domino intends to deliver any more unwelcome surprises, he holds off. Finally, I lift my head and face him again.

"Where are we going?"

His jaw remains clenched, and I recognize his trademark suspicion.

"I've trusted you this far, haven't I?" I softly point out.

His eyes narrow as if he wasn't prepared for that argument. Finally, he grates an answer through clenched teeth, "To Terra—via any means necessary. The most important thing is finding Pia's body. And," he adds, eyeing my throat. "Getting that damn thing off you."

Something in his tone reminds me of an accusation Jaguar made. *I'm sure Domino would recognize it…*

"You know who made this—or one like it at least—don't you?"

I'm holding my breath as I watch him process the question. I don't know what to expect, in all honesty. A lie?

Instead, he sighs. "Your father," he says. "He used a similar form of collar. I shouldn't have to explain in what context."

"And you copied him," I say thickly, envisioning the leather version he put on me at his estate. "Should I thank you that it wasn't explosive, at least?"

He frowns—that insult hit its mark. "A collar like that needs a specific charge to be released," he says, choosing not to address my accusation directly. "It's a small device. Your father would have one."

He doesn't explore just what that means. For now, I ignore it in favor of another pressing issue.

"So what now? We just drive through the gates and hope that Mateo doesn't detonate the truck?"

He scoffs at the suggestion. "No. Like your father, I also have a plan B."

"Which is?"

He hesitates a second time, but I don't have to prompt him to speak. "I don't think Mateo is in any position to turn down assistance with his merchandise. Not with two of his men dead. Securing his transport will ensure our way over the border—and fast. No explosions necessary."

I can't disguise my shock. "You'll still go along with his plan, after all this?"

As the seconds stretch into minutes, he doesn't reply. I could write it off as him being concerned about a pursuit, but there isn't a sign of another vehicle in sight, let alone one of Jaguar's. This must be a back road, far from the main highway leading to the border.

Which means no better time than the present to goad him into a conversation.

"You think Mateo will still even *want* your help?"

"Mateo would accept help from the Devil himself to secure his shipment. He won't have a choice," he adds, squaring his shoulders. "You should worry about what's next. We'll pass one town before we reach the border. We'll resupply there, get new clothes, and buy time to make the crossing."

"And what exactly are you shipping?"

His eyes cut to mine, narrowed in warning. "Don't ask questions you don't really want to know the answer to. When we get into Terra, you help me find Pia. Do that, and I'll keep my end of the bargain. Understood?"

"Tell me what I'm risking my life to help you smuggle, and we'll have a deal."

It's dangerous to make bargains with him. It's even more dangerous to test the limits of his patience. But hell, after tonight, I'm willing to gamble. Despite all odds, he came for me.

He hisses, gripping the wheel more tightly. I can see the gears turning in his mind. Trust me? Or keep pushing me away.

"Tell me you'll hear me out," he demands. "No fucking temper tantrums. No outburst. No whining. You listen."

"I will," I rasp. "Just tell me."

I shiver as he inclines his head my way. His smile is terrifying, tilted, and cold. "I haven't checked, but I assume the cargo holds drugs for now," he explains. "Once we reach the border town, it won't be anywhere near that tame."

My heart sinks, but I choke back my disgust. I'm done running from the truth.

"I want to hear you say it," I croak while meeting his gaze. After all, he's already hinted at what men like Jaguar and Mateo traffic in. "No more word games. No more double-talk."

"Women," he says. "Is that what you wanted to hear? Mateo wants me to smuggle a group of women, twenty at least, into Terra Rodea. From there, he can transport them throughout the country. I won't say what he plans to use them for, but I think you can figure that out on your own."

And I can.

I try to push my horror aside, fighting to get a grasp on the inner workings of his twisted world. Mateo. Jaguar. He claimed that they were all connected.

"I thought Jaguar trafficked in women."

"He does," he says carefully. "But more and more Mateo's been encroaching on his territory. A confrontation has been brewing between them both for a while. I suspect Jaguar hasn't helped things any."

"And you?" I question.

"What about me?" He inclines his head, and I realize that the shadows along his face are deeper than before—an observation that triggers a tendril of alarm down my spine.

"How did you get roped into their feud? After all, you claimed to hate my father because of his crimes, but this doesn't sound any better."

"I just want to get across the border," he insists, returning his focus to the road. "Spare me your comparisons until then."

This is one of those rare moments when I can sense more than just anger or annoyance from him. Something that prickles beyond the barriers of his apparent control, straining that nonplussed demeanor. He's uneasy.

That feeling grows more potent with every passing second. I can sense that he's not saying something. Something important.

CHAPTER EIGHTEEN

He parked Mateo's truck about an hour from where he found me. Cautiously, he takes time to inspect the sliding door to the cargo hold without ever testing the latch. Apparently satisfied that it hasn't blown up—yet—he steps back, heading for the driver's side. "Get in," he calls back to me.

I'm not so easily convinced. "And what if Mateo decides to hit his little detonator button while we're on the road?"

He shrugs and wrenches the driver's-side door open. "Then he kills me, loses the bounty on you as well as millions in merchandise. I think I'll take the risk."

I choke down my apprehension and follow him inside. Despite my doubt, we make it the first few miles without incident. Only then do I release the breath I wasn't aware I'd been holding. The further we make it without incident, the less tense I become. Soon, pockets of light pierce the darkness beyond the windshield, providing a newer worry to focus on. A town?

A small one, but I assume it's our destination because Domino veers left, venturing down a road so narrow the truck threatens to scrape the sides of either building. We travel at least three blocks before finally he turns into a gap in a barbed-wire fence, surrounding a structure made of gray cement bricks. A garage of some sort. One of the metal sliding doors is raised enough to reveal a modest workshop where two men mill about. The taller of the two has a rag dangling from his hip streaked with what looks like oil. He wipes his hands off on it, craning his neck curiously as Domino climbs from the truck.

"We're closed," he shouts in slightly accented English.

I watch Domino fearlessly circle around to my end, and I roll the window down in time to catch him say, "Change of plans. Get Mateo on the line. I need to talk to him. Now."

"The fuck?" The man's eyes narrow as he tosses his rag aside, rising to his full height. His right hand lowers to his pants pocket. From the peripheries of the property, at least three other men converge on the garage. "This ain't no office, and I certainly ain't a damn secretary."

"And if Mateo wants his merchandise over the border in time, he doesn't have a choice," Domino insists. His confidence is breathtaking, once again reinforcing just how easily he could fool not only my father, but everyone else with his bodyguard ruse. "Get him on the line."

The man's eyes cut to slits, but he jerks his chin, beckoning us inside. "It's your funeral."

"Let's go," Domino says to me.

I climb from the truck, only to feel a heavy hand land over my shoulder, providing enough stability to get my bearings.

"Stay close," he warns near my ear. This tone is different from the one he used just seconds ago, revealing a glimpse of his true unease. "If I tell you to, you run."

I don't need to be told twice. I lean into his touch, scanning the garage with every step we take. Two more men lurk in the background, carrying various boxes and items. They eye us guardedly, keeping their distance, while the man we're following leans against a counter strewn with tools. Head cocked, he inspects us, scowling. "You don't look like the usual team Mateo sends. How the fuck do I know you're not setting me up?"

"Call him," Domino commands.

The man fishes a cell phone from his pocket, dialing a number. He must put it on speaker, because I can clearly hear a gruff voice rasp from the other end, "This better be important."

"There's a bastard here who demands to speak with you—"

"I think your supply problems have doubled since the last time we spoke, Mateo," Domino says, stepping forward. "I've heard it's not polite to say, 'I told you so,' but I'll make an exception."

"You son of a bitch," Mateo growls, his voice broken by static. "Where the fuck are my men?"

"You should be worried about your merchandise," Domino counters. "I don't think Jaguar is content to let you keep your little sliver of the border after all. He'll make a move on you soon. Looks like you need a volunteer to secure your final shipment—and here I am. Lucky you."

"You think I'm that fucking stupid?" Mateo bites back.

"I don't think you have a choice. Tell your men to stand down, and I'll take your last shipment. For old time's sake."

"I should put a bullet through your skull—"

"But you haven't," Domino points out. "Tell your men to load the truck, and we'll be on our way."

Silence extends before Mateo finally barks out something in another language the man holding the phone must understand. Then the line goes dead.

"He says to let you through." The man cuts his gaze to me in a way that makes me feel stripped to the bone. "She doesn't look like the type to be in this line of work, though. If anything, she looks more like she should be on the other end of this little trip, if you know what I mean." His tone is anything but friendly, and Domino stiffens, his grip on me tightening.

"Yeah, I know what you mean. This one is for a special client."

"A client who likes his girls fucked up?" The man laughs but turns, shoving the phone into a drawer. "Though it's not my place to ask questions."

"No. It's not," Domino says. "She's not your concern. You can tell me about the other merchandise, though."

"You don't do this often, do you," the man replies, but his tone is harder. Suspicious? "No details worth knowing. You move the shipment over the border and bring it straight to the destination in Terra. No detours, and I shouldn't have to tell you that there is no peeking either. You keep your nose in your own fucking business. The truck is sealed for the crossing, so any tampering will draw attention from the agents. Though again, I shouldn't have to tell you this, should I?"

"Damn right you don't," Domino replies, releasing my arm. "But I guess you'll be wanting us to get a move on soon. What's the ETA on the loading?"

"You brought the first shipment?"

Domino nods.

"Then you leave it here, and—"

"Leo," a newer man calls from the doorway. "All clear. Everything's intact."

"Good." Leo, the man before us, sighs, though not all the suspicion leaves his gaze. "You won't be able to cross until tomorrow morning. Mateo forgot to mention that part."

"He did," Domino says, and that rare note of anger returns, disrupting the calm. "What happened to this being time sensitive?"

"It is," Leo replies. "But you happened to come at an unlucky time. The guards have changed out, and this new bastard is a stickler for a stricter, more orderly system when it comes to breaking the rules. He insists that he'll only ferry over Mateo's goods in the daytime, when you can slip in with the rest of the usual foot traffic and go unnoticed."

"So, what are we supposed to do until then?" Domino asks.

The man smiles, revealing a missing tooth near his back molars. "There's a motel up the street where you can stay, free of charge. You'll head out bright and early with the merchandise and just an hour or two until you're over on the other side. My man Marcos here will show you the way."

I can't tell what Domino thinks or if he feels the same increasing anxiety I do. Rather than argue, he nods and heads out toward the front of the garage, where Marcos stands, waiting.

"Lead the way."

He doesn't reach back for me this time, and I nearly run in my rush to catch up. By his side, I don't feel any safer. The noises of the quaint town echo loudly, seeming ten times more sinister than they had before. Every footfall, and barking dog serves to send my already heightened nerves skyrocketing. It's another harsh contrast to how sheltered my world was before. A carefully crafted cage of gilded mansions and social events. The few times I ventured beyond that beautiful illusion were in the backs of luxury vehicles parked alongside a random alleyway or back road.

But I've never been up close and personal to the grim reality that lies beyond Terra Rodea. Unsurprisingly, Domino doesn't seem as out of place here. He stands tall, cautiously surveying our surroundings. He's on edge, though it's barely noticeable. Still, I watch his hand near his pocket and wait for any outbreak of violence.

"This is it," the man leading us says, nodding toward a modest two-story building with neon lights spelling out the motel's name in glaring red font. It looks like the kind of place I wouldn't accept a one-night stand in.

"*Gracias*," Domino says as the man retreats. Then he grabs my hand, pulling me after him.

The interior turns out to be not much more appealing than the exterior. The walls are lime green, the floor a faded wood with peeling varnish. A lone woman stands behind the counter, scanning a magazine.

"One room," Domino says, flashing a wad of cash. "A tip if you can provide one with a view of the street."

With barely a glance from her magazine, the woman fishes a key from a hook on the wall behind her and tosses it to Domino. "To the left." She jerks her chin toward a nearby staircase.

Domino follows, dragging me after him and down a narrow hall.

Various noises seep through the walls—moaning, the hum of a television, and a shouted conversation between a man and a woman. In fact, judging from a giggling twosome we pass, most of these occupants seem to be couples.

When Domino finally slows near a room at the end of the hall, he unlocks the door and shoves me inside. "Wait here," he says before slamming the door—but with him on the other end.

"Wait!" By the time I wrestle the door open again, he's gone, and unease goes to war with my common sense. I've trusted him this far, haven't I?

Reluctantly, I reenter the room and lock the door behind me. Now, without the aid of adrenaline, the pain chooses to throb at full force. I spy a bathroom and enter it, grimacing as I finally face myself in the mirror above a small sink. Dried blood coats the side of my face, and the tender skin beneath promises a bruise.

Using a washcloth, I clean myself as best as I can. What I'm left with in the end, is a stranger I barely recognize, watching me with my father's gray eyes. It hits me now that Domino is right—I haven't stopped to assess what life I'd lead outside of being a Pavalos.

If I survive that long, anyway.

When I reenter the main room, Domino hasn't returned. All I can do is sit and wait, listening to the noises seeping through the thin walls. Finally, the doorknob turns, and I lurch to my feet.

“It’s me,” the intruder warns before slipping inside. Domino. In his arms, is a black plastic bag, the contents of which he dumps out onto the bed—a pair of women’s tennis shoes, a pair of gray sweats that might fit me, and a white shirt. There are also a few energy bars and a bag of chips that I assume constitute the closest thing he could come to regarding a meal.

Rather than explain, he pushes past me, turning his attention to the room’s lone window. He draws the blinds down, securing a pair of blue and yellow floral curtains over it next.

“I give it an hour, two tops,” he says in that hard, grim tone I know so well. The same he uses whenever he references Jaguar or my father. “Before reinforcements come. You noticed it too, didn’t you? The bastard was merely stalling. Should we make it through the night, we won’t be able to step foot near that garage without being ambushed.”

“How can you be so sure?” I ask.

“Because I know Mateo,” he declares gruffly. “Daytime only, my ass. He moves his merchandise at night.” He cranes his neck to eye an alarm clock on a nearby nightstand, conveying the time in blaring red numbers. “I bet they’ll wait until after midnight. That gives us some time, at least. You should eat—” He nods to the assortment of snack foods. “From here, we can see the road and know when they’ll head out. My guess is he knows better than to delay the shipment, and he'll have one of his men take the truck, while calling in backup to deal with us."

"If you knew that, why come here in the first place?" I'm floored once again by his convoluted thought process.

His amused chuckle, however, fully tips my mind into turmoil. "Because this is exactly what I counted on."

I sink onto the mattress, too exhausted to keep up with him. My feet are throbbing, my throat on fire. On top of the various aches and pains, hunger gnaws relentlessly at my belly. At random, I snatch an energy bar from the pile and devour it. Only as I set the wrapper aside do I realize what I've done.

I didn't stop to use my hunger as a weapon.

When I look up, he's watching me, dark eyes as alert as ever. I suspect he's aware of every petty thought in my head. All he does, though, is advance to grab another bar that he tosses toward me.

"Have this one too. You'll need the strength."

"I have an explosive collar around my neck, and you think eating is the most important thing right now?" I don't know if I'm joking or serious.

Either way. I'm caught off guard by the rich laugh escaping from him. It lasts only a heartbeat—just long enough to melt any doubts I might still harbor.

"Eat," he commands, his expression rigid despite the chuckle still edging his words. "Considering what I have in mind for you after we remove that damn collar, you'll be grateful you practiced swallowing."

He could have punched me, and I doubt my shock would be any less. His humor is as strange and twisted as every other aspect of him. Terrifying on the one hand. Irresistible, on the other.

Rather than counter him, I sigh, fiddling with the edge of the wrapper. I'm a coward for ignoring the obvious innuendo, but this moment feels too raw. Too delicate to risk ruining.

When I finally sneak a glance at him, he's looking away from me. "So, what do we do now?"

He returns to the window, scanning the street again. Looking over his shoulder, he smiles, and it's the most chillingly beautiful thing I've ever seen. "We wait," he says simply. He moves toward me only to snatch something from the mattress I didn't notice before—it must have come out of the same bag as the clothing.

He lifts it, and I recognize the shape—a cell phone, very basic in model compared to the previous ones I've seen him use. A burner?

He dials a number and sends me a searching glance as if debating whether or not to let me overhear. That fragile, burgeoning trust in me must win out.

He stays.

"It's me," he says gruffly into the receiver. "I'll be at the rendezvous point by daybreak for the handoff. Remember our agreement—no questions."

He hangs up and powers off the phone completely before removing the battery. Both he tosses into a wastebasket in the corner of the room.

"Are you going to tell me who that was?" I ask, not expecting an answer.

He surprises me with words rather than tense silence. "Soon. For now, get some sleep. You'll need it."

He stalks past the bed, returning to the window. Peeling up a sliver of the curtain, he peeks beyond, scouring for any hint of movement.

"I need you to tell me more," I say.

He inclines his head curiously, but doesn't even glance my way. "Do you think so?"

"Yes. *Please.*"

I can't see how he processes the plea initially. His back remains rigid, his gaze on the window. Suddenly, he lets the curtain fall from his grasp. Then he turns to face me, but I'm unprepared for the intensity of his expression. It's steely and impassive, like stone.

"You should wash up before we go," he says, jerking his chin toward the bathroom door.

"Wait," I start. "Can't we have one honest conversation—"

"Come on." Ruthlessly, he advances, herding me into the bathroom, where he strips the sodden remains of the dress Jaguar gave me. Naked, I step into the shower while he manipulates the faucet, much like he had at his bunker.

This time, he strips himself from the outset, squeezing into the narrow stall beside me. Gripping my chin, he tilts my head beneath the spray, watching me with those impassive dark eyes.

"I want you with me," he says gruffly. "Is that what you want to hear?"

"You want me to help you find Pia," I clarify, but I don't sound as sure of that as I thought I was.

"I've always wanted *you*. Ada-Maria Pavalos." He steps forward, moving slowly, his hands by his sides. One by one, he flexes them, extending the fingers before bending them so sharply the knuckles crack. "By my side. On my arm. In my bed. Whichever way I could get you. Because I knew the very first day I saw you, that you were the key to everything I desire. You once asked me what life I envision for myself. I'll tell you now. I want the life that was denied me. A beautiful woman. A beautiful home. A beautiful life."

His smile adds a cruel, mocking edge to his statement, but the hoarseness of his voice erases any doubt he isn't telling the truth. These words he means—every single one.

And I can see that, looking back. The beautiful, sprawling estate he maintained in the middle of the desert. All of the cryptic, guarded speech when it comes to me.

And right off the top of my head, I can think of several facts that prove his assertion for the lie it is.

"You have a funny way of proving your devotion to a woman you claim to…"

"Love?" he finishes—but that's too tame a word. Whatever he feels for me is something far more ominous, warped, and tainted by possession and perhaps some desire. I can't deny his lust—after all, I've experienced it firsthand. "Is that the word you were fishing for? The one you don't even know the meaning of, yet you seem to love throwing around in relation to what I couldn't possibly feel for you. Though I think we both established…" He hooks his hand loosely around the collar on my throat, forcing my chin into the air.

Defiantly, I hold his gaze, but the joke's on me. His eyes are practically on fire. The intensity takes my breath away. Literally. I'm left gasping as he flexes his grasp, tugging me against him.

"Neither of us know what love is. But if I had to describe it, I don't think it would resemble what you imagined that night, when you saw me as your savior, come to rescue Ada-Maria from herself. I'm not someone you should crave. If anything—" His breath fans my cheeks, his lips a hairsbreadth from mine. "You should fear what you do to me."

Something in his soft tone makes me bold enough to question. "And what is that?"

"You make me reckless," he declares without missing a beat. "Foolish enough to risk taking my attention from a potential target to play word games with you. You make me question everything. You always have."

"And yet, I can't seem to make you open up to me. Or tell me the truth. Or—"

"The truth is that I never intended to let you go. Though, I think you know that. You've always known it. From the day we met, you sensed what I couldn't even admit to myself until you were crouching at my feet, those beautiful eyes fixed on me. You were always mine, Ada-Maria."

Were these words uttered by any other man, I think they would come across as sweet. Some passionate, romantic confession. Voiced by Domino Valenciaga in his guttural rumble, the terse statement is anything but charming. It's a death sentence. A promised voice by a madman who truly has no intention of letting me go.

I think he enjoys watching that understanding wash over me. The same way he must enjoy running his finger along my pulse point, sensing how my heart races. Then stutters completely when I feel his lips graze mine.

The kiss is mesmerizing in its brutality. So sharp, aided by the grating scrape of his teeth. Then shockingly gentle as his tongue comes to swipe the sting away.

I'm in his arms before I know it, crushed against the wall of the stall, his heat insurmountable.

Large, his hands settle over my waist, snatching me to him. I suck in a breath, my heart racing. I've barely filled my lungs when he steps from the shower, still holding me captive.

The shift in temperature is a shock, but he seems unaffected, backing me into the bedroom.

"Should I demonstrate just what you do to me?" His voice is so guttural I don't just hear it—I *feel* it vibrating through my bones.

The promise of destruction glitters in those dark eyes as he inclines his head, taking my mouth with another kiss. The second I tilt my chin to match his savoring strokes, he pulls back, just enough to let me catch my breath. The look in his eye terrifies me. It's piercing enough to bolster every word he's said. And yet, no man could possibly claim to care for a woman, and yet look at her the way he's looking at me.

Like he only wants to devour me, body, and soul.

His lips settle over mine more firmly this time, easing them apart for his tongue to claim and devour. This should be painful with all my injuries taken into account.

But pain is merely a whisper in the face of him. His touch smothers it, his heat intoxicating enough to distract from everything else.

Even as his fingers ghost down my forearm, I'm powerless, swept away by the tide that is Domino Valenciaga. He lifts me by my waist, pivoting toward the bed. I land on the mattress face up as he looms above, flexing his fingers menacingly.

My breath catches as he crouches, cupping my calf in one hand before seizing the other. He spreads my legs slowly, moving to fill the space between them.

Images of the last time he was in this position flash through my mind. I feel my back arching in anticipation as his nails scratch along my skin.

"You are so beautiful." As he speaks, he runs his lips along my inner thigh, inching higher until…

I groan as what feels like his tongue lathes over me. This isn't like before—he's taking his time, tasting me with savoring laps.

Pleasure mounts ruthlessly, building with every groan he smothers into my skin. Every scrape of his nails on my flesh as he tightens his grip. His assault is maddening. Like a hot poker, I feel his tongue jab deep, wringing a cry from my throat.

"I want to hear you say it…" His voice echoes off the inside of my skull before I even see his lips move, repeating the request. "Tell me you trust me."

My heart lurches. I can't. After everything he's done, it's a bridge too far.

Or so I think until his teeth catch the edge of sensitive flesh and my thoughts go blank.

"Say it," he demands, verging on a growl. "You trust me."

"I…"

His fingers fan out, raking up the length of my leg to join the pressure of his tongue. I can't breathe as he eases the thick ridge of a knuckle inside me. Another. There's a daring edge to his motions—he's driving a little deeper than before, applying more pressure. More.

It's too much. My knees twitch, fighting to draw together, but his bulk prevents them from closing.

I'm at his mercy, a slave to his whims. Drawing in a ragged breath, he adds another finger, sinking both deep with a crooked motion that has me jerking over the mattress.

"Dom!" I clench my teeth over the rest of his name.

As if in punishment, he shoves those digits inside me again, grinding against my inner walls to sow friction.

"Please…"

"Say it."

He voices the words into me, churning my insides into an inferno. Even if I wanted to speak, I can't find the breath to.

Abruptly, he pulls away, letting the cool air baste the flesh he'd ravished a heartbeat ago. I barely shiver before he's on top of me, pinning me to the mattress. I can feel him, pulsing between my legs. One thrust, and he's inside me…

But only just. The tip? And yet, the fullness is damn near unbearable. Too much, and yet nowhere near enough. I never knew torture could be this cruel.

"Dom—"

He bucks his hip, sinking deeper—still only a fraction.

"Do you trust me?"

My eyelids flutter, fighting to keep him in view.

"Ada—" He thrusts again. Harder. Again. "Say it."

"I trust you." It's like he rips the words from my throat against my will, dragging out a confession I wasn't even aware of.

Yet, he still isn't satisfied. Teeth flashing, he growls, "Again."

This time, I physically push the words out. "I trust you."

He grunts, dragging his teeth across my collar bone. "More."

My mind reels. What more could he want? Then it clicks.

"I trust you, Domi—"

"No," he groans.

"Navid."

He bucks, driving himself so deep it hurts—but in the best way possible. The kind of pain only he has ever inspired within me.

A cruel, addictive agony.

CHAPTER NINETEEN

Our twisted peace doesn't last long. A sudden noise draws his notice and, within seconds, he's by the window, peering out through that sliver in the curtain. Whatever he sees makes him turn toward the bed and snatch his clothing from the floor.

"We need to leave." In a deft display of muscle, he tugs on his pants. "Get dressed."

He inclines his head toward a pile of fabric strewn over the floor—the sweatpants and shirt from earlier. I manage to pull the pants on one-handed, and Domino appears by my side to assist me with the shirt. I've barely shoved my feet into the shoes when I sense his mouth near my ear.

"We can't go out the front."

I don't know what that means. Not until he starts dragging me near the window.

It doesn't open fully—just wide enough for him to wedge his arm through the gap—apparently, that's all he needs. He jerks his wrist, and a wrenching squeal sounds from the hinges before the window flies open entirely.

Below is a loose grouping of trash cans, overflowing with rubbish and a narrow alley. From here, it's obvious that activity is happening at the garage, namely a bright yellow glow igniting the darkness. Headlights.

Domino positions himself behind me, palming my waist. I can sense his intentions even before he guides me to the windowsill. How exactly he intends for me to jump with only the use of one arm?

Apparently, by going first as an example. Lithe on his feet, he mounts the sill before I can. In a single leap, he lands hard in a crouch, one hand braced over the pavement. Just as quickly, he's upright again.

Low and gruff, his voice reaches up to me. "Jump."

I want to refuse. Then I see a flicker of movement beyond him—a flash of red light. Taillights. If there really is a truck of "merchandise" being loaded at the junkyard, it's on the move.

There isn't time to think. I just scramble onto the ledge and jump, bracing myself for the impact. The pain.

But it never comes.

He catches me with a grunt, cradling my right side against his chest to avoid jarring my shoulder. By the time I turn to see his face, he's set me down, nudging me toward the mouth of the alley.

"Let's go."

I pant, racing to keep up with him until, without warning, he stops short. "Get back."

We're near the garage now, but from a different angle, peering into the yard from behind a metal fence. In the darkness, I can see men moving about, as well as the glowing red taillights of Domino's truck.

"Stay here."

He inches closer, moving along the fence, then out of sight.

Not even a few seconds later, I hear a man cry out. Then a gunshot.

I go numb, my thoughts a frantic whirl—I can't move. Then another sound pierces the quiet. A shout, guttural and insistent. "Ada now!"

I lurch toward the sound of his voice, only to find him standing near the truck beside a man—a man whose head he has a gun against. "Get in the truck," he says to me.

I don't hesitate, scrambling into the cabin. My eyes, however, remain glued to him. He takes his gun, slamming the butt of it against the man's skull with a sickening thud. The thug goes down, and Domino rushes to claim the driver's seat.

It all barely lasted seconds, but plenty of time, apparently, for the other men at the garage to notice. A shout goes up, and someone rushes from the shadows.

"Get down," Domino warns. "Don't look up."

He must slam his foot on the gas, because the truck jerks forward, and I barely manage to lower my head before a monstrous crack echoes, so loud my eardrums throb in the aftermath. Another gunshot?

"Shit! Keep your head down!"

The vehicle swerves, so suddenly I lurch out of my seat and smack my head off the dashboard. The floor shakes beneath me as a monstrous crash resonates, followed by more shouts. I can sense the speed picking up, winding through the narrow streets.

"Mateo's crossing won't be open, after all," Domino says once I assume we're clear of the garage.

When I finally raise my head, we've gone beyond the town, tearing through the back roads of the desert.

His eyes aren't cold with defeat, but glittering with a cruel, devious gleam, I know well. "Luckily, I arranged for a contingency plan—"

"This is what you've wanted," I blurt out. It's an insane suspicion, but it only grows the more I see his face. "Whatever Mateo was transporting. You never intended to go along with him. You just wanted this…"

But judging from his past comments, whatever we're transporting in this truck isn't typical commercial merchandise.

"Do you plan to sell them to Jaguar?" I ask bluntly. Though if he is, would I even take offense to that?

Yes. The anger comes from nowhere, but I feel it more intensely than I think I've ever felt this kind of disgust. Hearing him claim my father participated in this trade was one thing. But I never saw it up close.

Not like this.

"Answer me—"

"If you even have to ask that fucking question, then you never knew me." He doesn't even take his eyes off the road, and yet I have no trouble picturing the full venom in his gaze. That cold glare.

"Fine," I say quickly, settling back into my seat. He told me that most of his "work" was a front. He always had an ulterior motive, but what could that be in this case? "You aren't planning to sell them," I say cautiously.

He's silent, still maneuvering through the open desert.

"Okay," I add warily. "So, you'll let them go? Won't Mateo's men come after us?"

"Mateo's been laying low," he replies. It isn't a direct answer either way, but his voice has lost that harsh edge. "The local authorities haven't taken too kindly to his business lately. Thanks to bribes from Jaguar, they won't do his bidding so easily, and he can't risk them finding any opening to probe deeper."

"And what about Jaguar?"

"He'll come, and soon," Domino says confidently. "I'm counting on it."

Suddenly, he brings the truck to a stop, kicking up a cloud of dust in our wake. As he climbs out, I scramble to follow.

He heads for the back, inspecting the lock on the bottom of the grate. He must take Mateo's threat seriously enough that he doesn't open the cargo hold.

But he doesn't have to.

I hear them anyway—soft, muffled cries emanating through the metal that twist my stomach into knots. A wave of emotion hits me all at once, and I turn away, gulping at the fresh air.

My father did this—or so Domino would have me believe. He facilitated this and cultivated a business that thrives on young women being brought into Terra for God knows what.

I want to deny it. God, I do.

As Domino has insinuated over and over, I know my father better than anyone. I know what he values above all, even his family. His own life.

Power, no matter the cost of maintaining it.

"What are you going to do now?" I croak, eyeing the wilderness stretching beyond. "Turn them over to Jaguar to make amends?"

"Get back in the truck—"

"No." I start walking, refusing to look back.

"We need to move. Before Jaguar's men catch our trail—"

"I won't be your accomplice." The words stick in my throat, because deep down, I know how shallow they are. I have no right to turn my nose up at any crime, after what I've done.

But maybe I've grown a new moral fiber in the time since I left Terra. I won't be a part of this. He'll have to lock me back there with the rest of his casualties of war.

"Ada-Maria." His voice sounds bitten out, a sign that he's at his limit. "Get in the truck—"

"I suggest you put me in the back, because that is the only way I'm going anywhere with you—"

"So that I can explain."

Curiosity robs my anger of its intensity. Dejected, I turn to find him watching me, but there is no smug grin to discern a lie from. Instead, his eyes meet mine coldly despite the distance, and I know in my gut that every word he'll utter next will be the truth.

"We're too close," he warns. "Don't let it fall apart now."

My throat tightens as I force down a hard swallow.

Slowly, I take a step toward him. Another—but in the same amount of time, he surges forward several, grabbing my arm to haul me back inside the front cabin.

"Speak," I demand, as he takes the wheel. "Now, or I swear to God!"

"I've arranged a meeting with another contact who can get us border access—and disable whatever bullshit bomb Mateo rigged to the back—but we need to move fast. Before Mateo realizes and sends us all sky high."

"Jaguar?" That pinching sense of unease returns, but I can't discern a single emotion from him. Not even guilt.

He remains fixated on the uneven terrain, navigating quickly. Almost too quickly. With every lurch and jerking of the wheel, my stomach dips.

If Mateo doesn't set off an explosion, Domino's driving might.

Finally, he sighs. "When we get over the border, you help me find Pia, and then you're free to go wherever the hell you want. Roy Pavalos or the moon. I only ask that you hear me out before then."

"Tell me who you're meeting with first."

"We're nearly there," he says gruffly. "You'll see for yourself. All I ask is that you trust me. Keep your head down and stay by my side. Afterward, you come with me to Terra. Can you do that? Can you promise me that?"

"I don't know," I admit, picking up on the tension wafting from him. It's different from his volatile anger when confronting Jaguar or Mateo. Whoever we're meeting is a new form of monster. "Why can't you just tell me…"

But as we crest the next ridge, the answer becomes obvious enough.

Three vans are parked in a line near what I assume to be a wall-less section of the border; their colors and insignia make their designation clear—federal agents.

"Oh my God," I croak.

Domino just drives, parking paces from them.

My heart races as he wrenches the keys from the ignition and raises his hands in a gesture of surrender.

"Remember what I said," he warns before climbing out. "Trust me."

"Keep your hands visible," one of the officers shouts.

Maybe they aren't who we're meant to meet. Could Domino's meeting have been hijacked?

But Domino approaches them fearlessly, and one of them steps forward to speak to him. The subtle familiarity betrays that they must have met before. Enough that Domino's posture, while tense, isn't anywhere near the state he enters when he's near Jaguar or Mateo.

Eventually, he nods toward the truck, and the men circle around to the back. Presumably, they work to disable whatever explosive Mateo rigged it with because, within seconds, a parade of women streams out one by one, visible in the side-view mirror.

My heart sinks at the grim confirmation. Maybe, some tiny part of me still clung to the faint hope that he might be wrong about all of it. Instead, the early morning glow illuminates the women in stark relief, undeniably real. They're pale, stick thin, each wearing a variation of plain clothing.

Kidnapped, a voice in my head whispers. They must have been taken from various locations without warning and packed into a truck like animals.

Ironically, much like how Domino stole me.

The officers approach them, seeming to take down their names while Domino slowly returns to the truck.

"We'll serve as a diversion," he explains. "They've left the tracker intact. We only need to drop it off at the checkpoint. Mateo won't realize for a while at least, that he's been set up."

He waits, but it's seconds before I understand what he's really doing—offering me the chance to refuse. Scream. Make a scene to draw notice and announce who I am.

But I don't—and not because of him. He's brought me all this way, and after everything I've been through, I deserve to see this through to the very end. The only way to find out for sure what exactly he's been after is to be there and witness the unveiling myself. I'm done being his willfully blind victim.

It's time to take my blinders off and face the reality awaiting me, no matter where it leads…

Or what I discover in the end.

"How long?" I ask instead.

Domino hides his shock expertly behind a guarded tilt of his head. "We should make it into the city around sundown. Then somehow get to the old Inglecias residence without arousing suspicion."

"And these agents will just let you prance off into the sunset?" I ask, eyeing the men warily.

"Like I said, they'll let us go. For now."

"So that is what you were doing all this time. Working for the very people trying to put my father in prison?"

He doesn't even dignify that with a response. His silence, however, speaks for itself.

"That's what you meant when you claimed that you were undermining him all along."

In reality, all those people he claimed to kill were instead ushered into protective custody.

"It's not a fairy tale, Ada-Maria," he warns. "There are no good sides in this story. Just sides. Theirs, your father's, and mine."

"You make it sound so hopeless."

He doesn't reply to that. Instead, he turns his attention to the windshield as one of the men advances, gesturing the truck forward. Rather than relieved, I feel even more uneasy.

Something has been left unsaid, and yet it lingers in the air regardless.

"I suggest you hold your questions for now," Domino advises as he takes off, down the seemingly abandoned road. "I can promise that you'll have far more by the time this is all over."

CHAPTER TWENTY

It's dark when I startle awake again—all while choking down a wave of guilt. Only a true monster, desensitized to the brutality around her, could find the capacity to sleep at a time like this.

Apart from a few minutes to utilize the bushes as a makeshift restroom, we haven't stopped. At least now, the vast landscape looks a lot more familiar. A view of rolling hills and manicured countryside sends a pang through my chest, and I sit straighter, scanning the road for a glimpse of the city.

"We're about an hour out," Domino says, explaining the absence of the skyscrapers I grew up surrounded by. "Once we enter Terra proper, I won't have a shot in hell at hiding you for longer than a day at most."

Which is as much of a warning as it is a blanket statement —*don't waste my time.*

I'm too tired to reassure him now. Instead, I watch the

world around us slowly morph into a familiar cage of concrete. The sight inspires an ache in my chest. Whether Domino realizes it or not, his secluded estate was much like a tiny piece of upscale Terra Rodea, planted in the middle of nowhere. Can he even make that connection himself?

All along, he's been building a miniature version of everything he claims to hate.

"So, what now?" I ask him.

"We need to drop this truck somewhere. I know a place. We'll get a smaller vehicle to navigate through the city in and buy more time."

"And then what?"

"Then?" He inclines his head as if he never had the question presented to him so directly before. "I finally enact my version of justice."

The promise doesn't conjure any of the warm, fuzzy feelings my father liked to inspire during his campaign speeches. In Domino Valenciaga's world, justice carries the same connotation as blood.

I WOULD HAVE THOUGHT THAT AFTER WEEKS OF captivity, I'd be relieved to return to Terra Rodea. That I would enter the city confines stronger, and with a sense of triumph over having survived my ordeal. In reality, I barely look up from the road as the rural desert gives way to crisp asphalt.

Something my mother said won't stop niggling at the back of my mind—*I want my daughter protected when Roy's lies inevitably catch up to him. He has far too many enemies. I can't protect her.*

She was afraid of more than just my father. Once Domino claims whatever information he's after, how much danger will I truly be in?

"We won't have long," Domino warns as if reading my mind. As suggested, we've left Mateo's semi in an abandoned industrial complex just outside the city, in favor of a smaller truck with a flatbed and a crew cab. "By now, Mateo must realize that the GPS location isn't where it should be. He'll attempt some attack out of revenge, I suspect—but Jaguar will be watching, if he isn't back in the city already."

"And then what?" I say, shifting my focus back to the present. "You get Pia's body, but my father is still alive, and Jaguar is angrier than ever. What do you even stand to gain?"

"Everything," he growls. That dangerous gleam ignites his gaze again, drawing a shiver from me.

"And then what?" Will he return to his estate?

His jaw clenches in that telltale way. Question time is over.

"We're almost there," he says, eyeing the road intently.

Sure enough, when I follow his line of sight beyond the windshield, I'm hit with a chilling nostalgia.

Ten years later, and somehow this sleepy neighborhood looks exactly the same now as it had then. My palms sweat as I note the small, square-shaped dwellings squeezed in beside each other. Until finally…

The brown house on the left-hand corner of this street comes into view. My throat tightens the second we pull into the driveway.

My palms are slick with sweat, my stomach in knots—but I can only imagine how Domino feels. He stares straight ahead, his expression stone. His eyes, however, are distant, gazing at something far beyond this narrow space. He's miles from me in a heartbeat, trapped somewhere I will never be able to follow.

"What do we do now?" I ask, hating myself for bothering him.

His jaw tenses as if he remembers I'm even here. Without a word, he exits the truck first, heading toward the flatbed. Unlike the one Mick and Ralph drove, this one has a covering over the bed, obscuring whatever might be on it. Like a rusted metal shovel, that Domino grabs one-handed. Where he found it, I can't even begin to guess—and I don't have the heart to ask as he approaches the house with slow, deliberate steps.

It's nearing sundown already, and the fading rays of sunlight bathe his body in a golden glow. I watch him, trying to reconcile this hulking figure with a sickly boy too weak to leave this very house. Soon though, my thoughts turn to my own sordid history with this dwelling. Being here in person is far different from pulling a potential burial spot out of nowhere. For the first time, the implications of what I've insinuated sink in—as well as the consequences if I'm wrong.

Left with no choice, I follow Domino out, skirting past the brown dwelling entirely until we reach a rusted gate barring the entrance to a minuscule backyard. In my few visits to the Inglecias house, I rarely set foot back here.

All these years later, it's surprisingly small. A lone tree guards the back of the space beside a weather-worn swing set.

"So, where should we start?" Domino asks as I draw even with him near the yard's entrance. His eyes blaze, raking over every inch of earth. "Under the flower beds? The swing set?"

"I..." My voice trails off as the folly of what I've done hits me like a punch to the chest. Seeing this place in person, it feels laughable that Domino could fit within the yard comfortably, let alone a body. "I'm sorry."

He doesn't react. Doesn't move. An irrational need to keep speaking infects me. I'm a broken record at this point, capable of repeating just one phrase. "I'm sorry—"

"I couldn't protect her," he says softly. At the same time, he grips the top of the gate, wrenching it open. "She needed me, and I couldn't even lift a finger to help her. And now? I'm still failing her."

"I don't know what to do."

"Tell me what happened." He crosses over to that lone tree at the back of the property, bracing his hand against the bark. "From the start. Just the truth. That's all I want."

"I… I just know that, I never wanted to hurt her."

It feels pathetic to admit, yet it's probably the most genuine thing I've ever said to him. There's no defensive hate. No excuses. Just guilt.

"I'm sorry—"

"We came all this way," he adds gruffly, turning his focus to the ground. "Just pick somewhere to dig, and we'll see if your 'hunch' is right. We can consider that your apology."

I can't tell if he's serious or not. Still, I choke down any reservations and copy him, eyeing the damp earth at our feet.

"Take your time," he says, his tone a fraction softer. "Where should we start?"

I inhale shakily while scanning the minuscule lot. There aren't many places to hide a body in retrospect. For some reason…

I can't take my eyes off the tree.

From the corner of my eye, I see Domino follow my gaze. Without any explanation, he hefts the shovel and starts digging, grunting with the effort. After the first few chunks of soil are removed, I crouch down, assisting with my bare hands.

We work mindlessly, in an eerie tandem. That inexplicable countdown I sensed while in Jaguar's domain returns with a vengeance—only this time, I suspect only seconds remain.

Ten.

Nine.

Six.

Four.

Two…

I hear it before I feel it—a clunk as the shovel strikes something too firm to be dirt. Whatever it is feels smooth beneath my probing fingers. Cylindrical…

"Let me." Domino crouches by my side, using his larger hands to brush the stray dirt away. The sun has fully set now, leaving the newborn moonlight as the only illumination. I have to blink several times just to make out anything against the dark earth. Then…

A flash of color. Fabric? I paw at it until I'm able to discern a hue, at least. Something pink. Or at least it used to be.

Pink like the clothing Pia Inglecias used to wear.

Including the last day I ever saw her alive.

I THINK I FALL. MY KNEES BUCKLE, AND I'M KNEELING over the cool, loose earth—but an unmistakable presence shrouds me from behind.

"It's alright. Don't look."

He moves to cover the hole we dug, presumably with the very shirt he was wearing. His bare back ripples as he stands, his head bowed, shoulders tense.

I choke down a hard swallow. "Is it—"

"You've done enough," he says, helping me to my feet. "Go wait for me in the truck. I'll finish up here."

There's genuine grit in his voice. As much as it pains me to revisit these memories, I can only imagine what he feels. Hate? Relief? Grief?

I look up, faced with his rigid back, and I can't discern a single emotion other than determination. With the reverence of a man in a church, he gently kneels over the disrupted earth, running his hands over the black cotton crumpled there. His head lowers, and I feel like a voyeur, spying on a private moment I have no right to witness.

Somehow, I manage to stagger back toward the truck unassisted. When I reach for the handle, however, I lack the strength to tug on it. It's as if everything I've been through decides to hit me all at once. The pain. The exhaustion. The guilt.

I wallow in it all, and I don't even react as someone approaches me from behind. For all I know, it could be Jaguar.

But no...

I smell him before I sense him round the back of the truck. In his arms, is a wad of fabric that he sets down gingerly beneath the cover. My stomach churns as I realize what might be wrapped inside the makeshift bundle.

"Is that—"

"I didn't want it to be her." His tone alone confirms the question I didn't finish asking. "Not like this. At least... I know she's finally safe."

"What will you do now?" I ask softly.

He faces me as stray strands of dark hair obscure his eyes. The green in them is sharper than ever, glowing in the semi-darkness. "Bury her," he says simply. "Someplace far nicer than here. It's what she deserves..."

He trails off, and I swallow down a reply. Now isn't the time to prod him for more answers. He needs this silence, so I let him have it for as long as possible. The only disturbances are the quiet chirping of insects in the background and the growing wail of police sirens in the distance.

"We should move," Domino says finally, glancing at the sky. "Something's off. I don't think we've been spotted yet, but I'd rather not stick around to find out. But you know what this means." He fixes me with the full brunt of that piercing stare. "*Who* is responsible," he adds ominously.

But do I? My conflicting memories keep replaying in my mind. Even my mother hinted at who she suspected might have played a role in whatever befell Pia—and not just my father. My thoughts race as I look down and spy something else, glinting in his palm.

"My mother's ring," I say softly.

Alarmed by my recognition of it, he curls his fist around the delicate piece of jewelry before securing the door to the back. When he faces me again, his expression is thoughtful rather than defensive.

"You see a ring. In reality, this is a blood diamond, taken years ago from a mine Don Roy and Carlos Domingas used to fund. Not only is it worth a fortune—" He uncurls his fingers one by one, revealing the item resting on his palm. Years buried in the earth haven't been kind to it. Its beautiful details caked in muck, the brilliant gemstone in the center dulled with grime. "But its origin would unearth a wealth of both Domingas and Pavalos secrets should anyone with power dare to look. Julian no doubt came to the same realization."

"Why didn't my father take it back?" I ask, musing out loud.

"He probably didn't realize. It's a clever trick, to conceal a weapon right beneath your enemy's nose. I'm sure Carlos thought your mother would slip it to a reporter or political rival who could bring the scandal to light. Instead…"

"Pia got a hold of it," I say grimly. "So, this is what my mother wanted you to find?"

It feels so foolish to say. All of this trouble for a stupid ring?

"You sound disappointed." Domino holds my gaze with a seriousness I don't expect. "You'll learn that power is mostly symbolic—and fragile. In the hands of a teenage girl, this ring is just a silly trinket. If Julian, on the other hand, can reclaim it? There's no telling just how he'll use it." He eyes the ring as he speaks. It looks so minuscule on his massive palm, too tiny to ever be of significance. "Your mother thought it was worth dying to find. I'm inclined to take her word on that."

Deep down, some part of me cringes at his faith in her. It's far more than he's ever been willing to have in me.

"Now you have what you're after," I say thickly. "What next?"

"This was only part of it." He comes closer, reaching out. Slowly, he fingers a lock of my shorn hair, frowning at the colored strands. For a heartbeat, I swear I see a glimpse of the man I used to watch from the shadows. "I wanted my sister's body," he says thickly. "But now I need to know the truth." His voice is the deepest I've heard it. For once, the cadence isn't cold—it's rippling with far too many emotions to decipher. "Tell me what happened."

The truth.

"What if I hurt her?" I demand. "Could you live with knowing that? If I was the one—"

"I know *you*," he insists. "Whatever you tell me, I'll believe."

My breath catches. I'm so caught off guard by the statement that I just blurt the first thing to come to mind without worrying about the consequences.

"I pushed her." My voice breaks over the confession. It's so surreal to hear it stated out loud with no excuse to soften the blow. "I pushed her. I don't remember much after that."

Luckily, my mother filled in the blanks. According to her, I became a different person afterward. A murderer?

"What if… What if I killed her?"

I can barely look at him, but he grips my chin, forcing me to.

"I can feel a part of me trying to remember," I admit. "But being here made me realize one thing. I was angry with her. So fucking angry. I—"

"Killed her?"

His voice… It's harsh, and yet at the same time devoid of the anger I'd expect. The hate.

"Before this mess?" He gestures wordlessly with his hands as if the concept is too damn vast to ever explain. "I would have believed that in a heartbeat. But now?"

He lashes out, cupping my chin again with a harsh gentleness that makes my stomach clench. Those ruthless eyes cut down to mine, piercing through me with a single searching glance.

"I don't believe you have it in you," he tells me.

I lick my lips, mustering enough air to reply. "To kill?"

"No. To lie." He releases me, frowning up at the sky, but I'm struck dumb by that simple admission.

He believes me.

"But what if—"

He raises a hand, and I finally notice what has him on edge. A noise, growing louder by the second. It's persistent, a mechanical whirl coming from above. A helicopter? I follow his gaze and realize I'm right. At least three circle the air not far away, nearing the city's downtown.

Could they be looking for me?

"We need to go," Domino warns, ushering me inside the truck.

When he joins me, he flips on the radio, hunting through the various stations until he finds one broadcasting what sounds like a news report. *"...civilians near West and Maple are to be on red alert. Defer to any police vehicles and follow all detour instructions."*

"Shit," Domino hisses. "You know where that is, don't you?"

"The hospital?" I don't grasp the significance at first. Not until I catch him eyeing my collar in a way that churns my stomach. "My father," I rasp. "Could something have happened?"

"I don't know." Taking the wheel, he pulls into the street, navigating through the neighborhood. "But we need to get that collar off your neck, and fast."

"How?" I ease the remote from my pocket, eyeing its metallic surface. In all the chaos, I'd almost forgotten my own dilemma. Perhaps this is karma for whatever happened to Pia.

I'm destined to have my life end in a similar violent way.

"Your father would know how," Domino admits. "But I always have a plan B."

His gaze warns me not to question him—but not out of secrecy like the previous times he kept me in the dark. I sense his motives this time are purely out of mercy.

Because whatever this "plan B" is, he knows I won't like it.

Not one damn bit.

CHAPTER TWENTY-ONE

With no resources to enter the hospital undetected, no allies, and, most importantly, no time, Domino's plan must be just a desperate way to console me before we both accept the inevitable.

I'm fucked.

The weight of the collar feels insurmountable—countered only by the strength in Domino's grip as he takes my hand, still driving with the other. Watching him, I don't even think he realizes he's doing it, giving me this one small shred of reassurance.

Maybe it's pathetic to cling to him so fiercely, tracing the contours of his knuckles beneath shaking fingertips. Even so, a part of me must feed off his stability because, with every passing second, I feel less…

Insane? In the resulting clarity, I don't find much bravery, however. Just resolve.

The issue of the collar aside, I'm ready to face my father and demand the truth I'm owed. No matter where the answers may lead...

But preparing myself mentally is a whole lot different than acknowledging the reality. As it stands, we won't make it within a mile of the hospital, let alone close enough to demand a damn thing from Roy Pavalos.

Domino, of course, knows as much. This drive through the winding city streets is merely for show, nothing more. Presumably, with a manhunt on my trail, it won't be long before we're discovered anyway.

Perhaps killing time is one last mercy he's willing to give me.

Which makes me an even bigger bitch for intruding on the silence by clearing my throat. "We don't even know which hospital he's in," I point out—one logistical flaw among many. "Or which room. Which floor. And if this commotion has something to do with him—" I gesture in the direction of the helicopters, though by now, they're barely audible in the distance. "We have no way of circumventing the security—"

"I know that." Domino's voice is eerily level, displaying the unnerving confidence he had when confronting Mick and Ralph in the desert, and again with Mateo. That patient, predatory calm. "I also know we're being followed. Don't forget that Mateo's truck still has its tracker intact. If Jaguar isn't already here waiting, then the bastard isn't half as intelligent as I give him credit for."

Here being a rundown industrial complex that resembles the place we left Mateo's truck initially. Unease grips my chest as my pulse begins to surge. Paranoia gnaws at the fragile part of me willing to trust him. Within seconds, that hope is battered beyond all recognition.

"Then why are we heading *toward* it?" I croak.

His fingers twitch in my grasp, and I loosen mine in anticipation of him pulling away—instead, he bears down harder, almost to the point of pain. His eyes gleam in the glow of a passing streetlight, fiercely determined.

"I need you to trust me," he grates, but it isn't a command or harsh order. It's a plea, coated in raw earnest. "No matter what. Can you promise me that?"

Can I? I eye our clasped hands, my throat so tight it hurts to breathe. "Tell me what your plan is."

"No." He didn't even hesitate. "You'd refuse outright on principle alone. But this could work. Just put your faith in me again."

His voice is deep enough to convey passion in that request despite everything in my logical mind warning me against it. Damn. It almost sounds romantic.

Putting my life in his hands for the umpteenth time.

Romantic, or insane.

"I need you to say it," he prompts, navigating around a wide, decrepit building with broken windows. "If you can't, we'll find another way."

From his steely gaze alone, I can sense for myself that there isn't another one. Not one he believes will work. Grim anticipation heightens every single second. I can almost hear the time counting down.

Ten.

Nine.

Three.

Two…

"Yes," I whisper, recalling the way he risked taking on Jaguar's convoy alone just to find me. As much as it chills me to admit, by that point, he didn't need me anymore. Not really. "I trust you."

He parks so suddenly the vehicle jolts—and in the same instant, everything goes to hell. Chaos is the only word that comes to mind as at least two dozen men race from the shadows, swarming the vehicle before Domino can even reach for his gun.

My hand aches in the absence of his touch, but that craving takes a back seat to terror as one figure steps forward, recognizable even in the dark.

"Speak of the devil." With that grim statement, Domino rolls down the window on his end, enough for the figure's guttural words to reach us.

"You both have been very, very naughty," Jaguar growls, still advancing. I figure few would notice the slight wobble in his steps; he carries himself so well otherwise. Warily, I look from him to Domino. Both must be cut from the same indestructible cloth.

Or perhaps Jaguar has his own secret vices that help him withstand a shitload of drugs.

"I'm surprised you've come crawling to face your punishment so eagerly," he adds. "I was hoping to savor the fun of tracking you down like rabid animals—"

"We came to make a deal," Domino cuts over him. "I suggest we cut through the bullshit and hash out the terms."

I'm stunned by the lack of inflection in his voice despite the numerous guns trained in our direction. Even so, he withdraws his own weapon, keeping it below Jaguar's view.

"No deal," Jaguar says, now close enough to make out the same dark outfit he wore in the van. His hair is mussed, his overall appearance less crisp, even in the glow of the vehicle's headlights. Rather than diminish him any, the fact just reinforces the suspicion that, from the very second he regained his senses, he's been hunting us down with the same zeal as his feline namesake. "I think I'd prefer to see your brains paint my walls instead. After we have an emergency family meeting on the importance of loyalty." He raises his hand, revealing the dark glint of his own pistol. "Now get the fuck out. Both of you. Preferably on your knees."

"Oh, I think you'll want to take me up on this offer—" Domino raises his weapon, twisting his body toward me in a fluid display of muscle. "Consider it non-negotiable."

The coldness I feel against my temple a heartbeat later could just be a stray gust of wind blowing in through the window. At least, if it weren't for the cruel promise dripping into my ear next. "She's no use to me with this collar on, and supposedly Roy Pavalos is the only one with the knowledge to open it. You get her free, then you get what you're after."

Jaguar's laugh is raucous and booming, clashing harshly with the tense atmosphere.

"You aren't in any position to be making threats, Dom-Dom—"

"You're the one who needs her alive," Domino counters. "Not me. I blow her brains out; you lose the only leverage you could ever hope to have over Roy Pavalos. Don't pretend like he isn't the real reason why you're here. What better time to strike than now when the bastard is wounded?"

"Confident of you to think you could even pull that trigger before my men have you in pieces," Jaguar points out.

"They fire on me, they fire on her," Domino replies coldly. "Which is why you haven't given them the order to. She dies, and it's nothing to me. But you'll risk losing your pesky bit of leverage."

"Wrong." Jaguar shrugs. "I could blow you both to pieces and take my sweet time picking through the mess to find the ring."

"You could. If it's even here, that is. You could always torture the answer from us," Domino adds, presumably suspecting Jaguar's next threat. "But that would take time. With Roy Pavalos regaining his strength by the minute, how long do you think you'll have?"

Jaguar's face is unreadable—apart from an almost imperceptible flicker of emotion across those dark, fathomless eyes.

"So, what would you have me do, Dom-Dom? Let you skip away merrily into the sunset?"

"No. Take us to Pavalos and get him to remove the collar. Then present him with the ring your damn self. That's my trade."

Jaguar barks out another coarse laugh, but this one is devoid of any mirth. "Always with the tricks," he scolds, waggling a finger. "That doesn't sound like a very fair exchange."

"I could always kill her now," Domino suggests, and the pressure on my temple increases.

I want to believe that he wouldn't. That it's all a lie. A lie…

That the conviction in his voice is merely for show—he's *that* damn good of an actor. The doubt barely has time to sink in when I swear I see his head jerk from the corner of my eye, though his gaze remains fixed on Jaguar. A message to me?

Don't worry.

But then he adjusts his grip on the gun. "Maybe I should—"

"It's your lucky day, Dom-Dom," Jaguar says, but happiness isn't the emotion I'd ascribe to the grit in his voice. "We were already on our way to a little tea party with Don Roy as the guest of honor. He even decided to leave his hospital bed for the occasion."

I frown. My father arranged to meet with Jaguar? Considering the swarm of legal trouble he's in, I doubt he'd be allowed to leave the hospital so easily. Without explanation, Jaguar reaches for the door to the back seat, opening it before the shock of his words can even set in.

"Roy," Domino says gruffly. "You know where he is?"

"You can drive," Jaguar tells Domino while climbing into the back. "Maybe I'll change my mind on the way there. Maybe not."

"You're too shrewd to give into the reckless impulse, Julian." With apparent confidence, Domino lowers his gun from my head and reclaims the wheel. Finally, I exhale but watching him, I don't sense the same relief. The set of his shoulders remains rigid, conveying an unease he can't hide. There might as well be a real jaguar crouched on the back seat. "At least not until you get what you're after."

"Enough chatter," Jaguar declares, keeping his gun trained on the back of Domino's skull. "It's time for a tearful family reunion, hosted by Don Roy himself. He's already waiting for us at his family's estate. *Vámonos!*"

His words chill me to my core. I don't doubt this reunion will be tearful.

And terrifying.

"You brought him here." Domino's incredulity matches mine as I eye the gates of my family's estate, barring the road before us.

"Are you insane? I'm assuming the helicopters are your doing? You took Roy Pavalos from the hospital?"

Jaguar's grated chuckle must serve as confirmation because Domino hisses, slamming his fist against the wheel. "Fuck, Julian! You didn't stop to consider that the police would check here first?"

"They won't be looking here," Jaguar says with a chilling laugh. "At least, not now. Thanks to a friendly tip, they believe Don Roy might have been taken hostage by one of his many enemies, heading outside of Terra in the hopes of a ransom. We have a few hours at least. The men I have planted within the Pavalos guard will see to that."

His breath sears my ear, startlingly hot. I don't have to turn to see why—he's directly behind me, ensuring I hear every word.

"What, Dom-Dom? Don't tell me you thought you were the only one who managed to embed yourself within the bosom of Don Roy?"

If Domino is surprised, I can't tell. That steely calm is impossible to crack, obscuring any real emotion lurking beneath.

With a cool tilt of his head, he addresses the man behind him. "I suppose you can have them let us in, then?"

From the corner of my eye, I see Jaguar roll down the back window and extend the arm sporting his tattoo.

Not even a second later, the gates up ahead begin to part. Usually, my father keeps at least two men staffed in the station manning the entrance, and a few more around the perimeter. Despite the supposed calamity taking place downtown, that arrangement seems unchanged as Domino pulls ahead through the outskirts of the property.

God. I can't describe what it feels like to be back here again. It's more visceral than emotional, resonating like a kick to the stomach as one by one the different aspects of the Pavalos Estate flash by. The tennis courts. The manicured lawns my mother spent so much of her time cultivating.

The house, with its winding balconies and the Spanish influence my father insisted the architecture have. Viewed now, with a gun to the back of my head, it all resembles nothing more than a glamorous cage. A façade in which I've lived most of my life under the shadow of violence and lies.

Looking back, it's hard to square those memories with the dwelling I see now. My father's influence is evident everywhere, infecting the beautiful landscape in a way that transcends even the sinister aura of Domino's estate.

“Home sweet home,” Jaguar singsongs as we pull up to the front of the house. “You ready to say hello to your Daddy after all your time away?”

He exits the vehicle, supposedly while keeping his gun on Domino.

When I look at the man beside me, his blank mask hasn’t faded any. “Let’s go.” His voice offers no hint of softness either, but when he reaches for my hand, his fingers give mine a firm squeeze that I feel down to my toes. I didn’t realize until now just how much I needed that sign. Craved it.

Just as quickly, he releases me to reclaim his gun before joining Jaguar outside of the truck.

Together they perform a strange, almost graceful dance of pointed weapons and fluid movement as Domino moves to my end and helps me out.

I’ve barely stood upright before Jaguar is already closing in. “Inside,” he commands.

Domino takes my uninjured arm, and I’m herded between both up the front steps leading to the home I grew up in.

It smells the same. How strange is that? Like the faint hint of flowers, the impeccable trace of lemon-scented cleaner, and cigar smoke.

My heart races, even though I know it shouldn’t be possible. I’ve been gone several weeks, but so has my father, according to Domino.

Still, as we mount the winding staircase, I'm flashed back to ten years ago when I did the same as a dazed teenager. God, it's so real. Realer than the scattered nightmares I've had since.

Trembling, I rounded this very corner and saw him…

It could be the shock of just being back here. Maybe it's a delusion conjured by dread. Whatever it is, more of that memory comes back to me.

I saw him. But he wasn't alone.

I don't know how I could have forgotten it. Or perhaps I just suppressed it…

Her voice. A low whimpering sound that didn't match the same fearless girl I knew.

"Did you think you could steal from me?" My father's voice was so cold, even the memory chills me to the core. "Did you think I wouldn't know it was you?"

A sound echoed, driving me onto the tips of my toes. From the hall, all I could see was his back, and a shadow flicker over the floor before a sharp crack resonated. Regardless, my cheek stung in sympathy as I recognized the sound.

A slap.

"You parade that damn ring around. Did you want her to see, was that it? You think you can threaten me? You can keep it."

Another sound came, but it was too loud. Too heavy.

Then a thud.

I don't know what drew me closer then, but when I crossed the threshold of his office, all I saw was red…

"Ada?" Domino's voice in my ear draws me back to the present.

I blink rapidly, struggling to adjust to the current reality. I'm shaking. Cold sweat drips down my neck, gluing the shirt to my skin. Ironically, I'm still lingering at the mouth of my father's office—but the vast difference between then and now is the only reason why I know I'm not hallucinating. In those days, my father stood tall, cigar in hand, his gray eyes indiscernible. Booming, his voice would reach me before I even set foot in the room.

Ada-Maria…

This time, there is no bellowed greeting. The man facing me now sits in the leather seat behind his desk, flanked by four armed men who don't seem alarmed by Jaguar's presence. They surround my father warily, their weapons poised at the ready.

To his credit, Roy Pavalos doesn't seem alarmed by the show of force—though a few glaring signs allude to whatever injury landed him in the hospital for so long. His right eye is slightly swollen, and a healing scratch mars his lip. From what Domino told me, my mother lured him into a "trap" that wound up with them both in a car accident. He must be injured enough that he can't stand.

And yet, he holds himself with every ounce of command I'm used to. With one look, I'm reduced to a fifteen-year-old girl again, and everyone else in this room fades away.

He says nothing. I don't know why I find that so strange. Silence, like violence, is only another weapon in his arsenal.

I feel it jabbing deep with every step I'm forced to take as Jaguar commands us forward. Then he stalks past us, leaning against a corner of the desk.

"Wonderful," he declares, clapping his hands. "What a beautiful, heartwarming reunion between father and daughter. Makes your fucking heart bleed, doesn't it, Dom-Dom? We'll cut to the chase, and I'll admit that I've already told Don Roy here all about your little betrayal. Though I'm sure we can let bygones be bygones. After all, Dom-Dom, you've just made my position ten times stronger by offering yourself up on a pretty little platter. Along with little Ada-Maria, here."

I barely hear him. I just watch, hating the mix of emotions that wash through me. Relief. Regret. Hope. Hope. Hope…

Domino was lying, after all. My father wouldn't do that to me. He wouldn't.

But I watch his eyes dart around the room—everywhere but at me. Domino is who he seems drawn to. Furious at.

Domino is the only one deemed worthy of his focus.

"Did you do it?" I don't know where the strength to speak even comes from. I must silence Jaguar mid-rant because I see his eyes cut to me, cold and narrowed.

Instantaneously, I sense Domino draw closer, radiating possession. His nearness alone gives me the strength to keep speaking.

"Did you tell him to kill me?"

Finally, my father shifts his attention to me, and I shudder. Shock isn't what I find in his gaze, nor alarm at the collar around my throat. No. In his eyes, I see the shadow of the girl I've always been. Worthless. Soulless. Desperate.

To him, I'm barely worth that wasted second of his time before he turns to Jaguar.

"You bother me for this?" he demands, and I flinch, shocked by how much softer his voice sounds, though still commanding. "You think to barter me down? Bring me something worth waging my life over—"

"Pia." A shiver runs through me as I hear my own voice echo. Never before would I ever interrupt my father. "Just tell me. Did you kill her?"

Or did I?

It's so damn pathetic to crave an answer from him after all this time, let alone expect one. And yet… He looks my way, and I suck in a breath.

"Interesting—" That voice isn't my father's. Jaguar instead, slinks around his desk to stand in front of him, his lips contorted into a chilling rendition of his usual grin. His eyes are ruthlessly cold, however. Merciless. "It looks like we've unearthed a bit of familial drama here," he drawls with a low chuckle. "Don't mind us. Continue—" Still smirking, he steps aside and gestures toward my father with a wave of his hand.

It's easier than it should be to ignore him. Instead, I focus on the pair of gray eyes identical to my own, blazing with every ounce of the cruel confidence I remember.

"I must have forgotten it," I say hoarsely. "But I saw you here that night. With her."

From the corner of my eye, I see Domino stiffen. Remarkably, he doesn't say a thing, though I know he's listening to every word.

"She was here, wasn't she?" My voice loses strength the longer I meet his gaze. It's as if the past ten years wash over me all at once. The fear he used to inspire in me with a single glance. The sting of his whip.

The pain of disobeying him.

My heart pounds as more sweat drips down my back. I'm swaying, rocking back and forth as my knees threaten to buckle. He doesn't have to say a single word for me to sense the danger building with every second I continue to face him like this.

But I'm not a scared teenager anymore. The memories in my head don't fade away beneath his glare—if anything, they feel more real by the second.

"You confronted her," I add, narrating the fragmented recollections as I recall them. "She had stolen the ring, and you were angry—"

"You look like hell, Ada-Maria." My father's voice rings out with all the authoritative clarity I remember. "You need rest —" He cuts his gaze to Jaguar. "Send her away."

"Oh, I don't think I will," Jaguar says, shaking his head. "In fact, it sounds like Ada-Maria here wants answers. I'm inclined to help her."

He crosses over to one of his guards and extends his hand. Obediently, the man withdraws a gun from his pocket and hands it over.

"Let's make things a little more interesting," Jaguar says, advancing toward me.

"What are you doing?" Domino pivots to block his path, but Jaguar laughs again.

"Relax." He nudges Domino aside and presents the gun to me on the flat of his palm. "I'm going to help the beautiful Ada get the answers she seeks. Don Roy speaks only one language," he tells me with mock seriousness. "Take it."

His tone leaves no room for argument. With trembling fingers, I grip the handle of the weapon one-handed. Its weight comes as a shock. It's almost too heavy for me to wield the way Jaguar and his men do, keeping their guns always trained on their targets.

I let my hand fall instead, taking care to avoid the trigger.

"Ah, that's no way to carry on a proper conversation," Jaguar scolds. "*This* is."

He aims his own gun squarely over my father's head. "I was hoping to remain civil here, but I'll try a question of my own. I would like to broaden my territory and expand into lovely Terra. To do that, I require 'cooperation' with whoever controls said territory. In this case, it happens to be you."

He lets that statement hang for a second before he chuckles. "I guess that isn't much of a question after all."

"You think this display is enough to rattle me?" my father asks. His tone is unaffected, his gaze harder than steel. "I've heard the rumors, but it seems you don't have much of your father in you after all. No balls to negotiate like a man on equal footing."

"We all know what 'negotiating' got my father," Jaguar counters, raising a dark eyebrow. "But how rude of me to interject. I cede the floor back to Ada-Maria."

He shifts his focus to me, and I swallow. The aches and pains battering my body choose now to assault me at full intensity. I hurt all over, and this childish voice in my head won't stop warning me to shut up. *Run. Hide. Don't make him angry.*

"I thought I might have done it," I say instead. "That I pushed her and hurt her. But it was you. Wasn't it?"

This time, my father's eyes narrow imperceptibly. I don't understand why at first—not until I register discomfort in my left hand. I've raised the gun without realizing it. Now the mouth of it is pointed somewhere over his chest. I flinch at the sight, but I can't seem to make myself lower the weapon.

"Just tell me. Please..." I've never begged him like this before, and yet he doesn't so much as flinch. As the seconds tick by, a demand wells within me, and I can't choke it down. "Answer me!"

"This isn't the time for your childish little tantrums," my father snaps.

There he is. This is the man I remember from that night—and nearly every day since whenever I dared to question him.

Faced with this fearsome glare, the person I used to be would have dropped her weapon and fled. Pleaded. Groveled.

I don't. "Just tell me," I croak, but despite how weak my voice sounds, I can't deny the strength in my tone that wasn't there before. "Just tell me the truth—"

"If you don't mind, let me interrupt again," Jaguar declares. He approaches my left side, ignoring Domino's warning hiss. "I'll be even more helpful. Don't forget our unfinished business, little minx," he adds.

It's a heartbeat before his meaning sinks in.

"You have a choice to make," he taunts, fingering a piece of my hair. "How convenient that both options are in this very room."

Domino or my father.

Despite his voice in my ear, I ignore him. This isn't about revenge, or hate, or even genuine curiosity. All along, I think I've known the real answer to this riddle anyway.

I just need to finally face it for myself.

"You killed her," I say, holding my father's gaze. "Why?"

He scoffs, but as it turns out, a verbal confession isn't even necessary. Written across his gaze is an answer more blatant than if he said it out loud. *What the hell do you think?*

"I want to hear you say it." I've never heard my voice this cold. Ice. My grip feels firmer, and the gun doesn't waver anymore. It feels dangerously light in my grasp, easier than ever to aim. "Why?"

"Why?" Suddenly, my father sits forward, slamming both hands onto the desk before him. "Because she thought she could get in my way. The little bitch thought she could blackmail me." His eyes slide to Jaguar before meeting mine again. "Don't make the same mistake." That command carries all the power I'm used to—but it rings hollow. In the next breath, he looks away, and I know in my soul this is all I will ever receive from him.

Silence and disdain.

Anger rises in me, more violent and twisted than anything I've ever felt. I swear, I see red, and the gun is even higher now. My wrist aches with the effort of holding it steady, but—without prompting from my brain—I can see my fingers adjust to find the trigger.

"Easy there," Jaguar interjects. His hand lands over my wrist. "I have my own loose ends to tie up," he adds, addressing my father and resuming whatever conversation they must have been in the middle of. "All I'm asking for is a few little territories—and all of Terra Rodea. A small piece of what you owe my family."

My father's lips curl back from his teeth as he spits. "You won't get shit from me."

"Oh?" Jaguar inclines his head, and a jolt of grim familiarity shoots through me. "Fair enough. I guess we don't have a deal after all. Not that it matters to me. After all, my father taught me the creed you two used to share—" He brandishes the gun with deceptive grace, finding the trigger without hesitation. "Always have a plan B."

It happens so fast I can't even cry out. All I see is the gun brandished in his hand before the sound rips through my eardrums.

"Don't look!" I'm in Domino's grasp, or so I assume, my face pressed to his chest. This time, I resist his touch and force myself to watch the scene unfolding before me.

Maybe it's the threat to my own life by way of the collar. Maybe I've already cried all the tears I had left.

Either way, even as the truth resonates through me, I don't feel a single tear fall. Instead, I find myself spinning to point the gun in my hand—only now, it isn't hard to aim it firmly over my target.

“Naughty, naughty,” Jaguar murmurs. In his eyes, I don’t find an ounce of fear. If anything… Excitement glimmers within their dark depths. He’s enjoying this. “I shouldn’t have to remind you that it’s five against two, do I?”

“Don’t—” The voice in my ear is grittier than I’m used to. With uncanny ease, Domino palms my wrist, easing the gun from my grasp. Rather than brandish it for himself, he tosses it onto the floor at my feet.

“Good boy,” Jaguar taunts, his eyes narrowing. “Now that the pesky housekeeping is out of the way. You give me what you fucking owe, or you can join good old Roy in hell.”

“The collar—” Domino spins me around, ensuring that I only see Jaguar and not the lifeless shape slumped behind my father’s desk. “Then we trade.”

“Dom, Dom, Dom. Always so damn bossy.” Jaguar seems to play with the gun, fiddling with it idly before he finally aims it squarely over Domino’s chest. “Give me the goddamn ring.”

“Shoot me,” Domino counters. “But then you won’t have shit.”

“I’ll have the lovely Ada-Maria,” Jaguar says with a chuckle. “And you can imagine all of the things I’ll do to her before sending her soul to join yours.”

“You could,” Domino counters. “But not before you hear my offer.”

“And what offer would that be? Another lie?”

"Take the collar off Ada, and you get the ring."

Jaguar shakes his head. "Not good enough—"

"And you get me. One favor. One chance to have me at your beck and call. That's what you've wanted from the fucking start, isn't it?"

Jaguar raises an eyebrow. "Why the hell would I believe even for a second that you would be so kind?"

"You can't take on Mateo alone," Domino counters. "Neither can you navigate the shitstorm you've just brought down on all our heads by killing Roy Pavalos in cold blood. But you put the word out that I killed him, I'll be indebted to you for protection."

"Like a good brother," Jaguar says, his smile callous. "But how can I be sure you won't change your mind?"

"You can't. But if it's between working with you or a murder charge, for now, I'll hedge my bets."

"Good old Dom," Jaguar snarls. "Always so damn honest."

He stalks forward, grabbing my chin with one hand while brandishing the gun in the other.

"Don't get impatient," he warns as Domino wavers in my peripheral vision.

I shudder as his thumb slides over the collar. I can't see what he does, but with a subtle click, the pressure relents.

"Why look at that," Jaguar says with a mocking bit of laughter. "I'll think about your little offer Dom-Dom,"

Jaguar says. "But you're right. Since *you* killed Roy Pavalos, you'll have a lot bigger problems on your ass than little old me."

"What are you playing at?" Domino demands in a coarse tone. "You're impulsive, but not stupid. You wouldn't accept using me as a patsy unless you don't have any other choice. You mentioned a plan B."

"Ah, that." Jaguar strokes his chin, smearing droplets of blood that must have splattered there. "Poor Don Roy was just a formality. There are several other promising candidates who can serve in his place as the Pavalos figurehead."

"Rodrigo," Domino says coldly. "You made a deal with him."

My uncle? I swivel my head toward him, but he remains fixated on the man across from us.

"Bingo," Jaguar says, but he isn't gloating anymore. "The bastard was tired of standing in the shadows, but aren't we all? Still, our arrangements might be a bit more amicable if he doesn't know I killed his brother directly."

"But with me serving as your so-called assassin, you get to use me as a scapegoat, but still keep Rodrigo in check."

Jaguar lifts his free hand in a mock salute. "Everybody wins, and you get to stay alive despite my better judgment. As a bonus, I think a few days on the run will give you plenty of time to reconsider stabbing me in the back again. But first… Where the fuck is the ring?"

Domino holds his gaze for a dangerous few seconds. Then slowly, he slips his hand into my pocket, withdrawing the tiny piece of jewelry. Without a word, he tosses it to Jaguar, who snatches it in his fist.

"I could kill you now," Jaguar says, drawing out the threat. "But I think I'd prefer to give you one last chance. After all, you'll be dead by sundown tomorrow without me. It seems as if you have no choice but to return to the fold, baby brother."

"You give me time to get underground," Domino reiterates. "Then I'm yours."

"Like you have a choice," Jaguar hisses. "By now, I'm sure some timid little maid has alerted the police. The bastards will be here soon, and I don't think the little game you played by ratting out Mateo will work a second time. Go."

He snaps his fingers, and Domino doesn't hesitate, snatching my wrist. His speed is impossible to keep pace with. Within seconds, we're outside, and he's shoving me into the passenger's side of the "borrowed" truck.

"What does this mean? What's happening?"

"Jaguar got his wish," Domino growls, claiming the driver's seat. "I'll return to the Domingas' fold. For now. I don't have much of a fucking choice."

"You did," I point out. "I could have shot him."

"No, you couldn't have. This is my fight. Not yours. I don't want that for you." The grit in his tone guts me. Paired with the dark, stormy look in his eye, I can see that this hurts him. It's more than just a simple setback.

This is his worst nightmare.

"And what about my uncle?" My voice comes out so soft. "Does that mean he was always working with Jaguar?"

It churns my stomach to consider it. Is anyone with the name Pavalos not scheming by nature? Even my mother seemed infected by my father's secretive nature.

"Probably." Domino stiffens as if remembering I'm even here. Then he sighs and faces forward, stoic once more. "The bastard just hedged his bets once he saw there might be an opening to claim your father's empire for himself. Either way, my original plan still stands," he continues while palming the wheel. A second later, we take off down the driveway. "Even if the timeline has been pushed back, Jaguar won't stand in my way for long. As for you… You could come with me. I'll need to regroup. Find Ines. Reclaim my territory and *our* villa."

His tone alludes to more than just an unknown future on the run.

This is a plea—one of the few he's ever voiced to me. It lurks beneath the gruff baritone, simple in essence—*come with me*? I'm so focused on his tone that it takes me a moment to notice his deliberate word choice.

"Our?"

"Yes, the villa has been in your mother's family for generations. That's why I thought you may remember it."

"Oh," I croak. It's all I can say.

Does it sting that he's revealed yet another snippet of my mother that I wasn't aware of? Yes. At the same time, it's another layer of honesty that I can't fault him for sharing. This revelation only proves there is so much I still don't know about the past. So many fucking questions that my brain hurts at the prospect of counting them all. I haven't even had the time to acknowledge my father's death, let alone decide what to do next.

But as I look into the eyes of the man beside me, I realize that I never had a choice.

From the start, I was always his, but in a way that differs from my father's brutal ownership. Domino Valenciaga doesn't require a collar to keep me close.

He never did.

From the start, I always *chose* to tether myself to him.

Even if it kills me.

~ The world continues in Blood Diamond Jaguar's first book ~

A WORD FROM THE AUTHOR

Hey there!

Thank you so much for reading! If you enjoyed the story, please leave a review and recommend the book to any friend you think would love this twisted world. You'd have my eternal gratitude. Even a short sentence goes a long way!

Then, come join the rest of us dark romance lovers in my Facebook Group where you can get snippets, sneak peeks of upcoming books and even help vote on aspects of future novels.

Come to the dark side:
https://www.facebook.com/groups/lanasbeautifulmonsters/

WANT MORE STUFF TO READ?
Join my newsletter and get a **free book**! Plus, you get to stay updated with any new releases, random giveaways and exclusive sneak peeks!
https://www.lanaskybooks.com/newsletter

Other Novels: https://lanaskybooks.com/

FREE BOOK - JOIN MY NEWSLETTER

Join my newsletter and get a **free book**! Plus, you get to stay updated with any new releases, random giveaways and exclusive sneak peeks!

https://www.lanaskybooks.com/newsletter

ABOUT THE AUTHOR

Lana Sky is a reclusive writer in the United States who spends most of her time daydreaming about complex male characters and parenting her Cockapoo Joey. She writes dark, twisted romance across several genres. Her titles include everything from mafia romance to vampires.

facebook.com/AuthorLanaSky
twitter.com/lanasky101
amazon.com/author/lanasky
pinterest.com/lanasky101
goodreads.com/lanasky
instagram.com/lanasky101
bookbub.com/authors/lana-sky

ALSO BY LANA SKY

For more titles by Lana Sky, please visit:

https://www.lanaskybooks.com

Made in the USA
Middletown, DE
23 May 2023

31298140R00192